CHRIST ON TRIAL

Christ on Trial

BY ROGER DIXON
based on the original story by
Basil Bova and Roger Dixon

COLLINS
St James's Place, London
1974

William Collins Sons & Co Ltd
London · Glasgow · Sydney · Auckland
Toronto · Johannesburg

First published in the United States of America 1973
by Pinnacle Books, New York
First published in Great Britain May 1974
by William Collins Sons & Co Ltd, London
Copyright © 1973 by Basil Bova and Roger Dixon
Reprinted September 1974

ISBN 0 00 221143 2

Set in Monotype Times
Made and printed in Great Britain by
William Collins Sons & Co Ltd, Glasgow

Chapter

1

The prisoner narrowed his eyes against the late morning sun, trying to see the expression on the face of the man standing above him at the top of the short, broad flight of marble steps that led from the large courtyard up into the city. Scarcely conscious of the heat, which had already turned the tightly packed courtyard of the governor's palace into an oven, nor of the growling crowd a few feet away, separated from him only by a line of soldiers, nor of the cuts and bruises on his body, nor of the thirst, he tried to read – so that he could remember, as long as he could remember anything – the face of the man who was afraid not to condemn him, the man who was speaking now to the hate-demented mob over his head.

'I find no fault in this just man.'

'No!' The crowd surged once more against the line of soldiers, which barely held. A centurion glanced anxiously at the speaker, wishing his chief would get it over with while he still had the situation more or less under control. Long years in this benighted land had taught the soldier to be prepared for anything.

At the moment, they were after the man who stood before them. 'Poor devil. From what I've heard he hasn't done any harm to anyone, but they're a funny lot – religious maniacs, every one of them!'

In spite of his pity, the centurion was glad they had someone else to hate for a while. But if the governor didn't give them what they wanted pretty soon, they were just as likely to turn on him and his men. He could hold them for a while, but he had only forty soldiers within call. They had not dared to spare any more from guarding the various other strong points throughout the city while everyone was in such an excited state, and anything was likely to happen. Forty men were scarcely enough in normal times; if the crowd turned really ugly now, they'd have their work cut out rescuing the governor – the prisoner would have to fend

5

for himself. At least four hundred people had managed to get into the courtyard, and there were thousands more outside. The centurion had already spotted several known zealots amongst them. Left to themselves they'd probably tear the accused man to pieces on the spot!

The din from the crowd was such that only the centurion, those standing close to the prisoner, and the prisoner himself heard what the governor said when he spoke again.

Once more the prisoner made no reply, and thinking, perhaps, that the man had not heard properly, Pilate came down the steps and stood only a few feet in front of him to repeat, more urgently now:

'Will you say nothing in answer to these charges they bring against you?'

The prisoner gazed at him; then the centurion saw him shake his head, almost imperceptibly.

The governor hesitated, uncertain. He knew what he should do for Rome – and for himself – but he was a superstitious man in spite of his outward sophistication, and his wife's warning earlier that morning still rang in his ears.

'Have nothing to do with that man, for I have dreamt many terrible things because of him!'

He glanced quickly at the mob, whose shouting rose even higher, then back at the prisoner. He remounted the steps and stood for a moment at the top with his back to the crowd before turning to face them. He raised his arms for silence. After a while, the hubbub subsided enough for him to be heard.

'At the time of the feast of the Passover it is customary to release a prisoner. Whom therefore shall I release to you: Barabbas the thief . . . or Jesus, whom some call Christ?'

A great shout went up. At first it was impossible to distinguish any words, but eventually a chant could be heard: 'Give us Barabbas. Give us Barabbas.'

Again Pilate held up his hand for silence. 'What then shall be done with the man who stands before you?'

Quite unexpectedly then, the sound died, until all stared at Jesus in silence. The soldiers eased their legs as the weight pressing on their backs diminished, but once more, the centurion

6

glanced anxiously at the governor. The silence was more ominous than the noise that had preceded it.

Finally, a voice from an unknown man somewhere in the middle of the crowd called out:

'Let him be crucified!'

Listening, Jesus thought that he recognized the voice, that it belonged to someone he knew – a young man who had once questioned him closely, become a follower, and then had fallen away. But he couldn't be sure. In any event, what did it matter now?

Another voice joined the first. Then he heard a woman crying out with a voice full of hatred, and presently everyone in the courtyard seemed to be shouting in unison.

'Let him be crucified! Let him be crucified!'

Jesus continued to look at the man standing above him and shouting, 'Why? What evil has he done?'

But his question was lost in the tumult.

Pilate turned and spoke to a servant standing behind him. The man nodded, then turned and hurried into the palace. He reappeared, less than half a minute later, carrying a towel and an earthenware basin half filled with water. The servant knelt in front of his master, holding the basin at a convenient height. To the crowd's amazement, the governor washed his hands. He then took the towel and turned to the sea of faces below him; this time, he had no difficulty in making himself heard.

'I wash my hands in token that I am innocent of the blood of this just person,' he said in a loud, clear voice that trembled only a little. 'Do with him what you will.'

While he was drying his hands some of the crowd began to chant again: 'Let him be crucified!' And others: 'Let his blood be on us . . . and on our children!'

Pilate handed the towel to his servant, who backed away. Then he nodded curtly at the centurion and turned to walk back into the palace, painfully conscious of the white faces of his wife and her maid watching him from an embrasure.

As soon as he disappeared, the sound from the crowd rose to a shout of triumph. The centurion nodded in turn to the captain of the guard, standing just behind the prisoner. In response, the

7

officer began to prod his charge towards the archway leading to the street outside.

At the summit of the hill two crosses were already in position. A third was laid alongside a hole between the others, by a man who had been forced by the soldiers to carry it when Jesus had collapsed beneath its weight and the curses and blows of those lining the route, many of whom had greeted him with adulation barely a week since.

The prisoner offered no resistance as he was lifted and placed along the upright, his arms forced outwards along the cross-pieces. Knowing what was coming, his throat constricted with revulsion, but when the first nail passed through his left hand and into the wood, he was barely aware it had happened. A second later, his head exploded in agony as first one foot, then the other, was shattered by a huge spike being driven between the bones. The pain made his mouth gape open in a silent scream. A few seconds later his right wrist was broken by another nail – and while he was still fighting for breath, the cross was raised and thudded into its socket with a jar that made his whole body cry out for mercy.

Slowly his brain cleared; in spite of the pain he felt almost a wave of relief. It had been a long road from Nazareth.

There was nothing more they could do to him now.

Lee stood, his hands clasped in front of him, looking up at the wooden image nailed to a cross. Once a polished brown, the cross was now blackened by the fumes of factories and the procession of steamers up and down the nearby Hudson River.

Lee had been born in Jersey City, in a house on this very street, just over forty years ago. The house had been torn down to make way for a laundry, but the small church where he had attended Sunday School and had been taken for his first mass was still here, as was the big cross outside (more remembered than the church), with its image of the would-be Saviour, eyes bulging heavenward from a tortured face.

Lee had often stood there as a child, wondering – trying to imagine what it must have been like to have nails hammered through your hands and feet. He would stand thinking about it

8

until suddenly his imagination became too real and he had to stop himself with a shudder. Father Mazzini – now long dead – had tried to explain what it was all about, but somehow Lee had never been able to reconcile the priest's words with the look of despair on the face of the image outside. Why was he looking up like that? Perhaps the sculptor had tried to capture the moment when Jesus had said: 'My God, my God, why hast Thou forsaken me?' But why should he have uttered such terrible words if he was truly the son of God?

The eyes of the image still rolled heavenward – corrosion adding, if anything, to the expression of grief. A ferryboat horn sounded from the river; it was a familiar sound, coupled forever in Lee's mind with the outstretched arms and pierced hands. The Christ gazed up, as he had as long as Lee could remember, at a sky now laden with clouds, but the only answer to his silent plea was, as always, the dull roar of traffic from the main highway at the end of the street.

What is Jesus doing in a side street in Jersey City, Lee had asked himself long ago, *in this place of shops and factories, of steamers on the river and skyscrapers rising from Manhattan across the water?* He had asked the same question again many times recently; now he was determined to try and find out, once and for all.

A voice spoke quietly, 'Father, forgive them, for they know not what they do.'

Lee started. He had not seen the young priest come out of the church, pause for a few seconds to look at him, then move to his side, eyes following Lee's gaze.

'What?'

'I'm sorry if I startled you,' the other smiled apologetically.

Lee let out his breath, then returned the smile and shook his head. 'I was daydreaming,' he admitted.

The priest nodded, then glanced back at the cross. 'You seemed to be staring so intently.' He paused, 'I often wonder what he must have thought.'

'I was thinking more of what he would say now.'

'Ah, yes.'

Lee hesitated, then said, 'Did you ever wonder what would happen if he came back?'

9

The priest's answer was gentle. 'I don't believe he ever left us.'

'I meant in the flesh.'

'We used to argue about that at college.'

Lee nodded slowly. 'I used to stand here wondering, when I was a kid.'

The other looked at him with new interest. 'You come from around here?' he asked.

Lee shook his head. 'Not any more,' he said. 'It was a long time ago.'

'Well . . . if you're still in the neighbourhood on Sunday, we'd be pleased to see you at mass.'

Lee inclined his head.

'Thanks . . . , but I've got to be going.' The priest nodded, and the two men stood for a moment looking at each other. 'Goodbye then,' Lee held out his hand.

The other took it, saying, 'We're always here if you need us.'

'I'll remember.' Lee gave a smile, then turned away, put on his hat, and walked to his car. He opened the door and was about to get in when the priest called after him.

'You didn't tell me your name.'

'Harrison,' Lee called back. 'Lee Harrison.'

The priest raised his hand in acknowledgment. 'I'll pray for you,' he said.

'Thank you, Father.' Lee paused a few more seconds, then got into the car, started the engine, and put the vehicle into a U-turn, which took him back towards the main road. He was conscious of the priest watching him until he turned the corner into the main stream of traffic headed towards the Lincoln tunnel.

Why he had stopped off there he couldn't explain to himself, except that he had been early for his appointment at NBC with Ray Burgh, at the company's offices in Rockefeller Center, and too nervous to want to hang around when he got there. Time was when Burgh would have been nervous about seeing *him*, but not any more. An independent producer was as good as his last success, and Lee had not had one for more than three years. Still, he was convinced his new idea, 'Christ on Trial,' was the best he had ever had. He had had plenty of time to think about it, lying in the hospital looking up at the ceiling, that was for sure. And

10

Ray must have been impressed from the little Lee had told him over the phone or he would not have agreed to see him.

More than likely it had started with the questions he had asked himself as a child. Maybe that was why he had to stop and get out – or maybe there was some other reason he didn't understand yet. But he had never had such a strong feeling of being swept along to some ultimate destiny.

Three years ago he had asked for the truth, but when the physician had told him it was cancer, his first reaction was of rank disbelief. The other had hurriedly gone on to say that there was more than an even chance they could do something about it.

Of course, they wouldn't be able to tell for certain, until the operation, but Lee had a good heart and wasn't overweight – that always helped. Besides, they knew a great deal more about it nowadays. The tragedy was that everyone knew someone who had died of cancer, but hardly anybody knew anyone who had been cured. This was largely because, in spite of everything, there was still a stigma attached to cancer, and people preferred not to talk about it. Also, there were literally thousands of people walking around, perfectly fit and healthy, who didn't even know they'd had it.

They had arranged for him to return for more tests and to visit the hospital for the first time the following week. Then Lee had joined the rush-hour traffic along the shore parkway, wondering if, after all, he was one of those who would have been better off not knowing. But by the time he had turned into his own driveway, he had decided that, on balance, he was less unhappy knowing than wondering but that he wouldn't tell anyone else, other than Dorothy.

One thing, with no children and with his wife having a career of her own, he had little to worry about if the doctors were wrong and he didn't come through it after all. With his life insurance and her job, Dorothy would be secure enough. Besides, she was still a fine-looking woman. She'd probably find someone else soon enough.

As he had parked the car, Lee had had no idea how soon his last thought was to come true.

11

He told her after dinner, and she listened to him in silence. As he went on, he became aware that she was looking at him with an expression closer to curiosity than concern.

When he had finished, she simply got up from the table where they had been facing each other over cups of coffee and, without a word, started to feed the dishes into the washer.

Lee had not been sure how she would react. Their marriage had not featured very prominently in the thinking of either of them, he imagined, for some years – they had just drifted along like most people. It was true they occupied separate bedrooms, had done so for some time, but that was only because their respective jobs called for irregular hours; they had agreed, five or six years ago, that if either of them was ever going to have a complete night's rest again, they had better stop trying to sleep in a double bed, the other half of which was, like as not, apt to be vacant, recently occupied, or about to be vacated. They still made love from time to time, usually after coming home from one of the rare occasions they were able to go out for an evening together. There was nothing earthshaking or particularly exciting about it any more, but Dorothy had a competent body, and it was invariably a pleasurable experience.

Perversely, watching her now through the kitchen door as she bent over the machine, Lee wanted her. He had heard before that the proximity of death often sharpens sexual desire, and he remembered a doctor friend of his once telling him how the marriage of two of his elderly patients – a record of more than fifty years' happiness – had been wrecked a few months before the husband died by his insisting on their resuming the physical side of their relationship after it had gradually faded into the background and finally disappeared more than fifteen years before.

Lee shuddered slightly and rose from the table. He involuntarily reached for a pack of cigarettes, then withdrew his hand, glancing down at the table for a moment before looking back at his wife. Dorothy was one of that rare breed of woman who look better – in the sense that their bodies seem better proportioned – nude than fully dressed. In spite of his morbid thoughts, he still wanted her like hell.

Lee moved into the kitchen and put his hands lightly on her hips. A woman gets to know by such familiar gestures that her mate desires her, and he in turn feels her probable response in almost the same moment. Without her turning around or moving at all, Lee felt her shrinking from him now. After a second he withdrew his hands, then moved to her side, forcing a smile to cover the rejection.

'I guess I thought you'd say something . . . if it was only good-bye!'

Dorothy closed her eyes for a second. Then without looking at him directly, she said: 'I'm frightened. You know how . . . "that" scares me.'

Lee nodded. Her mother had died of cancer when she was fourteen. He never knew if she had been very close to her – his wife had never been able to tell him about it, except in the most general terms. It was as if the experience of witnessing her mother's illness stood like a flaming sword between her 'now,' and possibly between earlier, happier memories. Suddenly Dorothy turned to him.

'I'm sorry,' she said.

Lee shook his head: 'There's no need to be. I understand. But don't be frightened on my account.'

'I know. You said the doctor said it was curable.'

'Sure.' Lee shrugged, then he smiled again. 'So what have we got to worry about? In a week or so I'll be up and about again, as good as new.'

She looked at him closely. 'What about your job? I thought you were putting a new series together?'

Lee nodded again. 'That's true, but it'll wait a while. Fortunately, everything else is running well, and there shouldn't be any problems Helen can't handle while I'm away.'

Helen was Lee's secretary, bartender, accountant, and perpetual buffer between him and those who would otherwise so pester him for work that he would never have time to do any of his own. She was a tall blonde (still), in her early forties, who adored Lee almost as much as the son who had just started college and for whom she had worked to keep in a manner to which she had not been accustomed at a similar age. The boy

13

had never known his father, who had flown safely through more than sixty missions over North Korea, only to be killed on a freeway the day after his return to the States. That he had died so soon had been a shock from which his young wife had taken a long time to recover – a shock almost equalled a few weeks later when she realized that she was pregnant. Kenny had come into the world fatherless.

'What about money?' Dorothy was asking. 'Have you got enough?'

Lee subconsciously registered the 'you,' and stopped thinking about how Helen would manage.

'I'm okay as far as the operation and hospital are concerned.' He shrugged. 'If everything goes as the doc says, there shouldn't be any problem.'

Dorothy nodded without speaking, then turned back to the machine and switched it on.

Unable to stop himself, Lee put his arms around her. His desire had gone, but now he felt terribly alone. He knew he had to face this by himself, but if she would only make him feel that it mattered whether he came through or not, not because people relied on him, needed him, for the driving force and ideas that had made him one of the most respected men in his profession, but because one person, at least, understood how frightened he really felt without being told. One person who would suffer with him, even weep at his passing, if it came to that.

Dorothy deliberately took a step back, so that he had to release her. He couldn't read her expression; there seemed to be too many emotions vying for attention to register on one face. Then she said, 'Lee . . . I know this is unforgivable, but I've got to tell you something.'

Why should he have known what she was going to say, right out of the blue? Some sharpened sense because of the illness? A trick of time – or just an inexplicable insight into the nature of this woman who he realized, all at the same moment, had become a total stranger.

'I know most people would wait, under the circumstances . . . but, please believe me when I tell you that I can't.'

14

Lee watched her struggling to find the words; unable, and to be truthful, unwilling to help.

'I'm leaving you,' she said eventually. 'I've fallen in love . . . I could see something like what you've just told me coming . . . but he wouldn't wait.'

'I see.'

'It's no one you know. There's no point in our discussing it . . . but even if it hadn't happened, I couldn't have gone on the way we were.' Suddenly she was crying. 'I'm sorry,' she choked, 'I feel so guilty about it now. I know how you must be feeling . . . but I can't help myself. I can't help loving him . . . and I'm terrified of sick people!'

So that's how it was. Helen drove him to the hospital ten days later and Dorothy moved out some time afterwards. True, she forced herself to come and see him a couple of times after the operation, but it was awful for both of them. He asked Helen to write, suggesting she not come any more and wishing her luck.

The doctor had been right in one respect. Lee came through, although he was told later that the growth had been more advanced than was suspected at the time. Then they started the radiation treatment to kill off any cells that the knife might have left and to ensure that no new growth would start. He had felt quite cheerful after the operation and not too uncomfortable, but after two or three treatments, things started to go wrong and his stomach began to feel as if they had poured acid on it.

He was wheeled along to a large room where he was left at the business end of something that looked like a fair-sized telescope. Then everyone retreated and watched him from behind a thick glass screen.

The pain built up to the point where it was agonizing. Doctors and specialists came to look at his broiled flesh – on which he couldn't even bear the weight of bedclothes – and eventually he was told that he was one of those unfortunates who were ultra-sensitive to radiation treatment. They explained that to continue on the present course would do more harm than good and that the only alternative was a new treatment based on drugs, which would take a good deal longer.

'How long?' Lee asked weakly.

The surgeon looked at him carefully. 'At least a year,' he said eventually. 'Possibly longer.' Then, before Lee could say anything, he went on, 'Of course, we shouldn't deal with it here. A nursing home would be more suitable.' He shrugged. 'Less expensive for one thing, and altogether more pleasant. Besides,' now he looked at him with a straight face, 'we need your bed for serious cases.'

It was arranged that Lee should be taken to a clinic near Virginia Beach. For a long time he was scarcely able to move while he was recovering from what amounted to radiation poisoning, the effects of which continued to mount for several weeks after the original treatment was stopped. In fact for a while Lee hung between life and death. He hardly remembered the move although his condition was not nearly so critical as it became later.

In his imagination, Lee received many visitors, but they told him later that only Helen had made the trip to sit with him one afternoon. It was a long way for her to come, but when he had recovered enough to talk, she came again and explained gently how she had had to cash his insurance policies to pay for the treatment and to provide him with enough reserve to see him through the succeeding months. Lee would have felt badly about it, but he had taken them out only for Dorothy and any children they might have had. Helen then went on to tell him that she had been forced to give up the office and take another job. She hoped he would understand, and of course she would leave and come back to him the minute he needed her. She had taken all his files and personal papers home with her, where they would be quite safe in the meantime.

She came to see him periodically after that, but it was a long way for her to travel and her new job gave her little time. He discovered later she had used quite a sizeable part of her own savings trying to keep the office going for him, but as time went on – six months had become a year, then two years – Helen's visits became less frequent. Finally she came to tell him that she had an opportunity to go to Hollywood with her new employers and she hoped he'd forgive her if she took it. By then, Lee's mind had recovered its old vigour but his body was taking a long time

16

catching up. He knew it would not have taken much persuasion for Helen to turn the job down – but he hadn't sunk that low. He sent her away with his blessing.

She put his papers and files in a deposit box in a New York bank and mailed him the key, after paying a year's rent in advance out of her own money. Looking at the key Lee wondered what use any of the things she had so carefully preserved for him would be by the time he got around to seeing them again. Things moved so fast in the entertainment business that you could drop out of sight and mind as fast as lead shot disappears down a well.

The matron who ran the little hospital, and who often came in to talk with him after her day's work was done, had warned Lee that one of the most difficult battles to win was against the apathy any long period of convalescence induced. He knew he owed much to her alternate goading and encouragement for reawakening his ambition.

And yet . . . his ambitions had changed, radically . . . and probably that was not surprising.

Lee could see that his money would outlast his period of recovery by about a thousand dollars. He was as good as back to the beginning – in more than one sense. But as time for his discharge approached, the only idea that kept nudging him seemed so wildly impractical that he began to despair. Yet he was incapable of turning his mind to anything else.

Lee had been brought up a Catholic, but like many of his friends, had gradually stopped going to mass and eventually had lost contact with the Church altogether. Despite this, in the end, before the operation, when everything else fell away, Lee knew it was that echo of hope in his memory – that death might not be the end of everything – which had enabled him to face the possibility with greater courage than he could have otherwise mustered.

Priests came to see him, first at the hospital, then at the nursing home. They had been simple, kindly men who had the power, sometimes, of bringing hope and peace to the dying, but failed unhappily to answer Lee's questions when he had recovered except by pointing to the virtue of faith.

'What sort of a God is it, then,' he demanded, 'who would create a creature with the desire and ability to ask questions, only to turn around and say he had no business wanting to know the answers?'

'But these are things we would all like to know,' an exasperated priest had retorted at the end of a particularly trying session with Lee. 'Only the Lord himself could give you such replies – or his Son, who spoke for him. Read your gospels!'

The 'idea' was a good one. Lee knew he was little different from most people, driven by the same hopes, threatened by the same fears. If only he could grasp the missing piece that would make it possible to turn the dream into reality, just this last once! To put his signature on the medium to which he had devoted his adult life in a way that would make up for the nothingness of most of it.

Not just for himself. What he had been through and seen others go through had taught him that pride and ambition were trivial qualities. But a longing for immortality was at the root of human existence. Let *his* be the memory of an event that moved at least a few, apart from himself, one step nearer understanding.

The idea lay embedded in his mind, apparently incapable of realization, but obliterating all rivals. If only he knew how to get it down on paper – but what writer was capable of such a thing? If it were possible, it would have been done long ago. Besides, the writer himself would have to know things hidden from all others.

At last, one night, less than a week before he was due to leave the nursing home, Lee prayed very hard before he went to sleep that either he would think of a way or be able to forget the whole thing.

Even as he was wearily getting up off his knees, the answer hit him with such blinding simplicity that he gasped and sat hurriedly on the edge of the bed as the implications hit him. No one need write it at all!

In spite of Lee's realistic assessment of his probable standing in the profession after an absence of almost three years, he was nonetheless shaken when he tried to telephone some of his old friends during his last few days at the nursing home. Many of those in power had lost their jobs during the shake-out after cigarette advertising was banned. He found it impossible to get past the secretaries of many of the remainder – most of whom were new to their jobs and had never heard of him. And it was obvious from the reactions of the two he did get to talk with – neither of whom could spare the time to listen while he outlined the idea – that he might as well be dead as far as they were concerned.

Lee took a deep breath and started again. He had known all along it was going to be tough – he was just going to have to use his imagination. Movements in the business worked both ways. If some of those he used to know had been axed, surely it was likely that others who had been in more lowly positions had moved up the field.

He began to think. This time he was lucky, hitting the target first time, although it was with slightly mixed feelings that he discovered that Ray Burgh was now a senior executive of NBC.

He was put through almost immediately.

Ray had first come to him about ten years ago, having heard of Lee's recent arrival in the first rank of independent producers through a coproduction deal with one of the big motion picture companies concerning an ambitious series called 'The World of . . .' The pilot programme had been 'The World of New York,' a hard-hitting piece of television journalism that at first had frightened potential sponsors to death. Eventually though, one sponsor, more courageous and farseeing than the others, had agreed to back it.

The viewing audience had been taken by the heels, and the series had never looked back. The first was followed by specials featuring most of the great cities of the world. All the programmes had caused exactly the same split in their respective establishments: on the one hand, there were those who became furious at having their dirty linen washed so penetratingly in public, and on the other, those who welcomed the comments of Lee and his directors as a means of cracking the crust of apathy that settles so easily over any 'civilized' community.

In his last few months in the nursing home, Lee had often wondered if it wasn't during his frequent absences while that series was being made that his marriage had started to fall apart. Dorothy had always been a bit strange for some days after he returned from one of the many trips he'd had to take during that period, but she had always seemed to recover and become her old self again.

Any successful producer, director, or whatever is bound to be inundated by people trying to sell themselves in one way or another. Lee's solution to this problem was to hire Helen.

Lee had been out when Ray had first called. And why she had made an appointment for Ray to come back and talk to Lee, Helen could never explain. Lee had put it down at the time to either a more convincing line on Ray's part or a fat bribe, but when he knew Helen better he realized it was certainly neither of these possibilities but probably the operation of that sixth sense of hers which enabled her to distinguish not only the genuine from the phony, but also those who could be of use to him from those who couldn't.

Lee had always made a point of honouring his secretary's commitment of his time if he could. This was not only a point of principle, but to have done anything else would clearly have undermined their relationship from the beginning.

In spite of a not-too-favourable beginning, Lee listened patiently to Burgh's ideas and agreed by the end of the interview to attend a screening of a pilot Burgh had made himself, having mortgaged everything he possessed in order to do it. The pilot was for a proposed series of programmes centred around interviews of children on matters of current interest to their parents. It wasn't so much the idea that was good, although the double possibility for humour – not only hearing the kids' opinions, but sneaking a secondhand report on what their mothers and fathers really thought about this and that – was valid enough. It was the way it had been executed that impressed Lee; he immediately recognized in Ray, who had done practically everything himself except hold the camera, a director of rare and sensitive talent.

20

As a result of the screening, Ray was given the chance to direct two of the last of 'The World of . . .' series. Everyone, including Lee, admitted afterwards that they were two of the best. Then Lee produced the children's series based on Ray's pilot, with Ray directing throughout.

This was also a smash. From then on Lee and Ray had worked as equals; not infrequently they worked alone, but whenever they collaborated, the result was sure to be above average.

They never became friends, but something happened at a party, given by one of the sponsors to celebrate the successful launching of the children's series, that burned itself into Lee's memory and warned him ever afterwards that he was dealing with a man whose immediate motives he might not understand but who was undoubtedly driven by an ambition as subtle as its horizons were probably limitless.

He had not really been in a party mood at all. Of course, he had been glad the series was a success, but he had been working too hard and was too tired to enjoy it. Besides, he was due on a plane for London the following morning and Dorothy had begged off coming with him in favour of a reception at the Waldorf for some big guns in her own field. This was before they were married, and she had gone to a lot of trouble to explain how important it was for her to attend. Lee had been patient and understanding at the time, but the more he thought about it afterwards, the more his own achievement seemed diminished, and he determined to leave as soon as he felt able to do so with good grace.

He stood, then sat, talking for a while, by which time the apartment was jam-packed. But just when he'd decided that the time had arrived for him to slip away unnoticed, he became aware that someone was standing in front of him. He had glanced up to see one of the most beautiful girls he had ever seen in his life smiling at him.

'Mr Harrison?' the girl had repeated.

Lee had got up so quickly that he'd spilled half his drink on to the carpet, but when she'd chuckled, he'd returned her smile without feeling embarrassed, as if this were a familiar joke between them.

'I'm sorry,' he had begun, looking up to face her after glancing down to see how much damage he had caused, 'I don't think . . .'

'We never met.'

'Thank God for that,' Lee had replied with heartfelt sincerity. 'If I'd forgotten, I should have no choice but to go out and kill myself!'

'I'd rather you danced with me.'

Somewhere in the semidarkness over on the other side of the room a few couples were moving slowly to music from a hidden source. The girl had held out her hand and Lee had allowed himself to be led across the party towards them, conscious that every male eye swivelled as they passed.

Edging on to the floor, the girl had turned to face him. As soon as he had taken her into his arms, her body curved into his with an immediacy that surprised him. Whatever he had been going to say died in his throat.

Her eyes were almost level with his. Seeing his expression, she had smiled, then put her head on his shoulder and said softly: 'Don't talk . . . just feel the rhythm.' Then, a few seconds later, she had whispered, 'And don't worry. I'm not after a part. I don't want anything, except to be with you.'

Realizing he was probably making a complete fool of himself, but no longer seeming to care, Lee had spent the rest of the evening on her terms. They hardly spoke at all, but danced, only occasionally pausing for a drink, during which time she hardly took her eyes from his face and never let go of his hand.

Lee had never before realized how much a woman could fill a man's consciousness, simply by standing beside him. How was it possible that this girl could simply walk up to him, and from then on make the whole world a more complete, more wonderful place just with her presence? Had he fallen in love with her? Surely it was not possible. Besides, he was too old for such foolishness . . . and what about the girl he was supposed to marry?

As time passed, Lee had found one part of his mind analysing the moment, as if trying to fix it in his memory forever, as one does during those rare moments when one knows extreme happiness.

Lee knew that what was happening between them had nothing to do with Dorothy, or any other woman – except that it had to do with all women and all men at the same time. As they moved together, he was conscious only of *her* – and it seemed they were drawn ever closer by that great force which demands only that two halves become one – the building block of creation.

They had left the party together with unspoken agreement and soon, in a place that had no importance in itself, had come together in a climax that reached out beyond ordinary awareness into new sounds and colours, before plunging them back with only a fast-fading memory of paradise.

The girl must have left while Lee slept. When he woke up in the morning there was a note in a small envelope on the dressing table – a note that must have been written before the party started and carried the whole evening in her handbag, waiting to be delivered. It said: '*Ray says thanks!*'

Chapter
2

Lee left the car at the Hertz offices on Fifth Avenue and took a cab from there to Rockefeller Center. Burgh's office was on the twenty-fifth floor, and going up in the elevator, Lee started to sweat. He had no doubt at all concerning the project he was about to try and put over, but he knew he had to sell it right the first time or he was dead.

On the door a bronze plaque read: *Ray Burgh: Programme Controller*. He knocked briefly and went inside.

The room was large and plush – obviously the outer office of a substantial suite. In the most prominent position an attractive woman in her early thirties sat behind a desk, talking on the telephone. An inner door probably led to Burgh's private office. On the other side of the room a young man in shirt sleeves was arguing with a girl over some schedules laid out on the desk between them.

The young woman facing him as he walked in was obviously Mary Bell, Burgh's secretary. Lee had spoken to her only once, on the telephone, but a lifetime's experience had taught him to remember the names of the secretaries of influential men. She glanced up as he came into the room and smiled briefly, nodding at the same time to indicate that she knew who he was, then turned back to continue her call.

Lee glanced around the room. He contemplated sitting in the chair opposite the desk but the call seemed to be coming to an end so he stood quietly instead, waiting for her to finish. The other two in the room ignored him completely.

Lee looked at Mary Bell more closely and liked what he saw. She had a high, intelligent forehead, nicely spaced brown eyes, and a flawless complexion. When she smiled she showed perfect teeth, and her voice had unexpected modulations that made it very pleasant indeed to listen to. Lee began to speculate that perhaps she had lived in Europe. Just then the call came to an end.

She replaced the receiver and looked up at him, but before either of them could say anything, the inner door opened and Burgh himself came out, carrying a hat and raincoat. He was the same age as Lee but had a larger build and looked considerably fitter. He was bald on top but deeply tanned, and his clothes, though conservative, were of the finest cloth. His entire appearance was in marked contrast to that of Lee, who had a permanently rumpled look these days. Burgh's whole manner spoke of a man who had 'made it' and intended to stay at the top. When he saw Lee, fleeting expressions of surprise, then irritation, crossed his face, but these were quickly swept aside by a practised smile. Lee, whose eyes had not forgotten to watch for such things, felt the familiar tightening of his stomach. Nevertheless he forced himself to smile and took the outstretched hand of the other as Burgh strode forward to greet him.

'Lee! How have you been?'

'Better thanks, Ray.'

Burgh's face switched to concern. 'Yeah, I was sorry to hear you hadn't been well.'

'It gave me time to think,' Lee smiled wryly.

'Well, that's what we could all use,' Burgh said, nodding and looking around the room for a few seconds before turning back. 'But look, fella, I'm sorry. I'll have to postpone our meeting.'

'Oh.'

'Something just came up.'

In spite of himself, Lee couldn't prevent showing his disappointment. Burgh put a hand on his shoulder.

'But from what you've told me it sounds like a great idea.' He glanced at Mary. 'Christ on trial – in a modern courtroom.' Then back to Lee: 'You know, I thought we might kick it around sometime as an idea for a special – to put out round about Easter.'

'That's what I said over the phone,' Lee began, but Burgh was not listening.

'Prestige show – sort of modern Passion play.'

'I'd like . . .' Lee began again.

'Only trouble is, you'd need a really big syndicate to sponsor a thing like that.'

'The way I thought . . . '

Burgh suddenly glanced at the clock on the wall and interrupted him again. 'Look at the time! Lee, I'm sorry, I really do have to go.' He turned back to face him. 'But we *are* interested. The only trouble is finding time to discuss it.'

Lee took a deep breath. 'I'm staying in New York now,' he said.

Burgh looked at him, impatience beginning to show again. 'Look,' he said, 'I tell you what – leave the script with Mary here, and I'll definitely read it over the weekend and call you next week. How's that?'

'There isn't a script.'

Burgh's mouth opened.

'That's the whole point,' Lee went on hurriedly. 'It doesn't call for one.'

'I see. Well . . . I don't know.'

'That's why I wanted to discuss it.'

'Yes, I see,' Burgh said doubtfully. 'Trouble is, sponsors aren't wild about unscripted programmes . . . unless they're panel games or something like that.'

'They'd go for this, once they knew the whole idea. I'm positive.'

Burgh nodded. 'Yeah,' he said, 'I see the sort of thing you have in mind.'

Lee hesitated a few seconds, then he said: 'Ray, I don't want to sound disrespectful, but I'm sure you haven't the remotest idea . . . and won't have until you give me a chance to explain properly.'

Burgh's eyes had started to wander away, but now he looked back. 'No script, you say?'

Lee changed his ground. 'We've done some good things together in the past, you and I,' he began.

Burgh nodded again. 'That's true. But you've been away, Lee. Tastes change.'

'The longing for truth never changes!'

The two in the background stopped talking and turned to look at them. Burgh stared at him intently, glanced up at the clock again for a moment, then back to Lee. 'Look,' he said, 'I don't know if we can do anything, but I would like to hear about it. I must go now, and I won't be back today. But if you'd explain it to Mary . . . I trust her judgment. She can fill me in later. If I think it has any possibilities at all, I promise I'll phone. In fact, I'll be in touch either way.' He paused for a few seconds, and when Lee didn't say anything went on apologetically, 'I'm sorry, it's the best I can do.'

Lee glanced at Mary, then turned back to Burgh. He smiled a little wearily. 'Then that's what it'll have to be, Ray. I won't kid you . . . I don't think anyone else'll listen to me.'

Burgh straightened up at once and smiled sympathetically. 'People remember Lee Harrison,' he said.

Lee shrugged. 'Well . . . I'll tell your secretary. Then I'll wait to hear from you.'

'Fine,' Burgh smiled and started to put on his raincoat.

'I'll wait as long as I can,' Lee went on, 'but it can't be too long . . . then I'll go.'

The other looked at him surprised. 'Where to?' he asked.

'Out of town. Away from this business.'

Burgh said: 'We can always use a man of your experience.'

Lee shook his head. 'No. I've had too long to think.' Then he smiled. 'But thanks, anyway. This is all I want to do. Afterwards,' he grinned slightly, 'I dunno. Maybe I'll grow peaches somewhere and sit in the sun!'

Burgh laughed at this. 'You have changed!' He finished buttoning up his raincoat, then held out his hand. 'Okay, Lee, we'll consider it, I promise.' The two men shook hands.

'Thank you.'

'It was nice seeing you again.'

Lee inclined his head: 'It was nice of you to see me.'

'Yeah . . . well, we'll be in touch.' Burgh patted Lee on the shoulder, then turned to his secretary. 'You know where I am if you want me?'

'Yes.' The girl nodded.

'Use my office if you want some peace and quiet.' He turned back to Lee and smiled. 'See you, then.' Burgh moved for the door.

'I hope so,' Lee said quietly.

Burgh opened the door but paused, looking back. 'By the way,' he said, 'how's Dorothy?'

Lee shrugged. 'Last I heard she was fine,' he said. 'Married to a guy in the garment business.'

Burgh looked at him, eyes unblinking. 'I see. Well . . . good-bye for now.' He went out, closing the door behind him.

After a few seconds Lee turned to Mary and smiled: 'Well . . . I suppose I was lucky to have him listen that much. Ray's an important man these days.'

'Oh, he's important all right!' The girl came round from behind the desk.

Lee looked at her. 'Do you think he's really interested?' he asked.

Mary shrugged. 'I don't know,' she said. 'He's got a nose for something good, but when you said you didn't have a script, he was going to brush you off.' She looked at him directly. 'Now he doesn't know why he didn't.' They paused for a few seconds, looking at each other. The young man in shirt sleeves on the other side of the room turned to the girl facing him.

'Okay,' he said. 'Come on, playtime's over. Let's get back to work.' The girl nodded.

Mary said: 'Would you like to go into the other office?'

'I'd rather have some coffee,' Lee said. 'I didn't feel like lunch.'

Mary nodded. 'Suits me fine,' she said. 'Shall we go downstairs?'

'Why not?' He opened the door for her and she went out, giving him a brief smile.

In the corridor, Mary waited for him to close the door, then they walked side by side to the elevator.

'Have you been with Ray long?' Lee asked.

'Just over a year.' Mary glanced sideways at him, curiously. 'I've heard of you,' she remarked.

Lee smiled. 'I'm flattered!'

They reached the elevator and Mary pressed the button before turning to him again. 'I heard you'd had an accident,' she said.

'Yeah. A head-on collision.' He paused for a few seconds before adding, 'With myself!'

Mary opened her mouth to say something but an elevator

arrived and they had to concentrate on squeezing into an already overcrowded car.

Downstairs, Mary went to sit at a table while Lee went up to the counter. By the time he joined her again, with a tray, two cups of coffee and a jug of cream, she had lit a cigarette.

'Are you sure you won't have anything to eat?' Lee asked.

Mary shook her head. 'No. But you go ahead.'

'I'll have something later.' He put the two cups down and set the jug of cream between them. Then he sat down, leaning the tray against the table leg.

'Cream?'

Mary shook her head. 'No, thanks.'

Lee picked up the jug and emptied it into his own cup, then stirred it slowly, looking at the woman facing him. 'I have a feeling you don't like the idea so far,' he said after a while.

Mary sipped her coffee, then put the cup down. 'What I think doesn't matter,' she said. 'I'll try and give a fair account.'

'I saw your expression – when we were discussing it upstairs.'

Mary smiled in spite of herself. 'Christ on trial – in a modern courtroom, yet!'

Lee drank his coffee, watching her over the rim of his cup. When he put it down he asked: 'What don't you like about it in principle?'

Mary shrugged. 'To be frank, I didn't like the idea when Ray first told me about it because it sounded like a smart-aleck idea.'

'By a smart aleck?' Lee interrupted.

He saw her eyes widen slightly. She drew on the cigarette before concluding, 'With a notion to make a comeback, no matter how.'

'And you care how?' Lee asked.

The woman looked back at him directly. 'I'm not a religious person, Mr Harrison,' she began, then hesitated, trying to pick her words. 'I imagine, like most people, I don't really have a religion, but deep down, I suppose, I still harbour some comforting thoughts that well . . .' she shrugged slightly, 'maybe there's something in it.'

'And you don't like the idea of these ideas being put on trial?' Lee persisted.

'Not if you put it like that. Certainly not in a way I suspect would be basically profane.'

Lee paused for a few seconds. 'Are you so sure of that?' he asked eventually.

Mary didn't answer immediately. 'I don't know,' she said at last. 'At least I'm beginning to think you're sincere.'

Lee smiled wryly. 'Hanging around death's door for a few weeks stimulates a remarkable growth in that quality.'

The girl smiled back. 'That still doesn't mean to say it's a good thing to do,' she said.

Lee nodded. 'I agree,' he said seriously. 'Sincerity alone is probably the worst qualification for doing anything.'

'Apart from which, I can't see how it can be done in a way that is not only sincere but also makes for compelling viewing.'

'And when all's said and done, that's what we're talking about if we want to get anywhere?'

Mary nodded slowly. 'Try finding the sort of sponsorship Ray was talking about upstairs for anything else.'

'I agree.'

'Besides,' Mary went on, 'you haven't a script . . . don't need one, you say. So what have you got? I mean, "Christ on Trial." It sounds dramatic, but where do you go from there?'

Lee pulled out a pack of cigarettes and lit one slowly. 'Well, I'll tell you,' he said carefully. 'I said upstairs that most people have a longing for truth. In a way, you said a similar thing yourself just now when you talked about the comforting ideas people cling to at the back of their minds, even when they have dropped all outward forms of religion.'

'I'd call them hopes,' Mary put in.

Lee nodded. 'All right,' he said. 'You *hope* Jesus Christ really was the son of God and died for our sins?' He had unconsciously raised his voice and Mary glanced uncomfortably at the nearby tables. 'It's all right,' Lee went on, 'they can't hear. I'm sorry if I'm embarrassing you, Miss Bell.'

Mary forced her attention back to him. 'I'm sorry,' she said, 'please go on.'

'It was such a long time ago,' Lee continued, lowering his

30

voice. 'So much has happened since. There are a million questions people would like to ask but can't.'

'What sort of questions?'

'About what really happened. Also, if Jesus really was the son of God, how would he level what he had to say with the state of modern scientific knowledge? And what relevance does his teaching have to life in, for example, New York today?'

Mary smiled faintly. 'I know some people who think they know the answers to those questions,' she said.

Lee nodded. 'So do I. The ones who have faith. But let's face it, what they have to say doesn't make much sense to the rest of us.'

'Perhaps they're just scared of the alternative.'

'Maybe. But if Christ *was* the son of God, then what he said must be right for us here and now.' He paused for a few seconds, then went on: 'So that's what I want to do. I'm confident of the outcome – for reasons I don't want to go into because they would only confuse the issue. I want to put the life and teaching of Jesus Christ on trial before a hundred million witnesses. I want him, and those who knew him, and those in possession of knowledge today relevant to the verdict, to present their evidence in the environment of a modern criminal court which, imperfect though it may be, is the finest instrument for weighing truth we have been able to forge in two thousand years.'

Mary's eyes widened with surprise. 'Criminal . . . ' she began.

'If Christ were guilty of misleading the thousands of millions who put their trust in him – many to the extent of sacrificing their lives – he was surely the worst who ever lived.'

Mary now seemed thoroughly shocked. 'But how?' she protested. 'You can't bring Christ back from . . . ' Her voice trailed away as she realized what she had been about to say. 'Well . . . you know what I mean,' she ended lamely.

Lee nodded. 'We can't produce him in court, or rather in a courtroom built in a television studio. Nor can we produce Mary, his mother, nor Peter, nor any of the others. But we can do the next best thing.'

'What?'

Lee paused for a few seconds, then asked, 'Have you ever seen a really great performance of Hamlet?'

Mary nodded. 'I think so,' she said.

'Then you have the beginning of the idea.'

'Acting?' Mary looked disappointed, but Lee shook his head at once. 'No,' he said, 'identification.'

Mary stared at him, her coffee growing cold in front of her. 'I remember reading,' Lee went on, 'that one of the greatest of all stage Hamlets once said he had identified to such an extent during the run of a particular production, he wasn't really acting at all. He had *become* the character, and if suddenly some of the others had started to alter the plot, he could have carried on indefinitely – knowing exactly how the mind of his own character would have reacted under any given circumstances.'

Mary nodded excitedly. 'Stanislavski, the man who invented that school of acting – where you seek total identity with the character you're portraying.'

'Yes! That's the idea! That's why there's no script.' He paused a few seconds, then went on: 'So that's how we do it. We build a modern courtroom in a television studio, brief the best attorneys possible for the prosecution and defence – attorneys who would base their cases not only on the gospel stories but on any other evidence concerning their credibility or otherwise.'

'And get professional actors and actresses to soak themselves in the various biblical characters?' Mary put in.

Lee nodded again. 'To the extent they would need to be called by either side.'

They looked at each other in silence. Mary's eyes were bright with excitement. 'You've really thought this out, haven't you?'

Lee smiled. 'I had plenty of time.'

'So I gathered.' Mary suddenly gave an involuntary shiver and looked around for a moment before turning back to him. 'Let's get out of here,' she said impulsively.

Lee looked surprised but agreed at once. 'Okay,' he said.

'Where?' They both stood up.

'Somewhere we can walk.'

'How about the park?'

'The park'll be fine.' Mary gave him a quick smile.

It was cold in the park but now the late afternoon sun had

broken through the clouds, striking gold against the office windows on the East Side, Lee and Mary walked slowly towards the bridge over the lake.

'You see now,' Lee was saying, 'although there's no script, there's no danger of it getting out of hand.'

Mary looked thoughtful. 'Because it's controlled like an ordinary court?'

'Exactly. By professional judge and counsel – in just the same way.'

'Yes, I do see,' she said.

They walked on a few more steps, reaching the bridge. Here Mary stopped and turned to face him, leaning against the railings and hugging her arms around herself to keep out the cold. She smiled up at him.

'Well?' Lee asked eventually. 'What do you think? You've been very quiet.'

Mary paused for a few seconds, then said: 'I think it's a really great idea, Lee. It's almost frightening!'

He nodded without smiling. 'I know what you mean.'

'But what about the powers that be?' Mary went on. 'Burgh and the others? When the implications of this sink in they'll be scared to death.'

Lee leaned against the railings beside her, looking across the water, and Mary turned in the same direction. 'That's what I figured,' he said, 'but when they hear who's going to play the part of Christ, they won't dare turn it down – assuming they listen that far.'

'I suppose you're going to say Olivier – or Burton. Somebody like that?'

Lee shook his head.

'Go on, then, surprise me.'

He paused for a few seconds, then said, 'John Burnard.'

In spite of herself, Mary's jaw gaped.

'Burnard!' she gasped. 'You must be mad!'

He turned to face her quickly. 'I don't think so.'

'But he's never out of the papers for one reason or another!'

'Exactly.'

'But not the way you want. He's always getting arrested. He's had six wives and about twenty paternity suits . . . '

'He also happens to be the greatest native born actor this country's ever produced,' Lee said, interrupting her.

'Maybe.' Mary paused for a few seconds, then went on: 'He's a legend in his own lifetime and all that sort of thing . . . but anyone less fitted to play the part of Christ, I can't imagine! I could tell you stories . . . '

'And I could tell you,' Lee interrupted again. 'Of course, how many of them are true . . . '

'Enough to make him *persona non grata* in most of South America.'

Lee shrugged. 'Well, I don't know,' he said. 'I think a lot of it's his own doing. He enjoys people thinking he's a bastard.'

Mary looked at him. 'The other explanation's more likely!' she said.

Lee paused a few seconds, then turned back to look out over the water. 'All the more surprising when the change takes place,' he said quietly.

'What change?' Mary looked at him, puzzled.

'When he gets into character.' He glanced at her. 'You don't believe he couldn't, do you?'

'No . . . ' Mary began doubtfully. 'But he'd never do it,' she went on after a moment. 'People have been trying to get him on television for years. He just won't.'

Lee straightened up. 'He'll do this,' he said simply.

'How do you know?'

There was a slight hesitation before Lee answered. 'Something I read about him when I was in the hospital.'

'You haven't got him already?'

Lee shook his head. 'No. But he'll be there when I need him.'

'How can you be sure?'

'I just am.'

Mary looked away for quite a while. When she turned back, Lee could see she had been doing some hard thinking.

'Then go to Hollywood and talk to him first!'

Lee stared at her. 'But what about your boss?'

'Don't worry. I'll keep him happy in the meantime.'

34

Lee went on looking at her, then suddenly he grinned and reached impulsively for her hand. Mary returned his smile.

He knew she was right. The only thing that had stopped him from going in the first place had been an acute lack of cash, but hearing her say it, he realized he was a fool to have gone to Burgh without Burnard's agreement already in his pocket.

Almost more important was that, after knowing him so short a time, Mary wanted him to win. It seemed a long time since anyone else had wanted that.

Chapter
3

Two persons, complete strangers to Lee and Mary but destined to play a vital role in the project they were discussing, were already in New York.

The first was Amos Brown, black middleweight champion, who at that particular moment was knocking the hell out of a sparring partner in Albert's Gymnasium on 105th Street. Once the crowd had loved Brown – but not any more. He used to do a clowning song-and-dance routine after he had won a fight, but now all they got was a clenched fist. The love had turned to hate, but still they came to watch, hoping one day to see somebody murder him. That was why, whenever Brown got into the ring these days, he was a killer.

His sparring partner tried to defend himself as best he could, but in spite of the protective headgear, Brown hammered him into the canvas. The other tried to get up but the champion floored him when he was still halfway. Again the young sparring partner tried to struggle up. Brown moved forward, but this time his trainer and two others leaped through the ropes and pulled him back.

'Enough! What are you trying to do – kill him?'

Brown's eyes seemed to come back from infinity, then he shook off the restraining hands and turned away in disgust.

'Get somebody who can stand up.'

His trainer called after him angrily: 'No one's going to get into a ring with you if you go on like this.'

Brown shrugged and ducked through the ropes. 'There's always someone who fancies their chances. You're paid to find 'em.'

The others watched him go, then looked at each other a moment before bending down to help his stricken opponent.

'I'm sorry, Mr Smith,' the boy said weakly. 'He came at me so hard, I wasn't ready.'

The trainer nodded sympathetically. 'That's all right, kid, don't worry about it.'

In the dressing room there was no one to help Brown; he had to use his teeth to unlace the gloves. He was fast losing the few old friends he had left. Even the Organization, which had seemed the best outlet for the hatred that had become the mainspring of his life, was beginning to wonder if the prestige his association undoubtedly brought was worth all the trouble his sullen lack of discipline caused.

Meanwhile, over on the other side of New York, in Brooklyn, lived a young novice nun. Her name was Anna Princi. On the surface she could hardly have been more different from Brown. God alone knew how close they really were.

At the moment that Brown was savagely tearing the laces off his gloves, Anna was on her way to answer a summons from the mother superior.

The mother superior's office was in a house a few hundred yards from the main part of the convent. Anna had to wait in the street until a nun, in answer to her ring, opened the gate that led into the front garden. She waited inside while the nun closed and bolted the gate, then was led along a pathway between two lawns and up some stone steps into the house itself.

The mother superior was at her desk, writing letters. Her face in repose was serene but when Anna knocked on the door and she looked up expectantly, her expression had much of the alertness and charm of her girlhood.

'Come in.'

The door opened and Anna entered. The mother superior smiled warmly. 'Ah, Anna. You got my message?'

'Yes, Mother.'

'You may close the door.'

The girl turned to do so and then turned back, looking apprehensive. The older woman glanced up at her, smiling. Anna was just eighteen and had a natural beauty that not even the unbecoming habit could totally hide.

'Come and sit down. There's nothing to worry about.' The

37

mother superior indicated a chair in front of the desk and Anna sat down quickly, holding herself stiffly.

'Relax, child. I'm not going to hurt you.'

Anna swallowed. 'I'm sorry,' she said. 'You don't usually send for anyone at this time of day unless something's wrong.'

The mother superior shook her head. 'That's when you notice,' she said. 'In point of fact I have people in and out of here all day, just like jack-in-the-boxes.' She frowned momentarily then looked up, eyes twinkling. 'Or should it be jacks-in-the-box?' Anna laughed in spite of herself, and the older woman smiled broadly. 'That's better. Now we can have a proper talk.'

She paused and the smile faded as she continued to look at Anna, although her expression remained kind. 'Anna,' she said, 'very shortly you are due to take your final vows.'

'Yes, Mother.'

'I needn't ask, although I must formally in due course, what your decision will be . . . because I'm sure you have made up your mind to serve God for the rest of your life.' She paused and Anna nodded without speaking.

'That being so,' the other went on, 'I want to tell you – and this will sound strange, perhaps even shocking, coming from me – that such a decision does not necessarily mean you should enter the Order. Nor does it, by itself, qualify you to do so.'

Anna did, indeed, look shocked. 'I don't understand,' she said tremulously.

The mother superior sighed. 'I knew this would be difficult.' She paused for a few moments, looking at the girl, then continued, 'Perhaps I shouldn't say this, but I dare not risk your misunderstanding. I have no doubt, from the point of view of the Order, that you are in many ways the most endearing and promising candidate we have. What I am not so sure of is that we are the most promising medium for you to channel all the love I know you feel in your heart.'

Anna shook her head slowly, looking bewildered. Then she said, 'I don't know what to say.'

The mother superior leaned forward across the desk, clasping her hands in front of her. 'What I'm trying to tell you, child, is that there is, or should be, a limit to the sacrifice those who are

38

called upon to be nuns are asked to make in giving up the world.' Her expression clouded. 'I'm not sure in my heart that yours might not be more, in the long run, than you could reasonably be asked to bear.' She spread her hands in front of her expressively. 'If that proved to be so, it would be a tragedy – and not only for you.'

'But . . .'

'Don't misunderstand,' the other went on, interrupting her. 'I'm not saying this is so – only expressing a doubt, which no amount of prayer has been able to resolve.'

Anna could contain herself no longer: 'But what have I done,' she burst out, 'or what haven't I done to put this doubt in your mind?'

'It's certainly not anything you have failed to do.'

'But please . . . how long have you felt like this?'

The mother superior hesitated. 'Almost from the beginning,' she said eventually. 'You came here at the earliest permissible age, shortly after your parents were killed. I suppose I had doubts then, but you needed love and that was easy to give. I thought the matter would resolve itself as the shock faded and your sense of security grew – that you would ask to leave; instead, your love for us and our way of life grew faster than the forces that would have pulled you away.'

Anna shook her head. 'What forces?' she asked, still bewildered. 'I just don't understand.'

The older woman looked at her, then asked gently, 'Don't you ever look in the mirror, child?'

Anna looked down at the hands clasped in front of her. 'Sometimes,' she admitted.

'Then don't you wonder what it would be like to have a husband and children of your own?'

Anna now looked up, her eyes burning. 'I don't allow myself to think such things.'

The mother superior took a deep breath and sat back in her chair. 'I watched you,' she said quietly, 'when we took those children to the beach last Sunday. When that little boy fell and hurt himself, you picked him up in your arms and held him.'

'I love children.'

The other nodded slowly. 'I know,' she said.

'But I love God, too,' Anna said passionately. 'I want to serve him here, and be like you and Sister Theresa and the others.'

The mother superior nodded understandingly, then she said gently, 'But none of us would hold a child in our arms after he had stopped crying, Anna . . . just for the joy of it.'

There was a long silence. Anna closed her eyes. When at last she spoke, it was almost in a whisper.

'It was that?'

'Not by itself . . . of course not. But I could give you a hundred other examples – small in themselves, yet all of which have warned me how hard it would be for you.'

Anna took a deep breath to try and force herself to be calm, but when she spoke her voice still shook. 'Am I to go?' she asked.

The older woman shook her head. 'I didn't say that.'

In an instant Anna's eyes widened. 'Then I can have another chance? Oh, Mother! I'll try so hard.' The other held up her hand and Anna's voice trailed away.

'It's not a question of you being given another chance, at least not by us, and certainly not by me.' She saw Anna's face fall and tears start into her eyes. 'I want you to give *yourself* a chance,' she went on more briskly, 'by going back into the world for, say, six months.'

'Six months!' Anna was aghast, but the mother superior continued. 'Then, if you still want to take your vows, I'll know my fears are groundless and nothing will stand in your way.'

'But six months!' Anna said desperately. 'Where would I go? How will I live?'

'Well, I've thought of that.' The mother superior rose from her desk and rested her hand for a moment on the girl's shoulder.

'You were training to be a dancer, weren't you, before you came here?'

Anna nodded.

'Then you can go and live with Sister Mary Pauline at our mission in Greenwich Village until you can find a job and a place of your own.' The mother superior smiled encouragingly. 'It should be a good base from which to look around,' she went on, 'and you can pay for your keep in the meantime by helping Sister in the evenings.'

After a while Anna looked up and tried to smile. 'It's such a long time since I practised,' she said.

'That doesn't matter. There's no hurry.' The older woman smiled down at her. 'Besides, you're young. You'll soon find your feet again.'

Anna hesitated for a few seconds, then stood up.

'Will I be able to visit you while I'm away?' she asked.

The other hesitated for a moment, then said gently, 'I think it best not. Not until the six months are up. Then, as I said, if you're still decided, there's no problem. And after that, even if you don't want to come back permanently, you can always visit us as often as you like.'

Anna nodded, then turned to the door. There she paused for a moment, saying, 'I can't imagine life away from here now.'

The older woman looked at her, fighting down an impulse to comfort her. At last, she shook her head slightly and said quietly, 'Yes, I know. That's what I've been trying to tell you.'

Chapter

4

The big jet took off at midday and, following the sun, landed five and a half hours later at Los Angeles early in the afternoon, local time.

Lee had no luggage except for the small bag he had carried aboard with him, so that it wasn't long before he found a phone booth in the terminal and started to dial the number Mary had given him before he left. She had come to see him off at Kennedy International and Lee knew she would do what was necessary, not only to stall Burgh until he got back but keep his interest going in the meantime. He knew also that he was lucky to have found such a strong ally. This was to say nothing of their other feelings for each other, not yet openly acknowledged, but recognized by both with secret pleasure and the happy certainty that wherever those feelings led was all right with the other.

The phone rang in the living room of John Burnard's house in Beverly Hills. After a while a beautiful girl, almost naked, came in from the terrace. She carried a drink in a tall, frosted glass in one hand and the top of her bikini in the other. She put the bikini top down on the table beside the instrument. Then she picked up the receiver and shook her dark, straight hair to one side before putting the phone to her ear.

'Hello?'

Lee spoke from the other end. 'May I speak to Mr Burnard, please?'

'I don't know – he's pretty busy right now.' The girl's voice had a childish quality.

'It'll take only a moment,' Lee persisted. 'I just want to know when it will be convenient to see him.'

'Who is this?' The girl frowned, then held the phone away from her ear to look at it as if expecting to see the speaker in the earpiece.

'My name is Lee Harrison.'

'What?' She started listening again.

'Lee Harrison,' Lee repeated. 'I'm a producer. I met Mr Burnard at a party in New York once, but he may not remember me.'

'He never remembers anybody.' Her voice took on a slight edge.

'Could I have a word, please?'

The girl shrugged. 'Just a minute, I'll ask him.' She put the phone down, then picked it up again.

'What's it about?'

'It's about a show I'm producing.'

'Oh . . . ' She put the receiver down on the table, picked up the top of her bikini and the drink, and went outside.

John Burnard was lying on a lounge beside the swimming pool, sunbathing, his eyes closed. His body, shining with oil, was finely proportioned and deeply tanned. His dark hair, now greying at the temples, was longish and curling at the back. The face in repose had a slightly flabby look, which was not apparent at other times. Enough of its original beauty remained to have conquered a second and third generation of women with as little effort as the first. Indeed, many who had known him for a long time would say that he was more compelling now than ever before – character more than compensating for the ravages of time. And then, of course, there was always the legend. There were so few superstars left. Perhaps Burnard was the greatest. In any event, it was impossible for most people to distinguish the man from everything that had been written about him during the past thirty years.

The girl stopped between his lounge and the vacant one she had obviously just been occupying. 'Why doesn't someone else answer the phone?' she complained. 'You pay enough people to look after you. Why does it always have to be me?'

She sank back on the vacant lounge and yawned. After a few seconds Burnard opened his eyes.

'Who was it, Jenny?'

Burnard's voice was perhaps his greatest asset. It had a natural quality God alone could bestow, but Burnard himself

43

had trained it over the years into a fine instrument, equally capable of projecting to the back of the largest theatre or intimately caressing every female in a cinema audience. Now it had a lazy purr that unconsciously emphasized the thinness of the voice of the girl beside him.

She said, 'I don't know. Some creep of a producer wants you to do something.'

'Oh.' Burnard closed his eyes again. 'Tell him to phone my agent.'

'You tell him. I'm tired.'

Burnard suddenly opened his eyes again and sat up, looking at her. As long as she kept her mouth shut, she was truly beautiful. He grinned.

'Worn you out, eh?'

'You'd wear anybody out.'

The star leaned forward and reached under the fragment of costume strung between the girl's legs. She opened her eyes and gasped as he leaned over her. 'Okay, baby, you rest. I want you to look good for the party.'

The girl nodded. 'I'll try,' she said breathlessly. Burnard kissed her lightly on the lips, then he leaned back, still looking at her, without removing his hand.

'What did you say his name was?'

'Harrison. Lee, I think.'

'Lee Harrison.'

'He said you met once in New York.'

Burnard frowned, then shook his head slightly and stood up. Even in his bare feet, he measured well over six feet. 'I don't remember,' he said.

'That's what I thought.'

'But the name seems familiar, somehow.' He paused, thinking, absent-mindedly groping for a cigarette among the glasses on a nearby table. He lit it as the girl asked, 'Hadn't you better go, if you're going?'

The star's eyes came back from focus infinity. He glanced down quickly and smiled. 'Sure.' He drew on a cigarette, then threw it into the pool, where it went out with a hiss, as he walked into the comparative darkness of the living room.

44

Burnard picked up the phone.

'Mr Harrison, what can I do for you?'

Lee had been looking at his watch and was half taken by surprise. 'Mr Burnard!' He straightened up, mentally pulling himself together at the same time. 'I've just flown in from New York hoping to talk with you about a television special I'm putting together for next Easter.'

'My secretary said you knew me.'

'Yes,' Lee said, 'we met once and . . . '.

'Then maybe you know I never appear on television,' Burnard interrupted him. 'I'm sorry you've had a wasted journey.'

Lee paused for a few seconds, 'I wrote to you about a month ago – when I was still in the hospital. It's to be called "Christ on Trial".'

Burnard frowned. 'Now I remember,' he said slowly. 'You didn't say too much about it.'

'Except that I want you to play the part of Jesus Christ.'

Burnard grinned: 'Yeah,' he said, 'I remember that. I thought you were some kind of nut!'

Lee also smiled. 'Maybe I am,' he admitted.

'My friends would die laughing, that's for sure.'

Lee paused a few more seconds before venturing, 'May I come and talk? It's like nothing you've ever done before in your life. Not just the part – but the whole idea.'

Burnard remained steadfast. 'I told you. I don't do television.'

Lee thought quickly. 'All right, Mr Burnard,' he said, 'I understand. But since I've come this far, wouldn't you be interested, at least, in hearing what you're turning down?'

The other scratched his head. 'Well, I guess there's no harm in that – as long as it's understood . . . '

'That you don't do television. Yes, sir. Can I come now?'

Burnard frowned. 'You mean this minute?'

'I knew that you'd read my letter.' Lee paused, then went on, 'And I'll tell you something else I've noticed, if you won't think it impertinent.'

Burnard glanced heavenward: 'Go right ahead!'

'Well, there's no one I've mentioned this to who hasn't wanted to hear the whole idea through to the end.'

'You're pretty confident.'

Again Lee hesitated before saying, 'Mr Burnard, if I had to sell my soul, I'd want a part in this.'

'You've certainly got me curious,' the star admitted.

'Thank you. Shall I come now?'

Now it was Burnard's turn to hesitate. He glanced briefly in the direction of the terrace. 'No,' he said, after a moment, 'not right now.'

'All right, when will it suit you?'

Burnard paused, thinking: 'I tell you what,' he said. 'I'm having a few friends in this evening. Come along then – any time you like.'

'Will we be able to talk?'

The star suppressed a grin. 'I expect we'll find a quiet moment,' he said lightly.

After the cab dropped him off, Lee had to pick his way through more than a hundred cars scattered around the house like confetti. His ears told him a party had been going on for some time. So many people had managed to get inside that he had to lean against the front door, when a servant managed to open it a crack, as if trying to board a subway train during the rush hour. Once inside, his hat and coat were whisked away and a drink was thrust into his hand. Lee downed this almost immediately, picked up another from a passing tray, and started to carry it towards the sound of a combo playing in another room at the end of a short corridor jammed with people ranging from those who looked like hippies to others who looked like stockbrokers. In any event, Lee noted, there seemed to be no difference in the behaviour of the two types – and that must say something.

As he pushed his way through, the sound of excited conversation on all sides almost engulfed the music, the source of which was his ultimate objective. As he brushed past one couple, the man turned away, leaving a tall blonde, with stringy hair and slightly prominent teeth, talking to herself. Seeing Lee she continued to address her remarks to him without batting an eyelid, without the slightest break in her flow of talk.

46

'. . . and I think it's so important to open one's pores to life, so to speak, don't you?'

Lee paused for a second to take a drink. 'Undoubtedly,' he said.

'I mean one's ears and eyes and so on,' the girl continued, 'just aren't enough, are they?'

Lee was going to say something but she suddenly looked up at the ceiling, ignoring him completely, and raising both arms above her head, poured the contents of her glass over a couple on the other side.

'I want it to flow through my body,' she exulted, 'so I can experience!'

Lee raised his eyebrows slightly and moved on through the doorway of what was obviously the main room of the house. The musicians were there, and on the opposite side of the room, Lee could now see his host, surrounded by a circle of apparently admiring friends, holding court. Lee pushed towards them, and as he got closer, began to hear what Burnard was saying.

'. . . if there's one thing I can't stand, it's a bad review. I just don't believe these guys who say it doesn't affect them . . . that everyone's entitled to an honest opinion . . . crap like that . . . '

Most of the circle seemed to be drawn from the more conventionally dressed members of the gathering – with the exception of a sensational looking girl, whom Lee took to be the 'secretary' he had spoken to earlier. She was wearing an openwork, evening cat-suit of thick, stranded wool, which wasn't so much see-through as see-past.

'I tell you,' Lee heard Burnard continue, resting a proprietary hand on the girl's shoulder, 'I've been in this business for more than thirty years, and if some jerk gives me a hard time just for laughs, it hurts . . . and anyone who says it doesn't is a goddamn liar!'

'Isn't that a sign of basic insecurity?' a young man in the group challenged. Burnard looked at him with distaste.

'Do you feel so secure?' he asked.

The other shrugged. 'Artistically,' he said, 'yes.'

Lee joined the circle unnoticed. 'And what the hell have you done, might I ask, to feel so confident about?' Burnard growled.

Knowing his reputation, Lee deduced he had probably drunk half as much again as anyone else, but it showed only in his temper.

The object of the attack opened his mouth, then shut it again, but the girl beside him said, 'Paul's just had his own exhibition in Chicago. The reviews were excellent.'

'Which just goes to show all the wind ain't down in the stockyards,' Burnard said, grinning suddenly and thickening his accent. Everyone but the artist and his girl friend laughed at this, and Lee saw the star gathering to kick his victim now that he was off balance. 'And I'll tell you another thing, kid . . . '

'Mr Burnard.' The star stopped in midsentence, looking around to see who had interrupted him. Those standing next to Lee edged away from him slightly, as if subconsciously avoiding a thunderbolt.

'And who might you be?' Burnard said, staring at him without interest.

Lee moved forward a step. 'Lee Harrison,' he said. 'You remember, I phoned you from the airport this afternoon.'

Burnard went on staring at him, then he nodded briefly. 'Oh yes,' he said. He paused for a few seconds, then went on more forcefully, 'Yes. Now, this is an interesting thing, ladies and gentlemen.' He glanced around to make sure everybody was listening. 'Mr Lee . . .'

'Harrison,' Lee put in.

'Mr Harrison is a producer who has flown all the way from New York to see me. What do you think about that?'

A small, bald, bespectacled man standing close to Burnard hurriedly straightened up and took the cigar out of his mouth, looking at Lee aggressively. 'Not much,' he said. 'Who is this guy? I never heard of him.'

Burnard smiled. 'Perhaps I should introduce you,' he said and turned back to Lee. 'This is Vince Story, my agent.'

Lee held out his hand, but the agent ignored it. 'This isn't another of your schemes, is it, John?' he asked plaintively. 'If so, I've got a right to know.'

'Not at all.' Burnard smiled broadly. 'Coming here was Mr Harrison's idea entirely.'

48

Story turned back to Lee. 'You should've come to me first,' he said.

Lee looked at him for a moment, then back to Burnard. Some agents you had to take notice of and some you didn't. With Lee's experience he could tell one from the other in a few seconds. 'I don't have too much time,' he said.

'That's no excuse,' the other began.

'But reasonable,' Burnard interrupted with an expansive gesture. He glanced wickedly at the others. 'Who talks to the jackal when the lion listens?' The others laughed at this, except Lee, who was thinking that this was all he needed to confirm his snap assessment.

'Besides,' Burnard went on, 'Mr Harrison has a rather unusual part to offer me.'

'I want to discuss it,' Lee said carefully.

'I see.' Burnard looked around again. 'Perhaps I shall have to give an audition!'

The agent moved closer to Lee. 'What part?' he demanded.

Lee hesitated.

'Go on,' Burnard told him. 'Don't be shy. Why don't you tell them?' Lee didn't answer immediately.

'Very well,' Burnard said with a shrug. 'I shall tell them myself.' He paused for a few seconds to make sure everyone was listening before announcing: 'Mr Harrison wants me to play none other than – Jesus Christ!'

There was a moment's stunned silence before those within earshot burst out laughing. Burnard turned to Lee. His mouth wore a smile but his eyes were serious: 'You see,' he said, 'what did I tell you?'

'Can we talk about it later?'

'What's wrong with here and now? I thought you were in a hurry.'

The girl beside Burnard looked at Lee sympathetically. 'John, why don't you leave the poor guy alone?'

'Why?' The star looked down at her, then at Lee. 'By the way, Mr Harrison, this is my secretary, Miss Jenny Simak. You spoke to her earlier.'

Lee inclined his head in acknowledgment as the girl turned

back to him. 'It's no good, Mr Harrison,' she said, 'you're wasting your time. I know him.'

Burnard pulled a cigarette from a glass on a nearby table and at once three hands appeared with outstretched lighters. 'Good advice, my dear,' he said, bending down to light his cigarette from the nearest flame without bothering to look up at the person holding it. 'But probably Mr Harrison knows that in his heart already.' He straightened up, drew on the cigarette, and exhaled slowly, looking at Lee. 'Nevertheless,' he went on, 'I'm prepared to bet he stays, swallowing any humiliation I may care to offer in the meantime, because whatever details he may have up his sleeve, I've already learned by making a couple of phone calls that no one's going to back him unless I agree to play ball. Am I right, Mr Harrison? May I call you Lee?'

Lee looked at him for a few seconds. He was sure the other was lying – probably for effect – but it was not impossible that he was telling the truth, and a wrong word at the present time could ruin everything. 'You called?' he said eventually. 'Who?'

'You're surprised?'

The girl saved him from having to answer by turning to Burnard: 'When did you call?' she demanded.

The star hesitated just a split second too long. 'While you were getting dressed,' he said. Lee breathed an inward sigh of relief, but obviously he was in a delicate position.

'You didn't think I'd let you come here without checking, did you?' Burnard was saying. 'So tell us all about it.'

Lee took another deep breath. To go on in these circumstances was obviously pointless, but he dared not anger the star nor risk humiliating him.

'Mr Burnard,' he said eventually, 'I can't explain a thing like this in this sort of atmosphere. I thought we could talk afterwards.'

The agent poked him in the ribs with the butt end of his cigar. 'Talk now if you know what's good for you,' he said unpleasantly.

Burnard looked at Lee, amused. 'Perhaps Lee has changed his mind about my doing the part,' he said. 'It's not difficult to see he's wondering if it's worth it.' He paused for a few moments, then continued, 'Well, do we get to hear about it or don't we?'

Lee glanced briefly around the waiting circle, then turned back. 'Mr Burnard,' he said quietly, 'in my opinion you are the only man who could not only do justice to the role I came here to discuss, but attract a wide enough audience to complement what I believe will be a production that will be remembered and talked about for a very long time, possibly forever.' He looked around again quickly and apologized. 'I'm sorry if that sounds extravagant.' He turned back to Burnard. 'I don't know whom you talked to – but you're right about one thing: without you, "Christ on Trial" probably will never see the light of day. However, you're wrong about me. I've swallowed plenty of the sort of thing you're handing out tonight, but I won't stay here and let you pour contempt on this idea. Not just because of what I feel about it but because if you are to do what I hope, you must come into it with the right attitude, and your chance of doing so will be destroyed by continuing this conversation.'

Story looked at him, amazed, then shut his mouth like a trap. 'Listen, you creep,' he began, 'who the hell . . . '

'Shut up!' Burnard snapped, his eyes never leaving Lee's face.

'I'll leave word with your servants as to where you can reach me in the morning,' Lee went on. 'I'm catching the four o'clock plane back to New York tomorrow afternoon. If I haven't heard from you by then, I shall tell the network the deal's off as soon as I get back.' He paused for a few more seconds, looking around, then nodded. 'Goodnight.'

Lee turned on his heel and disappeared into the throng. The group stared after him, wide-eyed.

'The nerve!' Story began indignantly. At once there was a chorus of agreement, but Burnard handed his drink to the girl, pushed his way through to the terrace door, and went outside.

Burnard moved swiftly across the garden to the front of the house. He caught Lee just coming out of the front door: 'Where do you think you're going?' he demanded.

Lee looked at him quickly to see if he was about to get a punch in the nose, then decided otherwise. 'Back to the hotel,' he answered.

He started to walk away from the house, but Burnard fell into step beside him. 'Have you got a car?'

Lee shook his head. 'No,' he admitted.

'You'll never get a cab around here. Come on.' He took Lee by the elbow and steered him to a big convertible with the roof down.

'Get in,' said Burnard, opening the passenger door.

Lee hesitated for a few seconds, eyebrows raised, then shrugged and did what he was told. Burnard slammed the door and walked around to the driver's side.

'You don't have to do this,' Lee began as the other sank into the seat beside him.

'Shut up!' Burnard peered at the controls.

'Is this your car?' Lee asked.

'I don't have a car right now.'

'Oh.'

The star glanced at him briefly and grinned slyly. 'Practically every time I went out I smashed it up,' he said, 'so I just gave up.'

'I see. What about your guests?'

Burnard shrugged. 'Let 'em drive their own cars.' He reached forward to press the starter and the engine roared into life.

'Where are we going?' Lee said, raising his voice.

The car leaped back, crashing into the one behind. Burnard glanced around, only mildly interested, and changed gear. 'What?' he said.

'I'd as soon walk.'

The engine roared again.

'Nonsense. We're going somewhere quiet, then you can tell me all about it.'

Lee opened his mouth to say something else, but suddenly the car jumped forward, tyres squealing. They seemed about to crash into a white Cadillac badly parked across the entrance to the driveway, but Burnard wrenched the steering wheel savagely to the right, flinging the convertible through the narrow gap and out to the road. Lee decided to concentrate on holding on to his seat and to keep any further remark until they arrived wherever they were going.

They ended up in a downtown bar where the star, obviously

well known, was enthusiastically welcomed. Once he had bought drinks all around, however, the two were left alone to talk.

Just after two o'clock Lee drove the convertible back to the hotel, leaving Burnard to find a cab. The other had insisted on this, and seeing how much liquor Burnard had consumed while they were talking, Lee had not argued. He still hadn't received an answer – that was promised for the following afternoon, when Lee would return the car.

Burnard stood on the edge of the sidewalk, watching the car disappear into the distance. He felt strange – in a way he would have found hard to describe. The cooler air outdoors and the feel of the hard edge of the curbstone under his foot were comforting. Undoubtedly the liquor had had a lot to do with it, but it wasn't only that. The talk of the last couple of hours had left him on a plane of excitement he hadn't experienced in a long time. Eventually he began to walk back, roughly in the right direction, unwilling to shatter the mood by returning to the party too soon.

As he strode past the unlighted windows of shops and offices, Burnard breathed deeply and felt his head begin to clear. But the feeling of excitement – of being on the verge of something really great – was not diminished in any way. On the contrary, the movement, ·the disciplining of muscles to walk even faster, brought his body more in tune with his thoughts, so that they in turn raced away into the possibilities suggested by Lee.

There were still quite a few people about, most of whom glanced curiously at the giant of a man who strode so purposefully through the night, looking neither to right nor left, as if setting out on some great adventure. A few recognized him, and everyone in his direct path stepped out of the way hurriedly to let him pass.

Burnard didn't even notice them or the effect his passage was producing, but when he reached a shabby warehouse district, where the shops were mainly liquor stores, a police car glided up beside him. The patrolman in the passenger seat wound down the window.

'I wouldn't hang around here, Mr Burnard, if I were you.' Burnard looked at him more closely and recognized one of the four policemen it had taken to bring him in – during his most recent brawl at Dino's.

Burnard was well known to the force. Despite this, he always made it up to them in some way after any trouble, no matter what the judge said, and he was a sure touch for any benefit that happened to be short of funds. And so, between rounds, as it were, he and the law were on reasonably good terms – except for a few officers down at headquarters with an eye on their careers, who disapproved of him on principle.

The policeman's expression was friendly now, and Burnard smiled back as he bent down to talk to him. 'Matter of fact, I was just going to look for a cab,' he admitted. The other shook his head and pulled a face. 'You won't find one around here,' he said. 'Do you want to go home?'

'Yeah.'

'Okay. That's no problem.' The cop jerked his head, indicating the back of the car. 'Get in.'

'Thanks.'

The driver swung the car round in an illegal U-turn and accelerated in the opposite direction.

When they reached Burnard's house, there were still enough cars around to make the policeman glance back in surprise.

'Unlike you to miss one of your own parties,' he remarked.

Burnard grinned as he stepped out of the police car. 'I decided I was a bad influence,' he cracked, and the other chuckled. 'What about coming in for a while?' But the cop shook his head.

'Sorry. Another time. We've got to get back.'

'Okay. I understand.'

The policeman smiled. 'Look after yourself.'

Burnard shrugged. 'With service like you fellas give, I should see to myself?'

'All right. Take it easy!'

'Thanks for the ride.'

'Our pleasure.'

The cop raised his hand in salute as the car moved down the hill. Burnard waved back, then turned to enter the house. Suddenly he felt tired and not at all in the mood for what he knew was probably waiting for him.

As he let himself in, there were only two couples draped around the hall and passageway leading to the main living room. One woman in her late forties was lying on her back on the floor with her eyes closed. Two younger men lay on either side, propped on their elbows, talking over her recumbent form in desultory fashion. Each fondled one of her massive breasts, which had burst their restraining bonds some time earlier, probably after their owner had passed out and one or the other of her present attendants had sabotaged some vital link in her super-structure.

Burnard could hear music still coming from the far room. Picking his way over the horizontal trio, he made his way through.

As he suspected, the party had progressed considerably since he had left. The air was thick with the smell of marijuana, and practically everyone in the room was partially undressed. Looking from the doorway at the by-no-means unfamiliar scene, it suddenly reminded him of a snake pit and he couldn't think why he had never seen it that way before. He was unable to see Jenny, and hoped she had gone to her room. She usually felt sick if she drank too much, but that saved a lot of trouble.

Over on the far side of the room Burnard recognized the wife of one of the studio managers, clad only in panties and bra, standing on a coffee table and swaying unsteadily to the music, her eyes closed. Her lower jaw was slack and she was obviously stoned out of her mind. That no one took any notice of her, despite the fact that she was a beautiful girl, was a sign the party was well into its third stage. He turned to the light switches beside the door and snapped them all on.

'Okay, everybody. Get dressed and go home. The party's over!'

There is nothing more certain to kill an atmosphere that has been slowly generated by soft lights and sweet music than the sudden termination of the music and a violent alteration in the lighting. The immediate effect was like lifting a stone covering an ants' nest, with the more mobile struggling into a modicum of cover while the less able writhed like white maggots. It took a good half hour to clear everyone out, resolve the arguments over

55

clothing, and persuade tearful wives and jealous husbands to postpone their fights until they got home.

Burnard opened the door of Jenny's room and was relieved to see her fast asleep on the bed – alone. He closed the door quietly, then went back to the task of shepherding everyone off the premises. He paid the musicians their usual fee plus a generous tip, but when everyone had apparently left, there was still one car in the driveway and it wasn't Jenny's. Hers, he knew, was in the garage.

Suddenly a thought clicked and he turned back into the house and flung open the door of the guest room.

Story, his agent, wheeled from the foot of the bed in shocked surprise, the strap still tightly grasped in his upraised hand. A naked girl lay on the bed, her wrists and ankles tied to the bedposts with cords from the robe and pyjamas that were always kept in the adjoining dressing room.

She had been gagged with a face cloth that had been rolled into the shape of a sausage. A Japanese vibrator had been thrust into her body, its muffled hum sounding like a bumble bee in a jam jar. Burnard grasped the entire scene in less than a second. The girl's eyes were wide and terrified and there were red marks where Story had whipped her stomach, thighs and breasts. He strode forward and snatched the belt out of the agent's hands.

'I told you what I'd do if ever I caught you doing this in my house again,' he said angrily.

Story's shocked face lapsed into a weak grin and he shrugged helplessly.

'I'm sorry, John. You know how it is. This dame heard I like to do things. She crashed the party just to see me.' His voice took on a whining quality as Burnard started to untie the cords.

'It wasn't my fault. Honest. I had no intention . . . '

Burnard removed the gag and started to massage the girl's wrists. She started to weep like a half-drowned kitten.

'A promise is a promise,' Story pleaded. 'You know me, I always try to keep a promise, but she came right up to me and started whispering until I couldn't stand it.'

In spite of his feelings at that moment, Burnard could believe him. Once the weakness of any man in a position to help ambitious actresses became known, there was no limit to the lengths some of them would go to for a favour.

He removed the rest of the cords, turned and pushed Story out of the room, pausing only to pick up the girl's clothes and throw them at her. 'Get dressed,' he ordered. Then he glanced at the thing that still buzzed between her legs.

'And take out that . . . object!'

The girl stopped crying and looked at him in a sudden, calculating way, before reaching down to obey him. Burnard slammed the door shut.

When he turned around, Story was straightening his tie and looking at him uncertainly.

'How did you get on with that jerk?' he asked, trying to sound normal.

Burnard closed his eyes for a second and ran his fingers wearily through his hair.

'We all thought you'd gone after him to punch him in the nose,' the other continued.

Burnard shook his head. 'Not now, Vince,' he said. 'I'm tired. Just go home. We'll talk later.'

Story nodded. 'Okay, John. Anything you say. But, uh . . . what about . . . what's-her-name in there?' He looked anxious again. 'I'd better wait . . . '

'I'll take her home. Just go.'

The other looked at him, wondering whether to risk a crack, but wisely thought better of it. Instead he jerked his head in the direction of the door.

'I'm, er . . . sorry, about that.'

'Vince!'

'Okay.' Story backed towards the front door. 'But I'd just like you to know I'm sorry. And it'll never happen again. Never. I promise.' Burnard stared at him without smiling.

'Goodnight, Vince.'

'Goodnight, John. Uh . . . it was a swell party. Thanks!'

He raised his hand, then opened the front door and left quickly, closing the door behind him.

Burnard heard the car leave just as the door behind him

57

opened and the girl came out. Seeing him standing there alone, she looked around quickly.

'Where's Mr Story?'

'Gone. I'm taking you home.'

The girl looked at him for a moment, then grinned broadly and moved towards him.

'Well! That's all right by me, Mr Burnard.'

She put her arms around his neck and thrust her tongue into his mouth. He stood quite still for a second, then bit – not too hard, but enough to make her yelp. She backed away from him, looking up into his face. Then she grinned again.

'Oh. I get it.' She nodded in the direction of the bedroom. 'You want some too . . . is that it?'

'Do you have a coat?' Burnard's voice was hard. The girl shook her head. 'Then let's go.' He turned and walked to the front door, then held it open for her. She stopped opposite him.

'There's no one at my place. I share an apartment with three other girls.'

'It doesn't matter.'

'All right.' The girl shrugged and walked out the door. She waited while he got Jenny's convertible out of the garage.

It took half an hour to reach her place. Burnard pulled into the curb, then reached across and opened the door on her side without killing the engine. They had driven most of the way in silence, apart from the directions she had given him.

For a few seconds she did not move, then she turned to face him, her voice brittle.

'So that's it, is it? No good-byes. No date. Your little chum has had his fun. Now you don't even want to know my name.'

Burnard looked at her. 'No one asked you to come,' he pointed out.

'I hurt all over.'

'I'm sorry.'

'Sorry doesn't help!'

Burnard sighed and reached into his inner pocket. 'Okay,' he said, 'I guess you have something coming to you.' He pulled out two fifties and held them out. The girl looked at him, then snatched them angrily and got out, slamming the door hard.

'I've a good mind to call the cops and show them what that guy did to me.'

Burnard looked back at her without blinking. 'Don't,' he said quietly. 'And don't phone Mr Story . . . or my office, for that matter, for whatever reason.'

'I could put the screws on him after this if I wanted to. Don't tell me what to do.'

'Before you do anything, just think about why I should bring you back myself, not just call a cab.'

'Why? Because you didn't want your little friend to get into trouble!'

Burnard smiled for the first time, but his eyes were ice. 'On the contrary,' he said. 'I wanted to know where some friends of mine could reach you in a hurry . . . if anything happened.' The girl looked at him, then backed away. She seemed frightened.

'What do you mean?' she demanded. 'Are you threatening me?'

'Not at all.' Burnard shook his head slowly. 'But if I read about you in the papers in the near future, make sure it's in the entertainment pages, not the obituaries.'

The girl's jaw sagged; as he drove off, her mouth was still open.

After he turned the corner Burnard enjoyed a few seconds of amusement. He judged that she was too young to have recognized the scene she had just unwittingly participated in, a scene from a film that was so rotten, apart from his own performance as a cheap hood, that it hadn't even been shown on television. He sighed as he remembered how long it had taken him to break away from the type. Then the smile faded as he rejoined the freeway and remembered why it had been necessary to drive her home. One of these days he was going to break with Vince. The agent represented a part of him he had to leave behind sometime, before it was too late.

Burnard parked the car, then let himself back into the house. He opened Jenny's door quietly and found she had changed into a nightdress and was just getting back into bed, having been sick in the bathroom. He came and sat on the edge of the bed, looking down at her. Her face was white and her hair was damp with perspiration.

59

'I must look dreadful,' she croaked.

He smiled gently and put a cool hand on her forehead, shaking his head slightly.

'Pretty dreadful,' he agreed.

Jenny closed her eyes and pressed his hand more firmly against her forehead with her own.

'Feel pretty bad?' he asked tenderly. 'You shouldn't drink so much. You know it upsets you.'

'I know. Never again!'

'You always say that.'

Jenny opened her eyes to look up at him.

'I want to be what you want me to be,' she whispered. Burnard frowned, then he shook his head again.

'I just want you to be yourself.'

Jenny continued to stare at him, then, suddenly, her eyes welled with tears, and she turned her face into the pillow. 'I'm so sorry,' she croaked. 'I don't blame you, going off with other people when I'm so hopeless!'

'You're not hopeless at all!' He looked down at her, troubled in a way he couldn't explain.

'Yes I am.' Jenny twisted herself around and pulled a hand-kerchief from under the pillow. She blew her nose, then said: 'If I hadn't passed out, you wouldn't have taken that girl home.'

'How do you know about that?'

'I heard you getting my car out of the garage. You wouldn't have done it unless you planned to make love to her.'

Burnard smiled in spite of himself.

'Very smart! And how long ago was that, Watson?'

'Don't make fun of me.'

'I'm not making fun of you, Jenny, but you've got it all wrong.'

She looked at him for a moment. 'Well, I don't know exactly. I went back to sleep again after it woke me up.'

Burnard glanced at his watch.

'If you want to know, I was gone exactly one hour and three minutes. Which is half an hour each way and three minutes to frighten some girl half to death so she wouldn't call the cops and show them Vince's signature.'

'Oh, no. Not that again!' Then he saw doubt begin to gather in her eyes once more.

'Who did you spend the evening with after you got back?'

'No one. The cops didn't bring me home till after two.'

'Oh, my God, John!'

'It's all right.' He held up his hand to calm her. 'No trouble. They just gave me a lift. I let Lee have the car.'

'Lee?'

'You know, the guy who suddenly appeared in our midst like the spectre at the feast.'

'Oh, that creep!' He saw her relax.

'As a matter of fact, he's quite a guy!'

Jenny closed her eyes and winced as a skewer of pain plunged through her temples. Burnard put his hand on her forehead again.

'Still pretty bad?'

She nodded without opening her eyes. 'My stomach's okay now that I threw up. But my head!'

'All right. Just try to relax and I'll massage it for you until you go to sleep.'

The girl nodded. Gently but firmly he kneaded her temples and forehead. Then he made her lie on her side while he massaged the back of her neck.

Just before falling asleep, Jenny mumbled, 'John?'

'Yes, Jenny?'

There was a long pause. He thought she had gone to sleep, but she murmured, 'I do . . . love you.'

He didn't answer, and a moment or two later she was asleep.

He stopped slowly, so that the break in rhythm wouldn't wake her. Then he stood up and paused for a moment, looking down at her. She was twenty-three, young enough to be his daughter. At the moment she looked about fifteen! But she loved him – he knew that was true. And whether he loved her or not, he was responsible for her. He paused a moment longer, then turned off the bedside lamp and left the room, closing the door behind him quietly.

Burnard opened the french windows and walked out on to the balcony along the side of the house, from which he could see the ocean and the lights of the city stretching away into the

61

distance. He was responsible for Jenny in a special sort of way. She had said she wanted to be the way he wanted her. That was a terrible responsibility and one he couldn't avoid, without running away from it altogether. And even then the escape was problematical.

What sort of person did she think he wanted her to become? Whether he liked it or not, she was trying to mould herself in his image. Which came back to the question: What sort of a person had he himself become . . . and was that really what he wanted to be?

Usually, self-questioning plunged him into depression – a depression he ordinarily dispelled with a stiff drink – but now, the memory of his talk with Lee fresh in his mind, he found himself strangely detached from the questions, perhaps because he felt, for the first time in many long years, that maybe there was a chance after all.

This was nonsense! Burnard pulled himself up sharply. He was getting everything out of proportion.

That Harrison! He certainly knew how to sell a bill of goods! But Burnard wasn't making up his mind yet.

He glanced at his watch. It was a little after four. Five hours before the shops opened. He had some checking to do before he faced Lee again. So far it had all been on one side.

Burnard took a shower, lay down naked on the top of his bed, and telling himself to wake up in four hours, began to drift into sleep.

He supposed everyone was responsible for everyone else, really. That's why he had felt bound to take the girl home and to try to protect his agent at the same time, although, in truth, he didn't at all care about either of them.

Love just sharpened the feeling of responsibility. Maybe that's why all the world's great religions set such store on everyone loving everyone else.

But, in order to love everyone, you'd have to be God himself, wouldn't you?

Lee drove the car up the drive, parked and got out. He rang the bell. After an interval the door was opened slowly by Jenny, who was wearing a beach robe and dark glasses. She winced at the light, but when she saw Lee, stood back and beckoned him in.

He waited in the entryway while she closed the door; then she directed him along the corridor to the living room.

'He's expecting you.'

'After you,' Lee said, politely.

'I'm going to lie down. I don't feel well.'

'I'm sorry.'

'He's been up since eight o'clock.'

'That didn't give much time for sleep,' Lee admitted.

'You can say that again. He went out to buy books.'

Lee's interest quickened, but he said, 'I'm sorry if it disturbed you.'

'Drop dead!' Jenny turned and went into another room, closing the door behind her. He was left standing alone in the hallway. After hesitating for a few seconds, he walked along the corridor and knocked on a half-open door. It was opened almost immediately by a servant on his way out, carrying a tray of lunch things.

'Mr Burnard?' Lee asked.

The servant nodded and smiled, indicating that Lee should go in, and stood aside to let him pass.

The curtains were drawn over the windows. After the glare outdoors, the room seemed almost in darkness except for the area where Burnard sat in a large armchair under a reading lamp. He glanced up briefly as Lee entered the room and smiled.

'Come in, Lee.'

'Good afternoon.'

'Is it?'

Lee moved closer and saw that Burnard, wearing a pair of thick, horn-rimmed glasses, held a book in his lap. He continued to read for a few seconds. More books were piled on a small table beside the chair.

Burnard suddenly shut the book and took off his glasses, looking up at Lee. 'You're in good time,' he said. 'Sit down.'

'Thanks.' Lee sat in a chair opposite. The other looked at him for a moment then glanced at the pile of books, waving his glasses at them. 'As you can see, I've been doing some homework.'

Lee smiled. 'Looks like it,' he answered.

'I'm ashamed to say we didn't have a Bible in the house,' Burnard continued, 'so while I was at it, I bought a couple of new translations.'

Lee nodded. 'I had one in the hospital.'

'Yes, I remembered.' Burnard paused for a few seconds. 'I agree with you,' he went on eventually, 'they certainly bring everything to life in a way I would not have dreamt possible.' He put the glasses down on the table, then picked up and glanced at two more books. 'I also got a couple of the others you mentioned.' He held them out for Lee to inspect, then put them back on the table. Both men looked at each other searchingly.

'Well?' Lee said, after a while.

Burnard took a breath and changed his position so that his right leg hung over the side of the chair. 'You've explained how important this is to you,' he began. 'You didn't say why, but that's your privilege. Just as it's mine to make a few guesses.' He grinned, then went on, 'As you know, I've never done this sort of thing before.'

'I don't think anyone has.'

The other nodded slowly. 'Which is certainly an attraction,' he agreed. 'So . . . I don't like television, but I guess we should all try everything once. And that being so, if I'm to meet the monster face to face, I could scarcely arm myself with a better role!'

Lee leaned forward in his chair intently. 'You'll do it?' he asked. But Burnard held up his hand.

'I haven't said so.' He paused for what seemed an eternity, but Lee forced himself to wait without saying anything.

'The only thing stopping me,' Burnard began again, 'and why the hell I should confess this to you I don't know, except that if you're prepared to trust me with this, I guess I'd better return the compliment.' He shrugged. 'Anyway, since this morning considerable doubts have been forming in my mind about my ability to do it the way you want.' He grinned suddenly. 'And it's been a long time since I bothered about a producer's conception of a part I was considering!'

Lee smiled, acknowledging the joke, then began, 'I'm . . . '

'Don't say flattered,' Burnard interrupted, but Lee shook his head.

'I wasn't going to,' he said. 'I was trying to think of a word that combined gratitude with relief . . . and happiness. Now I *know* you'll do it.'

The other looked at him curiously. 'Because I've fallen under the spell?'

'If you like.'

'Then first you should hear this: My real name is not the one you know me by.' Burnard changed position again and sat forward in the chair, thoughtfully pulling a cigarette from a case on the table and lighting it with the built-in lighter. 'That was given me by the casting people in the first picture company that gave me a job.' Lee nodded and Burnard glanced at him. 'Don't ask my real name,' he went on, 'it's none of your goddamn business. But I think you *should* know I'm not a Christian.' He exhaled smoke, watching Lee carefully.

Lee paused for a few seconds. 'I never thought about it,' he admitted. 'What are you, Jewish?'

Burnard shrugged. 'I'm not anything,' he said, 'but I was brought up as a Jew. It's certainly the only religion I have any experience of at all.'

'That's why you have doubts?'

Burnard shrugged slightly. 'It's not illogical,' he said.

Lee felt an almost unbearable excitement beginning, as the implication of what he had just been told sank in. Suddenly he leaned forward in his chair. 'But it is,' he said. 'When you think about it, Christ wasn't a Christian either!' Burnard looked at him for a moment, then flung back his head and roared with laughter. Lee watched him, smiling, but he went on even more forcefully. 'He wasn't. He was a Jew!'

Burnard stopped laughing.

'After all, what is a Christian? Someone who was brought up in the Christian faith. But that was not true of Christ. Allowing for differences in time, he was brought up just like you, according to the Mosaic law. His whole idea was to *fulfil* the law, not to destroy it.'

Unable to restrain himself, Lee got up and started to pace about the room. 'I never thought about it before,' he said, 'but it's so obvious! What better starting point could there be than that you both had the same religion?'

Burnard continued to look at him without answering.

'Now, take it from there,' Lee went on. 'Read and absorb the story. What convinced Jesus that he was the Messiah? What must he have felt when the full realization took possession of him? What was he to do to fulfil his destiny? And how did he turn, in the end, to face death?' As he spoke, Lee stopped in front of Burnard's chair, looking down at him. 'This is what you've got to imagine,' he said, 'until it becomes second nature – not anything about the religion that grew up later. Identify with the man – and justify only the faith he had in himself. Everything else follows.'

Chapter

5

With Burnard agreeing to the leading role, the network, as Mary had predicted, did not have the nerve to turn the programme down. Having stuck their necks out, they decided to run 'Christ on Trial' over three evenings, from Good Friday to Easter Sunday.

The publicity machine started to roll with the signing of the star. Three weeks after Lee returned to New York, a large, chauffeur-driven limousine drew up in Rockefeller Plaza with Burnard riding in the back. A prearranged group of pressmen with several television cameras waited at the entrance of the main building. These had been joined by a crowd of onlookers who surged forward as soon as the star was recognized, so that Burgh and two of the network directors had to fight their way through to welcome him.

A conference room on the third floor had been set up for the signing. There was a long table with contracts already laid out, a battery of microphones for speeches, and still more television cameras. Thirty or forty reporters packed the room – a tribute to Burgh's staff-work – together with a reception committee of network executives and potential sponsors. The dozens of others present may or may not have had any business there other than the free drinks provided by the bar that had been set up in one corner of the room.

To Lee it seemed more like the finale of a summit conference, but he supposed the network had a right to protect its interests. He watched the president of the network shake hands with the star and saw him introduced to the sponsors – at least, he hoped that's what they would be. Burgh had been right – the sponsors were not too happy with the idea of a scriptless show, but Lee was reasonably confident they would come through. He stood next to Mary, trying to keep her from being trampled to death, and amused himself with the thought that although it was his idea, and so far he had done most of the work, he was probably the last person anyone was interested in at the present time. Not that he had any illusions. If you wanted to get anywhere in this business, you had to play it the only way there was. He was going to be in charge of production – that was all he really cared about. And in the end he had Burnard to thank for that too. When it came to it, Burgh had wanted to be the producer himself. Lee supposed they would have let him in somewhere, but the star had said he would work with Lee or not at all. Then Lee had insisted that Mary be his assistant – so it all worked out.

Once the ballyhoo was over, Burnard went back to California to start immersing himself in the role of Christ, and the production team really got down to work. Burgh contented himself with launching the long-term campaign that would bring public interest to a climax just before the programmes went out. For Lee, the first order of business was to persuade two attorneys, who would have to be outstanding in their profession, to lead the prosecution and defence.

Ever since the idea for 'Christ on Trial' had crystallized, one man alone had stood out in Lee's mind for the role of prosecutor: Maxwell Baal, well-known television commentator on legal matters and Yale law professor. During his long convalescence, Lee had watched Baal many times. He saw a man with a mind like a rapier. Moreover, Lee liked the fact that Baal was a declared agnostic. If he could be persuaded to take the part, Lee was sure he'd do a superb job. For defence counsel, however, he had no idea at all.

At this point Mary did some research and came up with the name of another well-known lawyer, Arthur Lang – a recent runner-up for the governorship of New Hampshire.

Lang was a big man, in every sense, whose outwardly lazy manner disguised one of the ablest brains in the profession. His easy-going façade had led many an accomplished liar, lulled into a sense of false security to betray himself on the witness stand. In addition, Mary ascertained that Lang was a lay preacher of reportedly deep conviction. Lee felt that this was essential in the circumstances and that Lang would be the perfect match for Baal, whose only real advantage would appear to be his sharper sense of humour. Counterbalancing this would be Lang's wider experience and possibly deeper compassion.

Lang was frequently in New York, where he maintained an office, and Lee had no difficulty in getting to see him. When he outlined the project, Lang was full of enthusiasm and readily agreed to accept the part. On the contrary, Baal was non-committal. He had no plans to visit New York in the near future. Just as Lee was beginning to think all was lost, the attorney suddenly invited Mary and him to his home in Weston, Connecticut, suggesting the following Thursday and adding that he and his family would be happy to have them stay overnight.

Mary didn't say anything immediately when Lee told her he had accepted the invitation on her behalf, and he realized at once that, in his anxiety to persuade the attorney, he had acted without thinking. There was an obvious implication in their taking such a trip together. No matter how small, it implied a development in their relationship neither of them had discussed. But after hesitating for a few seconds, Mary said it would be all right. Lee knew the step had been taken, almost before either of them knew it.

Perhaps that was the best way. To think about these things – to plan, sometimes spoiled them in advance. Afterwards, dwelling on what had happened, Lee realized that, natural as the idea of them taking a trip together had seemed once it was accepted, if Mary had refused – which she was perfectly entitled to do – it would have been much more significant and would probably have killed their relationship.

They left New York about four o'clock the following Thursday afternoon, just as it was starting to get dark but before the rush hour traffic made driving difficult. The sky was overcast, and before they had even joined the turnpike, it began to sleet. A radio announcer, interrupting a programme of music, informed them that heavy snow was forecast and that the level of pollution in the air over Manhattan had reached an unacceptable level.

Lee chuckled as he switched to another station. 'I guess that means we should all hold our breath for twenty-four hours!'

But the forecast was accurate enough, and before another

69

half hour had elapsed he was having to slow down because the wipers couldn't cope.

Mary looked at him a little anxiously but knew better than to suggest that they might have difficulty once they turned off the main highway. Lee turned the windshield heater up full blast, and that helped; but once they left the turnpike near Bridgeport, they had trouble finding the right road.

By six o'clock they reached Westport, then took a wrong turn which led them down to the beach instead of inland. Lee cursed and reversed the car too quickly, backing it into a hollow. From then onwards, no matter what, the car stuck fast.

Mary took the wheel and Lee pushed, but that was no better and finally Lee opened the door and collapsed on to the seat, gasping for breath.

Mary kept the engine running for the sake of the heater and wisely said nothing while he recovered. It was now six-thirty – past the time they were due to arrive. It was snowing more heavily than ever, and their chances of getting out seemed practically nil.

Lee turned to Mary, anguish written all over his face. She looked back at him, speechless, then away for a few seconds. Finally she turned to him and said in a voice that shook slightly: 'We could always invite them to meet us here!'

They looked at each other in silence a moment longer, then both of them exploded with laughter and hung on to each other until they recovered.

Lee wiped his eyes with the back of his hand, still grinning. 'Actually, it's not a bad idea at that!' he admitted. He wiped the steam from the inside of the side window and tried to peer through it. 'Most of these picnic places have a phone,' he said eventually. 'We could at least let them know what's happened.'

'Always supposing you can find it.'

'And it's still working,' Lee added. 'But . . . ah!' He reached forward into the glove compartment and produced a flashlight. 'What have we here? Miracle of miracles! It actually works!'

He demonstrated, flashing the light into Mary's face, making her blink.

70

'Okay,' she said after a moment. 'But don't go out of sight of the car. I don't want to spend the night here by myself.'

Lee grinned. 'You never know, you might be molested by a passing Eskimo!'

'Ha, ha. Very funny!' Mary put her tongue out. 'You know what I mean!'

'All right. Don't worry.' He put his hand on the door handle. 'If I don't have any luck pretty soon, I'll be back.'

'Take care.' Mary suddenly leaned across and kissed him, the smile gone from her face.

Lee looked at her. 'Hey! I think you really are worried about me.'

She pulled another face. 'This isn't exactly what I had in mind when I accepted your kind invitation!'

They looked into each other's eyes, then Lee grinned reassuringly and got out, slamming the door hurriedly behind him.

From then on, things began to improve. Lee found a row of telephones behind some buildings he guessed acted as the centre of an open-air restaurant in the summer. At last he found a phone that had been overlooked by vandals.

Baal's wife told Lee her husband hadn't made it back from New Haven himself yet. When Lee explained their predicament, she told him that one of the boys would come for them in the Land-Rover.

The vehicle arrived within twenty minutes, driven by an enormous young man dressed in lumberjack fashion. This proved to be Fred, the oldest son, who was following in his father's footsteps at Yale. With the aid of the vehicle's four-wheel drive and a piece of rope, the car was soon out of the hollow and back on the main road, headed in the right direction.

They drove on through Weston, following Fred, who very considerately went slowly. After another mile, the Land-Rover pulled over to the side of the road and Fred jumped out and ran back to them. Lee wound down the window.

'You'll have to leave your car at the bottom of Hill Drive, Mr Harrison,' the boy told him. 'I see that my father's home now, so you can park your car beside his.'

'Oh . . . fine,' Lee said.

'Don't worry about blocking the entrance. There's only our house up there, beside Miss Galliard's, and she doesn't have a car.'

'All right.'

Lee waited for the boy to get back into the Land-Rover, then followed him into the driveway entrance, stopping beside another car parked just inside.

Fred halted the Land-Rover again, then came dashing back to open Mary's door. She smiled her thanks as she got out, taking the arm he proffered to help her into the waiting vehicle. Meanwhile Lee killed the engine and reached into the back seat for their overnight bags.

He was amazed at the ease with which the Land-Rover climbed the two hundred or so yards to the house through snow already lying quite thick. Before another minute had elapsed, they were inside being greeted by Baal, his wife and the whole family (another boy of seventeen, a girl about a year younger, a boy and girl about eleven and twelve respectively, and Tilly, a huge black labrador) with a warmth that soon had them feeling as if they'd returned to old friends after a long absence.

Whatever Lee had been expecting from their host proved to be totally wrong, demonstrating, not for the first time, what a false impression a public image can convey of the man behind it. More often than not, in Lee's experience, the reality was a disappointment; but the warmth and power of Baal's personality captured both Mary and him at once and gave them that rare but sure feeling of being in the presence of someone they would never forget as long as they lived, even if they never met again.

Ellen Baal was a pretty woman who stood at least half a head taller than her husband. It was obviously from her that the children took their stature – both older boys towering over their father – but it was equally certain that he dominated them all without effort and that they loved him for it.

The house itself, which Ellen Baal told them later was pre-Revolutionary, was without a view because of the surrounding trees. The following morning she took them outdoors to show them the square central chimney with the characteristic roof – smoke coming from its sides. But she admitted regretfully that apart from the stack and chimney pot, little remained of the original house; it had rotted away when it had stood empty for almost twenty years between the wars.

Lee and Mary had tactfully been given adjoining rooms at the top of the house. The door between had been left locked but with the key on Mary's side so that she could adjust their sleeping arrangements to suit their relationship. Nothing was said, but it was typical of the sensitivity they were soon to realize was the hallmark of this family – a sensitivity that stemmed, of course, from the parents. They were, as Lee discovered when he had known them a little longer, the most genuinely happily married couple he had ever met. What particularly impressed him was that they seemed completely oblivious of their good fortune – unlike others of his acquaintance who never ceased to parade their devotion in public, which always made him suspect that in private they hated each other's guts!

They were joined at dinner by the Miss Galliard whom Fred had referred to earlier as having the only other house on the hill. She arrived just as they were about to sit down, wearing a man's shapeless felt hat, huge rubber boots, and a heavy raincoat over a thick tweed jacket which, she told Mary and Ellen with some pride as they helped her remove some of her outer garments in the hallway, she had bought in the Scottish Highlands during an appearance with her company at the festival in Edinburgh some years ago.

Lee could tell from Mary's expression, although she smiled politely, that this didn't really mean very much, but as he looked at the face of the woman now emerging – a surprisingly thin butterfly – from the cocoon of assorted clothing, he recognized one of the all-time greats of the American legitimate theatre. Lee thought she must be seventy-five by now, if she was a day, and remembered that Eva Galliard had once ranked with the Barrymores and had been in some ways even more remarkable in that she had been the first woman ever to have combined the role of international actress with those of director *and* producer.

She smiled at him as they were introduced. Her face in close-up proved to be interlaced by dozens of fine lines, like a piece of valuable porcelain, but her grip was as firm as a man's.

73

'I'm delighted to meet you, Mr Harrison,' she said, continuing to hold his hand after they had finished the initial greeting. 'When I heard the purpose of your visit, I bullied Maxwell into inviting me to dinner. I do so want to hear more about your proposed programme.'

Lee smiled. 'I'm very flattered. Of course, I recognized you at once.'

'Ah!' The old woman nodded briefly. 'Not many people do nowadays.'

'I'm sorry . . . ' Mary began uncertainly, but Miss Galliard let go of Lee's hand and put a hand on her arm.

'Don't be,' she said, smiling. 'You're far too young to remember an old stager like me.' Then she looked at Baal who was standing, smiling at both of them, and said impatiently, 'Come along, Maxwell. Let's go and sit down. I shan't wait to hear more from Mr Harrison.'

'Dinner's ready,' Ellen said. 'Go right on in.'

Baal led the way into the dining room where a long, Swedish style, refectory table stretched down the centre of the room, offering seating for at least a dozen. Mary followed Ellen into the kitchen to offer her services, and Miss Galliard took Lee's arm so that they went in together.

The meal consisted of an Indonesian dish. Baal explained that his wife's parents were Dutch and that she had been born and brought up in Java where the family had lived until their escape from the Japanese in 1941. After a short period in Australia, they had come to the United States and had eventually settled in San Francisco. (This explained the very slight accent Lee had already noticed whenever Ellen pronounced anything with a long 'a.') A huge bank of rice formed the centrepiece, and they were all given plates and told to help themselves from the dozens of bowls of spiced meats and vegetables that surrounded the rice and from the smaller plates of dried fruit and chutneys that were distributed around the table.

'The trick is not to take too much of any one thing until you know whether you like it or not,' Baal explained. 'Some things are hotter than others!'

The food was delicious, and with Ellen's encouragement,

74

Lee and Mary came back several times for more of the things they particularly liked. Baal and the children needed no such encouragement, nor did Miss Galliard, who amazed Mary with the prodigious quantities her seemingly frail body could hold.

There was comparatively little talk during the first stage of the meal, but eventually the four younger children left the table. Ellen went into the kitchen to fetch coffee and Baal sat back in his chair and lit cigarettes for himself and the two women flanking him. Then he looked across the table at Lee and smiled.

'Well, Mr Harrison. You told me a little of your idea over the telephone. As I understand it, you want me to participate as prosecutor in a mock trial of Jesus Christ for television. Now you tell me you've persuaded Arthur Lang to act for the defence so there must be more in it than I thought. But I must say my first impression was that either it was going to be so deep I would be out of my depth – as you know, I've never been a religious man – or it might cheapen a faith which I don't happen to hold myself, but which undeniably makes bearable the otherwise intolerable lives of many.'

Lee saw there was nothing for it but to go right back to the beginning.

The attorney neither interrupted nor commented in any way while Lee was talking. He sat listening with obvious intensity, but Lee became aware that he was not acquitting himself well. He had explained the project more times than he could remember, but people had always interrupted to ask questions or to challenge something he had said. Without any sort of resistance, Lee felt he was stumbling in the dark. Yet, he had to find the right words because now more than ever he was convinced that Baal was the man he needed.

When he finished, the other let the silence hang for a while, then he asked quietly, in a voice totally devoid of hostility, 'Why is this so important to you?'

Lee knew exactly what was meant, but before he had a chance to answer, Ellen came back with a tray and put steaming cups of coffee in front of them.

Miss Galliard drew on her cigarette and remarked, 'To me, the answer has always lain in the hidden years. You know, that period between the time Jesus is last heard of as a boy of twelve, and the beginning of his ministry. Did you ever wonder why he waited that long?' She looked around briefly, before continuing. 'Was it all preparation? If so, why were we never told about it? Or could it have been that he was not sure himself?'

Lee said, 'You mean, whether he had a unique relationship with God or not?'

'If you like.'

Lee nodded, then he turned back to Baal. 'You're right,' he said. 'This does mean much more to me than simply producing a good programme – even one that will re-establish my reputation in the profession.' He glanced around. 'In case anyone didn't know, I've been away!'

Baal nodded. 'Oh, yes,' he said, 'we knew. Or rather, Eva and I knew.'

Ellen looked at him with a hint of reproach. 'You never told me,' she accused.

Her husband shrugged. 'I just thought it was something Lee would rather not talk about; at least, not tonight.' He smiled at Lee. 'If my wife had known you'd only just come out of the hospital, we should have talked about nothing else all evening!'

'I wouldn't.' Ellen made a face at him, but Lee realized that some unspoken message had passed between them, and that their concern for him, a complete stranger, was somehow involved.

He followed her example by not pursuing the matter. Instead, he looked directly at Baal and said, 'I thought for a while, maybe it would be a new sort of target to aim at. If you like, a crown to set on whatever I've managed to achieve so far. But the more I tried to explain it to other people, the more I realized how deeply I was concerned, not just as a producer, but as a human being.'

'Then aren't you taking a hell of a risk?' Baal asked gently. 'It's one thing to lay your reputation on the line with a project like this. But it seems to me you'll be putting up your whole philosophy – everything that makes you what you are.'

Lee thought for a moment. 'Not long ago, I might have agreed with you. If we're shouting into an empty cave when we pray, if no one really gives a damn what happens to us, if the death of a human being is no more than the falling of a leaf in

76

the autumn, the end of all endeavour, all imagination and, most terrible of all, love, then perhaps it would be better to go on living in a fool's paradise or maybe I should say, in total inconsequence, made tolerable by ignorance. But my answer would be that our journey towards a verdict will be something apart from the verdict itself.'

Lee became aware that the younger children had re-entered the room, and he turned to greet them with a smile.

'Hi!'

'Sit down,' their father said quietly, and they obeyed immediately. Baal then turned back to Lee.

'Please go on,' he said. 'You were saying, I think, that the evidence will have a significance beyond the immediate verdict?'

Lee nodded. 'I think that what I'm groping towards is that I believe Jesus Christ, above all men, learned something about what I have been saying that went beyond the knowledge of any other man who ever lived.' He looked around before continuing and shrugged slightly. 'Perhaps there was nothing particularly unique in his teaching. Buddha, Mohammed, and above all, Moses and the Old Testament prophets taught the sacrifice of self to the common good and the disciplining of personal behaviour towards the highest imaginable ideal – called "God" by all of them. But only Jesus of Nazareth claimed affinity with that ideal, and called him "Father." '

Lee paused again, inviting comment, but the others remained silent, as if afraid to disturb his train of thought. Only Miss Galliard at the opposite end of the table nodded slowly. Their eyes met for a moment and he saw that she wished him to continue.

'I know much was written about his life shortly after he died,' Lee said. 'Perhaps this was sufficient for those who knew him, or lived at the same time and in the same environment. But I think that, with the best will in the world, something was left out. Not necessarily a particular event or saying, but some key that we were not expected to do without.' Mary stared at him wide-eyed as Lee went on, now with mounting confidence:

'Whether the conclusion is that Jesus was the son of God or not, the image that has filtered down to us through two thousand years, which the vast majority of us find so removed from everyday life, will be shown to be incomplete. What I pray is that, during what amounts to the re-creation of his life, we shall rekindle the flame and warm ourselves once more, as did those countless thousands before history got in the way. That we shall learn, once more, why so many followed him to their deaths – not in ignorance but with understanding – an understanding that we have lost.'

Baal took a deep breath, then asked, 'Have you any idea at all of the nature of this "missing piece," if I may call it that?'

There was a long silence, then Lee shook his head slowly.

'None. Except that it is something of the heart rather than of the mind – some truth that others, before us, half understood. It became so much a part of Christ's personality that he forged a bond with the Creator, which I believe he wished all men to share – not to set him apart.'

There was another long pause, then Baal cleared his throat. 'Yes,' he said quietly, 'I'm beginning to understand.' He smiled at Lee, then glanced at his wife before continuing: 'Very well. If you want me, I'll do it.' His expression became serious. 'Nevertheless, I still think your hopes are founded on sand. And once I start I shall attempt to prove so to the utmost of my ability!'

Lee held his eyes steadily for a few moments before answering. 'That's all I ask. Thank you.'

'I like you, Lee. I hope we'll still be friends when this is all over.'

'I hope so, too.'

Then the two men smiled at each other, and the tension eased. Fred wanted to know if his father was coming up for the football game next Saturday. Lee talked to Ellen about some of the stars who had been in his shows in the past, and he heard Miss Galliard telling Mary about one of the times she had taken her company to the Soviet Union.

Later, when the children had left the table, either to go to bed or to watch television in the other room, Ellen brought more coffee and they sat talking for a long while. Miss Galliard brought the conversation back to the 'hidden years' – evidently a favourite topic – about which she proved to be something of an authority. She told Lee and Mary that she had sketched out a rough projection of what she imagined must have happened during those twenty-three years, with the idea of writing a book one day. When Mary asked why she had never done so, the older woman explained that the difficulty had always been to know how and where to set that moment of revelation she felt certain must have occurred when Jesus knew for sure who he was.

By the time they all went to bed, it was past one o'clock. Lee glanced out of his bedroom window and saw that it had stopped snowing.

The door between the two rooms remained locked that night, and Lee was grateful. He knew Mary understood that his mind would be racing with excitement because Baal had accepted the part and that he would want to be left alone to think. He loved her all the more for it and knew with greater certainty how closely their lives were being drawn together. The time for final commitment might have been delayed but when it did come, as Lee knew it must, soon, it would gain everything from those other bonds that became stronger with each passing day.

The network had allotted Lee a fairly luxurious office, with an excellent view of Sixth Avenue, for the duration of the production. Three days after he moved into it, Lee called the first meeting of the two attorneys to hammer out a mutually acceptable format for the 'trial.'

Lang arrived first, closely followed by Baal. After some preliminary banter, the four of them sat down, Lee behind his desk with Mary at his side, the two attorneys in easy chairs facing them.

'Gentlemen,' Lee began. 'As we have three consecutive programmes, I was going to suggest that we concentrate our attention on one particular aspect of the case each night.'

Lang glanced at Baal beside him, then said, 'Well, since there is a time limit, I suppose that makes sense.' Baal nodded after a brief pause.

'We don't want to rush through the earlier evidence,' Lee explained, 'in order to be sure of finishing by the end of the

79

third programme, then possibly have the problem of spinning it out.'

'By the way, Lee,' Baal asked, 'how *are* we to obtain a verdict? I don't think we covered the point in our earlier discussion.'

Lee sat back in his chair. 'Ray Burgh had in mind to ballot for the right to be in the studio audience as part of the publicity run-up,' he told them. 'I thought we might choose a jury from them.'

'How?' Baal asked.

'We won't have time to examine them, surely?'

'That's true,' Lee nodded. He looked from one to the other. 'Why don't we give each member of the audience a number as they come in, then pick six men and six women at random. How would you feel about that?'

Lang said, 'Well, I guess under the circumstances it's as fair as we're likely to get.' Again he turned to the man beside him. 'Mr Baal?'

'It heightens the element of luck,' the other pointed out.

Lang nodded. 'That's true.' He looked back at Lee. 'What exactly is the charge?'

Lee glanced at Mary who read from her notes: 'Fraud . . . in that the Accused did misrepresent himself as being the son of God.'

The smaller of the two men opposite laughed lightly. 'Sounds legal,' he remarked.

Lee smiled. 'Would you like to suggest any rewording?'

The two attorneys looked at each other, then back to Lee. Both shook their heads slightly.

'No, I don't think so,' Lang said. 'It certainly goes to the heart of the matter.'

'What about the method of choosing the jury?' Mary asked.

'I certainly can't think of anything better on the spur of the moment,' Baal admitted, 'but may we come back to it if we have any ideas in the meantime?'

'By all means,' Lee answered, pausing for a few seconds to glance down at his notes before continuing. 'Now. As to phasing the trial into three parts, what I had in mind was something like this . . . ' He waited for Mary to hand each of them a sheet of paper before reading from the copy in front of him.

'The first will deal with the bringing of the charge, the opening speeches, the calling of witnesses, modern and historical, concerned with the birth of the Accused.' Lee glanced up for a second but, on receiving no comment, continued. 'The second day – or night, rather – will deal with the Accused's ministry, and the third, with the crucifixion, the closing speeches, and the jury's verdict.'

Both men studied the summary Mary had given them. This time it was Baal who nodded and looked up first. 'It seems a fair enough basis to work on,' he said. 'I take it that this framework will not be totally inelastic?'

'And that we will be able to make suggestions for improvements later,' Lang put in, 'if any ideas occur.'

Lee said, 'We're open to any suggestions. I just feel, to make the most impact, each evening should have a definite shape of its own.'

'Who's going to control all this once we're on the air?' Baal asked.

'A judge – whom we have yet to secure, by the way – just like a normal court.'

'And the usual rules of evidence and procedure will apply?' Lang asked.

Lee nodded. 'That is one of the most important aspects.'

'To make up for the lamentable lack of both in the original, I presume?' the other said, smiling.

'Partially.' Lee returned the smile, then glanced at Mary, who looked down at her notes.

'The main thing left to discuss is the witnesses,' she told him.

'Right.' Lee nodded and turned back to face the two attorneys. 'As we agreed, gentlemen, you are free to call anyone you wish. You yourselves can arrange for modern expert witnesses, but I should like a list from each of you now, as Miss Bell advised you when she arranged this meeting, of those biblical characters you will want to call, so that the parts can be cast and as much time as possible given to the actors concerned for study.'

Lee decided to hold public auditions. This met with opposition from the network, which would have preferred to play safe with actors and actresses they knew. But Lee was determined that with the exception of Burnard, the parts would go to unknowns. It always made him sad to think of all the talent that went to waste in New York.

When the doors opened the first morning, there was already a long queue outside the rehearsal rooms Lee had chosen for the auditions. The actors filed in, some laughing and joking, others serious and tense. Lee thought to himself that this was probably only one of several auditions being held that morning.

Anna came down the stairs into the mission hallway carrying a small case. She now had on ordinary clothes but wore no makeup. A year or two earlier she would have looked odd in her borrowed, second-hand clothes. But fashions change and now the effect was slightly hippie, except for her beautifully brushed, shining black hair, which was combed back from her face and tied with a single ribbon. This style would have been too severe for most girls but Anna had such lovely features that it highlighted her beauty.

She paused at the bottom of the stairs and looked through an inner doorway leading off the hall. 'I'm going now, Sister Mary Pauline,' she called. Almost immediately a nun came out and looked her up and down. She was about fifty years old and had a severe expression except when actually smiling – which she often was.

'Let's have a look at you.' Anna stood back obediently to be inspected and the nun nodded. 'Turn around,' she ordered. The girl did so slowly, then turned back to face her examiner.

'Well?'

The old nun's face suddenly cracked into a broad grin. 'You look lovely, child,' she said.

Anna, however, was still doubtful. 'You don't think . . . ?' she began.

'Think what?'

'You don't think I look . . . well . . . ' she shrugged, 'you know?'

Sister Mary Pauline sighed. 'Now then,' she said, 'don't let's

82

start on all that again. You're a beautiful young girl, praise God, and there's nothing wrong with that. Do you think the Lord doesn't know what He's about?'

Anna smiled. 'Well,' she said, 'wish me luck.'

Again, the sister's severe expression softened into a smile and she held out her arms to kiss Anna on the cheek. 'All the luck in the world,' she said, then held Anna at arm's length looking at her. 'If you dance as well as you look, they'll give you a part for sure!'

Anna frowned. 'I've practised as hard as I could,' she said. 'I'm so stiff when I wake up in the morning!'

'Well, never mind. Do your best, and if you don't succeed, there's always another day.'

'Thank you.'

Sister Mary Pauline glanced at the clock on the wall behind Anna's head and lowered her arms hurriedly. 'You must go or you'll be late,' she said.

Anna opened the front door and went out, followed by Sister Mary Pauline. When the girl reached the bottom of the steps, she turned to look back.

'You won't be disappointed if I don't get the job?'

Sister shook her head severely. 'Certainly not,' she said. 'More fool *they!*'

Anna smiled and started towards the bus stop. She reached the street corner, turned one last time to wave, then saw the uptown bus coming and dashed out of sight.

The bus was crowded and Anna could barely find room to stand. Suddenly she realized that the old man seated in front of her was staring at her, his grin made even more horrible by the fact that it was toothless. She glanced about, looking for a way to escape, but she was hemmed in. Just as the old man reached forward to touch her leg, the bus pulled to the kerb for its next stop, its doors opened, and in the ensuing shuffle, Anna was able to move away and slip into a just vacant seat.

Sharing the seat was a young black man. He smiled at her, simply because she was a pretty girl who had happened to sit next to him. Anna smiled back and the boy said, 'Hi!'

'Hi!'

'You going to work?'

Anna nodded. 'I hope so,' she said.

'Goin' for a job?'

'Yes.'

The boy looked at her, nodding and smiling. 'Good luck, then,' he said.

'Thank you.' They both smiled but did not talk again, and Anna gazed out of the window with mixed feelings of excitement and apprehension. She was going to the audition of a new musical play she had seen advertised in *Variety*.

The auditions were held on the bare stage of an empty theatre. Each girl in turn had to dance to the music of an upright piano on one side of the stage. Sitting in the darkened auditorium were the producer and director of the forthcoming show with another man, evidently a friend. Anna, now wearing a practice suit, stood in the wings with a group of other hopefuls, waiting to be called on stage by the stage manager who carried a clipboard with lists of their names and previous experience.

The girl now auditioning had been directly ahead of Anna. She watched her pirouetting about the stage, improvising to some classical-type music. Suddenly the music broke into a modern tempo which the girl followed with complete change of style until the producer shouted, 'Okay, Miss Ansell, that's fine. Stay behind, will you?'

The girl nodded and smiled, then joined the small group of successful applicants on the other side of the stage. The stage manager turned and looked at Anna. 'You're next,' he said.

Anna swallowed but walked quickly out to the front of the stage and spoke to the producer, as they had been told to do by the stage manager.

'Anna Princi.'

The producer turned to the man beside him. 'Quite a dish,' he remarked. The other nodded, staring at Anna admiringly.

Anna took up a position at the back of the stage. The music began and she started to dance, managing the classical section well enough. But a few seconds after the music broke into the other tempo, she realized that it was beyond her. She stopped.

84

'I'm sorry,' she apologized, 'I don't have much experience in modern dancing.'

The director frowned and crossed her name off the list.

'We don't have time for you to learn,' the producer told her, not unkindly.

Anna nodded. 'I understand,' she said and started to turn away.

'Better luck next time,' the director said automatically, but the producer called after her, 'If you'd like to stick around, we'll have a talk afterwards.' Anna hesitated for a few seconds, then nodded briefly and walked off into the wings.

The producer turned to wink at the director as the next hopeful came on.

'Josie Lane,' the girl announced.

'All right, Miss Lane, let's see what you can do.'

The girl started to dance. Unnoticed by the other two, the third man slipped out of his seat and went backstage.

He found Anna, already in her coat, changing her shoes. He stopped in front of her, smiling sympathetically.

'That was tough!'

Anna looked up and saw a small man in his early fifties. She smiled back.

'Not really, I've been away too long.'

'Is that right?' Anna noticed he had a nervous way of talking, as if expecting to have to eat his words at a moment's notice.

'I need a lot more practice,' she admitted, 'and some lessons.'

'Yeah, maybe.' He glanced at the empty chair beside her. 'Mind if I sit down?' Anna shook her head and he did so, looking at her keenly. 'If you'll forgive me for saying so, Miss . . ?'

'Princi,' Anna told him.

'Miss Princi . . . I think you're barking up the wrong tree. I mean . . . there are so many dancers and so few jobs these days.' He shrugged, spreading his hands: 'Okay, I dare say you'll get one in time, but where's that going to lead?'

'I don't know,' Anna admitted.

'Well, let me tell you,' the other said, his voice taking on fresh confidence, 'nowhere!'

'I want a job only for six months,' Anna told him.

85

'Why?' He paused for a few seconds, then asked, 'You getting married?'

Anna hesitated, then she said softly, 'You could put it like that.'

The other nodded vigorously. 'I see!' he said in a tone which seemed to indicate she had just revealed one of life's mysteries. He paused for a moment before asking suddenly, 'Who's the lucky guy?'

'He's quite well known.'

Her questioner's eyes widened knowingly. 'I get it,' he said, 'doesn't want the news to get out right now?'

'There wouldn't be much point.'

'And you don't want to take money from him until you're married, is that it?'

His questions were so pressing that Anna felt like telling him to mind his own business, but it was obviously just his way. His concern for her seemed so genuine that she simply looked at him again and said gently, 'Mr . . . ?'

'Aberello,' the other said at once. 'Sorry, I should've introduced myself.' He grinned suddenly. 'Everyone calls me Herb.'

'Well . . . Herb, I really don't want to talk about it, if you don't mind.' She was glad she hadn't said any more because the smile dropped from his face at once.

'Oh . . . sure, sure. Listen . . . I wasn't trying to be nosy.'

He looked so worried that Anna said hurriedly, 'I realize that.'

'It's just that . . . I wondered what you were going to do now.' His face was practically tying itself into knots.

Anna shrugged. 'Try again, I suppose,' she said.

Aberello paused for a few seconds, looking in the direction of the stage, then turned back to her.

'Listen, I shouldn't say this 'cause George is a friend of mine.'

Anna finished changing her shoes, put her dancing pumps in her small case, then stood up.

'Who's George?' she asked.

Aberello also stood, then jerked his thumb in the direction of the music. 'The guy in there,' he said, 'the producer.'

'Oh.'

'I just wouldn't hang around, that's all.'

Anna smiled. 'Thank you,' she said. 'I wasn't going to.'

Aberello nodded again as if his life had just been spared. 'Good!' Then suddenly he grinned again. 'Actually, I didn't think you were the type.'

Anna paused for a moment, then she said, 'Well . . . if you'll excuse me,' and half turned in the direction of the stage door.

'Oh sure, you gotta go.'

'Someone is expecting me.'

'Your guy, eh?'

'Not this time.'

'Oh.' Aberello paused, then grinned again. 'There I go – minding your business!'·

Anna smiled back. 'It doesn't matter,' she said.

'Which way are you going?'

'Just to the corner to get a bus.'

'Mind if I walk with you?'

'If you haven't anything better to do.'

'Not at all.'

They walked along the corridor towards the stage door, Herb still talking ninety to the dozen. At the last minute he dashed forward with unaccustomed gallantry and opened the door for her. Anna gave him a smile as she went out.

A few seconds later, they were walking towards the corner of the block where the traffic roared down one of the main avenues. For a few seconds Aberello was silent, then he said, 'Listen . . . I was thinking. If you want a job only for six months, you don't want to spend most of the time looking.'

'Not if I can help it,' Anna admitted.

' 'Course not . . . so I was wondering if you'd consider something different.'

Anna looked at him. 'But I'm not trained for anything else,' she said.

He looked back at her with open admiration. 'That doesn't mean you ain't, I mean, you aren't, qualified, does it?'

Anna frowned slightly. 'What sort of job?' she asked.

'Well . . . I got friends all over. I happen to know, for example, they're auditioning for some minor parts up at NBC day after tomorrow.'

Anna's eyes widened. 'Television?'

'Yeah. After all, you speak well . . . and you know how to move.' He shrugged. 'With your looks, what else do you need?'

They walked on a few more steps before Anna said, 'But I don't have any acting experience.'

Aberello grinned. 'This ain't acting,' he said . . . 'It's for one of them soap operas! You know the sort of thing?'

Anna nodded. 'I guess so,' she said doubtfully.

Finally, they reached a corner and stopped. Herb delved into his inner pocket and brought out a card. 'Here,' he said, 'there's a guy called Joe Shand. Can you remember that?'

'I think so.'

'Write it down when you get wherever you're going. He's the studio manager. Give him this and tell him I sent you. He'll see that you get a chance.'

Anna looked at the card. 'Where are they having them?' she asked.

'The auditions? Rockefeller Center. The show's called 'Game of Life' or 'View of Life'! You know, something like that. Just ask in the lobby which studio they're using.'

Anna put the card in her pocket. 'It's very kind of you,' she said.

'Think nothing of it.' He stood grinning at her like a well-meaning sheep dog.

'I won't promise to go,' Anna told him. 'I'd like to talk it over first.'

Herb suddenly looked worried. 'Perhaps you'd better not mention my name, then. Say it's all your own idea.'

Anna laughed softly and touched him on the arm for a second. 'Don't worry, Herb,' she said, 'and thank you.'

The other brightened at once. 'It's been a real pleasure!'

Anna glanced up the avenue and saw a bus coming. 'I have to go now,' she told him.

The other nodded. 'Okay,' he said. 'Maybe we'll meet again?'

'I hope so,' Anna said. 'Good-bye, Herb.' She held out her hand, which Herb pumped gratefully. 'And thanks again for trying to help.'

'Any time!' He eventually let go of her hand.

'Bye!' Anna gave him a last smile, then turned to go.

Aberello watched her hurry to get on the bus and stopped to wave as it went past, hoping to catch a glimpse of her, but she had taken a seat on the other side. He watched the bus disappearing into the traffic, the smile slowly fading. He shook his head and turned away, puzzled.

'Must be going soft in the head,' he muttered to himself. 'Didn't even try and get her phone number.'

'Tough luck, buddy!' Herb looked up and noticed for the first time a cop who had been standing on the corner and who had evidently overheard the entire conversation. Aberello gave him a sour look and opened his mouth to offer some obscenity, but thought better of it and walked slowly back to the theatre.

Later that night, Anna stood in her bedroom gazing at her reflection in the mirror. After a while, there was a brief knock on the door and Sister Mary Pauline came in. Anna turned to face her quickly.

'Did I make you jump?' the nun asked, smiling.

Anna returned the smile, but took a deep breath. 'It's all right,' she said.

'I was wondering what was keeping you so long.'

'I'm sorry,' Anna said, but she made no move. The nun looked at her, frowning.

'Well, come on then,' she said, 'if you're ready. Father's waiting for us.'

The girl still held back. 'Sister . . . '

Sister Mary Pauline, who was heading towards the door, turned back to look at her.

'Yes?'

'That man I spoke to you about.'

The nun frowned. 'Him again! I've told you what I think. If it's honest work, it doesn't matter what it is.' But Anna still looked unhappy.

'I didn't tell you everything he said.' She shrugged slightly. 'I thought it would sound proud, but now it's worrying me.'

Sister Mary Pauline took a deep breath to control her impatience. 'Go on, then,' she said.

'He said . . . he suggested I might get the job – not because of what I can do, but the way I look.'

Sister Mary Pauline looked at her pityingly. 'The trouble with you is you've been around nuns too long!' Her eyes twinkled despite the severity of her tone, and Anna had to laugh. 'Listen,' the other went on, 'does a bunch of flowers have to be ashamed of itself? I mean . . . did you ever ask yourself – what is the *point* of a bunch of flowers?'

'It's not quite the same, is it?' Anna asked.

Sister Mary Pauline shrugged impatiently. 'Nobody said it was,' she said. 'With people, what really matters is what they look like inside. And only the good Lord can see that, so stop worrying!'

Chapter

6

A few days later Lee sat at a table in Mary's favourite restaurant, just round the corner from Rockefeller Center. A drink was on the table in front of him. Although he was studying the menu, Lee saw Mary as she entered and stood up to beckon to her.

'Hi!'

Mary smiled apologetically. 'I'm sorry I'm late. There was a call from my mother just as I was leaving.'

Lee helped her into a chair. 'Nothing wrong, I hope?'

Mary shrugged slightly as she pulled off her gloves and put them on the table beside her. 'It's always difficult to tell, but I'm afraid I shall have to spend the night with her.'

'Oh.'

Seeing his expression, Mary put her hand over his. 'I'm sorry, darling.'

Lee put his other hand on top of hers and smiled. 'That's okay.'

'She's a lot better than she was,' Mary went on. 'When my father died I had to go out there practically every night. She couldn't bear being alone in the house. But she's got over that, thank heavens.'

'Shall I get a car and run you out there?'

Mary smiled at him gratefully: 'That's very sweet of you,' she said, 'but I think it's best not. She's always pestering me about getting married again! It would only lead to complications. Besides, I don't want you to get overtired. You've a lot on your mind at the moment.'

'Well, okay . . . if that's what you want. But I'd like to do it, really.'

'I know.' Mary took both his hands in hers. 'And I want you to meet her. In spite of everything I've said about her, she's a very intelligent and sweet person – you'll love her. But

91

I don't want you to see her for the first time when she's in one of her depressed moods.'

Lee smiled ruefully. 'Whatever you say.' They went on holding hands, looking into each other's eyes for a few more seconds, then a waiter appeared at Mary's elbow.

'Good evening, Miss Bell.'

Mary looked up and smiled. 'Hello, Brad,' she said. 'How's your son?' The man expanded visibly.

'Just finished his hundredth mission. We're expecting him home any day.'

'That's wonderful.' Mary turned to Lee. 'Brad's son is one of the most decorated flyers in the navy.'

Lee nodded and smiled. 'I hope he gets home safe,' he said.

The waiter inclined his head graciously. 'Thanks. He won't be going back, thank God. He's done his share.' Mary nodded in agreement. 'More than his share.'

'Yeah.' The man paused thoughtfully, then smiled at them: 'Well,' he said, 'what'll it be?'

Lee had already made up his mind. 'I think I'll have the special.' He glanced at Mary. 'What about you?'

Mary perused the menu, then shrugged and put it down. 'I guess I'll have my usual steak,' she said half apologetically. The waiter nodded.

'Okay.' He took the menus away. 'One special and one steak, medium rare.' He glanced at Mary. 'Right?'

Mary nodded. 'Right!'

'With a tossed salad and Roquefort dressing?'

'Right again!'

The waiter turned to move away but Lee held up his glass. 'Brad, I'd like another, please.'

Mary said, 'I thought you weren't supposed . . . '.

The waiter held up his hand. 'Don't worry, it's something Mac dreamed up. Strictly no alcohol!'

'Oh.'

'Just to kid myself into believing I've got insides like other people,' Lee said.

'All right.' Mary looked back at Brad. 'Then I think I'll have a vodka and tonic, just to balance things up.'

'Coming right up.'

Mary glanced at Lee with a grin. 'Unless you'd rather I sat here and concentrated on feeling sorry for you.'

Lee looked at the waiter with mock severity. 'Fetch the drinks, Bradley!'

'Sure.' The waiter grinned and went off into the kitchen, leaving the two of them smiling at each other.

'Well?' Mary said after a while. 'Tell me how it went – seeing I've been stuck in the office all day doing your dirty work.'

'You mean the auditions?'

'What else?'

Lee nodded slowly. 'We got some wonderful characters,' he began, then hesitated.

'What's the matter?' Mary asked.

Lee shrugged, 'Oh, I dunno,' he said. 'I guess it was stupid to think casting would be that easy.'

'You've only had a few days!'

'Yes, I know. But while we could have cast some characters in half a dozen different ways, we don't seem to have got anywhere near casting others.'

Mary frowned. 'Which?' she asked.

The waiter put their drinks on the table and went away again without a word.

Lee said. 'Three, principally. Judas, Peter, and Mary, Jesus' mother.' He took a sip from his glass, then looked back at her. 'I suppose the real trouble is I'm not clear in my own mind what sort of people they really were. I thought I was, but several people came close enough to my original ideas to make me realize how phony they were.'

Mary looked at him, concerned. 'How?' she asked.

'Well, take Judas, for example. I think most people imagine him as a cross between Shylock and Fagin.' Mary couldn't help smiling as Lee went on. 'But if that were so, why did Christ choose him in the first place?' He looked at her directly, and when Mary didn't answer, he continued. 'He risked his life with the others, and Jesus must've thought he was made of the same stuff in his own way – unless you're going to claim that Jesus made a hopeless blunder right at the beginning, which sowed the seeds of his own destruction.'

'Perhaps, he chose one deliberately to betray him,' Mary said without much conviction, but Lee shook his head.

'No, that doesn't stand up at all. Jesus knew what was going to happen, but until the very end I don't think he had the remotest idea that one of his own disciples would betray him.'

Mary nodded and took a drink from her glass. 'I see what you mean,' she said thoughtfully. They looked at each other in silence for a few moments until Bradley set their food in front of them.

'What's the matter?' he demanded. 'You both look like the Russians are in Yonkers!' Lee and Mary smiled. 'That's better. Pain in the stomach *after* the special's bad enough!'

'Okay.' Lee nodded.

'Bon appetit!'

'Thanks!' The waiter walked briskly to another table and both Lee and Mary started to eat.

'Changing the subject,' Lee said after a while, 'how do you think our two legal beavers are shaping up?'

'I think they were pleased that you managed to get Haald to umpire.'

'*Judge* Haald!' Lee said, smiling. 'Do you mind?'

'Sorry!'

He paused thoughtfully, then said: 'Oh . . . I dunno!'

'Anyway,' Mary went on, 'having a European high court judge taking part has removed any lingering fears that they might be demeaning themselves in some way.'

When they left the restaurant, Lee managed to get a cab for Mary quite easily. After he had closed the door for her, she wound down the window.

'What will you do now?'

Lee said, 'I think I'll just walk for a bit – do some thinking.'

Mary nodded. 'Take care,' she said.

Lee looked at her fondly. 'You, too.'

The driver pulled the newly installed bulletproof glass partition

to one side and growled impatiently over his shoulder. 'Look . . .
where to, lady?'

'Grand Central,' Lee told him.

The driver put the car into gear. 'Okay,' he said, 'let's go,' and
slammed the partition shut.

'See you in the morning,' Lee called and Mary nodded.

'Bye!'

The cab roared into the traffic. Lee stood for a few seconds
watching, then started to walk back along 52nd Street, turning
left into Seventh Avenue, and heading towards Times Square.

For a while he wandered aimlessly through the throng of
late shoppers and theatregoers, until he came face to face with
a poster, advertising a middleweight contest, plastered to the
boarding around a new construction site. There was a big picture
of Amos Brown, the middleweight champion, and a sticker
across the whole poster, 'TONIGHT!'

Lee studied the poster for a while, glanced at his watch,
paused a few more seconds, and following an impulse that his
experiences over the past weeks had taught him to ignore at
his peril, called a cab.

It was one of the smaller arenas. By the time Lee reached
his seat, the main contest had already been called. Brown was
facing a younger, slightly bigger opponent. For the first three
rounds both men circled each other warily, exchanging only an
occasional left jab until the crowd began to whistle and boo
impatiently. Having followed Brown's career pretty closely,
Lee deduced he was acting under orders to keep the fight going
for a few rounds. Lee was right. The bell for the fourth had
hardly rung when the fighter sprang from his corner and started
to drive his less experienced opponent around the ring. The
crowd roared. Lee was too far away to hear what was said but
he could see the trainer shouting at Brown from his corner.
He glanced back into the centre of the ring just in time to see
the younger man change his balance slightly and, evidently
unseen by the referee and judges, knee Brown skilfully in the
groin – not to put him down, but to make him drop his guard
long enough for the other to fetch him a right uppercut to the
heart, which sent the champion staggering back against the ropes.

The crowd screamed with delight as the other fighter sprang on him like a tiger. Within a few seconds Brown was down.

Now the crowd went mad with joy as the referee began to count. The champion staggered to his feet but the count continued to eight before the fight was allowed to continue. The younger fighter tried to get in close again, but Brown had recovered sufficiently to hold him off until the bell.

Brown's seconds had obviously done a good job between rounds, because when he came out for the fifth, there was never any further doubt about the outcome of the fight. After two preliminary left hooks that sent his opponent's head smacking back on his neck, Brown landed a perfectly timed right-cross, which put the other man down for good.

The referee counted him out, then held up the champion's hand, but there were more boos than cheers. Somebody shouted, 'Give us a song, Amos,' and a few others joined in, but Brown glared briefly in their direction and ducked his way out of the ring.

Lee sat for a few seconds, an oasis of quiet amidst the turmoil raging around him, but his mind was a whirlpool. He knew Brown of old, having done a documentary about him in the fighter's earlier days, when Lee himself was still struggling. Sitting there during the last few seconds, he had suddenly been possessed by a quite incredible thought. He paused a few moments longer, then got up and pushed his way towards the dressing rooms.

He was stopped at the entrance to the tunnel by an official. 'Other way, bud.'

'I want to speak to the champ.'

'Some other time.'

'I'm from NBC. The name's Harrison.' The official looked at Lee with new respect. 'Well, I'm sorry, Mr Harrison, but the champ don't give interviews. My orders are to keep everyone out.'

'He'll see me,' Lee told him. 'We did a feature some years ago when he was still a contender.' He paused for a few seconds, then added, 'I know it helped at the time.'

The official shrugged uncomfortably. 'Well . . . I'll ask,' he said, 'but don't be upset if he won't see you. He's changed.'

Lee nodded briefly. 'So I gathered,' he said.

'All right, Mr Harrison. Please wait here.'

The man turned and disappeared along the corridor. Lee glanced around for a few seconds, then followed. The man in front of him disappeared into a doorway. As Lee approached he heard Brown's angry voice.

'What're you going to do about that punk?'

'What can I do?' he heard someone else say – probably the trainer.

'He's not getting away with it!'

The official came out of the doorway just as Lee reached it. He shrugged and jerked his head towards the voices. 'I'm sorry, Mr Harrison. He's got other things on his mind.'

'I heard.' Lee paused for a few seconds. 'Maybe I can help.'

The other looked at him, then stepped out of his way. 'Suit yourself. I've got other things to do.' He walked down the corridor and out into the arena.

Brown was lying on a couch being massaged by one of his seconds. Lee recognized the trainer, an old man, standing at the head of the couch looking down.

'How come nobody saw it?' Brown was saying angrily. The other shrugged.

'I saw.'

One of the seconds nodded. 'Me, too.' But Brown turned his head to snarl at him.

'I meant the judges, bird-brain!'

The trainer said quietly, 'Maybe they saw, too.' Brown sat up to face him.

'Well, now you're talking!' Suddenly he caught sight of Lee standing in the doorway and glared. Lee smiled.

'Hi!'

'What's he doing here?' The others turned and the trainer moved towards Lee, who held up his hand.

'Lee Harrison, NBC.'

'Get him out of here,' Brown shouted.

Lee side-stepped so that he could speak to Brown directly. 'Don't you remember me, Amos?' he asked. 'It must've been six years ago.'

The trainer looked at Lee, frowning, then he glanced back at Brown doubtfully. The latter stared at Lee for a few seconds before his face relaxed slightly. 'Yeah,' he said, 'I remember.' He flopped back on the couch and the second glanced quickly at the trainer, who nodded.

Lee took a few steps closer to the couch as the second resumed the massage. 'I caught the fight,' he said.

'Then you saw what happened?'

The trainer looked at him as Lee shrugged. 'Of course I saw.'

Brown glared up at the others. 'There you are,' he began, but Lee added pointedly, 'Everyone saw.'

'What do you mean?' Brown growled.

Lee shrugged again. 'I mean everyone saw. But nobody cared.' He paused for a few more seconds before going on. 'I doubt if anyone in the whole arena,' he glanced around, 'present company excepted, wanted you to win.'

The trainer nodded quietly. 'He's right, Amos. I've been trying to tell you this for months.'

'So what do you want me to do – quit?' Brown snarled.

Lee shook his head. 'That's not for me to say.' He paused a moment longer, then went on, 'But an idea hit me suddenly – while I was watching you out there.'

'Like what?'

Lee eyed him quizzically. 'I wondered if you might want to try something else for a change.'

It was the trainer's turn to look surprised. 'Why?' he began to demand as Lee turned to him.

'I don't know. Maybe I need him,' Lee said slowly, his eyes unwavering, 'but maybe he needs to do this more.'

Brown shook off the second's hands and stood up. 'What you talking about, mister?' he said.

Lee turned back to face him. 'You've fought for yourself most of your life. I'd like you to try being someone who took on the whole world.'

The following day Lee borrowed one of the company's cars and drove down to the Lincoln Tunnel.

From the moment the idea of 'Christ on Trial' had come

98

into his mind, he had believed in its essential rightness. If he had any doubts at all, they were only in his ability to do it justice. But now it seemed providence had taken a hand. Lee had never had such a strong feeling in all his life and knew better than to try and interfere. Following the same instinct, he had left everything in Mary's hands just after midday, so that he could revisit the district where he had lived as a child. He wanted to seek out the young priest he had spoken to on the day he had returned to New York.

He parked the car outside the church, paused to glance up at the figure of Christ, then went in through the side entrance. He knew that Father O'Connell would be waiting for him in his study, since Mary had telephoned earlier that morning.

After they had sat down, the priest listened carefully while Lee explained the project to him, then said, 'How can I help you, Mr Harrison? Do you want some advice?'

Lee smiled: 'I'd be happy for your opinion any time, Father. But that's not why I came.' He paused for a moment, looking at O'Connell. 'I wondered if you would give evidence on behalf of one of the witnesses?'

The other raised his eyebrows with surprise. 'Take part, you mean?' Lee nodded. 'But Mr Harrison, I'm no actor!'

'This does not call for an actor in the ordinary sense,' Lee assured him. 'Just someone who is so familiar with the story that he can imagine how his particular character would react in any given circumstances.'

The priest nodded. 'Yes,' he said. 'You explained that. Identification, I think you called it?'

'That's right.'

'But I still assumed that some sort of experience would be necessary.'

'It is,' Lee told him. 'But not necessarily acting. After all, you're used to speaking before an audience.'

'You could put it like that,' the priest smiled.

'So there's no reason why you should get tongue-tied or anything.'

'I suppose not!'

99

'And there are no lines to learn. In fact, in your case, nothing to learn at all. You know it all already.'

The priest frowned slightly. 'Well,' he said, 'I wouldn't say that.'

Lee spread out his hands in front of him. 'All right,' he said, 'we never stop learning. But you know what I mean.'

Father O'Connell was silent for a few moments. He was obviously thinking hard, and Lee watched him intently. Finally the priest said, 'It might do no harm to meditate on one of the gospel saints.' Then his expression lightened. 'Might be very interesting and instructive, in fact.'

Lee nodded. 'We're all going to learn something.'

He spoke with more feeling than the priest could possibly have understood, but O'Connell inclined his head, nevertheless. 'Yes,' he said, 'it could be very interesting.'

'Added to which,' Lee went on, 'I can arrange a fee.' He glanced briefly out the window. 'Which might go some way, perhaps, towards helping – whatever you're trying to do around here.'

At this the other sighed. 'Ah, yes,' he said, 'we can always use money. I often think we have to spend far too much of our time thinking about that instead of getting on with the real job in hand.'

Lee paused, then he said, 'I understand you've started a drug rehabilitation centre?'

'That's a grand phrase for a modest effort!'

'Perhaps two thousand dollars would help make it less modest?'

Father O'Connell looked at him, visibly shaken. 'Two thousand!' he repeated, obviously dazed at the size of the figure. As Lee waited in silence for what seemed a very long time, he wondered if he had made a bad mistake, but finally the priest asked, 'How long would it take?'

'Just three nights, plus a couple of meetings beforehand to make sure everything runs smoothly.' The other nodded, and Lee went on, 'There won't be any rehearsals, as such, but I want to make sure everyone knows exactly what's expected of him.'

'Of course.'

The last night, of course, will be on a Sunday – Easter Sunday.'

'Yes, I understand.'

Lee waited for him to go on. When he didn't, Lee added: 'Costumes and makeup will be dealt with individually, but that shouldn't take more than a few hours to decide.'

The priest hesitated while Lee watched him keenly, then he took a deep breath. 'What part do you want me to represent?' Then he smiled faintly. 'One of the apostles, I hope – that would be very instructive.'

Lee said quietly, 'I want you to play . . . Judas Iscariot.'

Had he hit Father O'Connell in the face he could hardly have shocked him more. It was quiet some time before the priest was able to speak.

'Judas! Mr Harrison, is this a joke?'

Lee shook his head firmly. 'Not at all,' he said.

'But you can't be serious.'

'Why not?' Lee looked at him calmly.

'You can't expect an ordained priest to portray the man who betrayed our Saviour!'

'I thought an ordained priest might be one of the few people who would understand how he had really felt . . . and what made him do it.'

Father O'Connell stared at him. His lips moved as the beginnings of a dozen answers flew through his mind. Finally he shook his head. 'No. I couldn't!'

Lee had been expecting this. He sat forward intently. 'Why not?' he demanded. 'Will there be no forgiveness for Judas on the Last Day?'

'I don't know.' The other shook his head once more, closing his eyes briefly.

'Perhaps doing this might help you to find out. After all, Judas was only the first. Many men have betrayed Jesus down the pages of history.' Lee paused for a few seconds, then went on. 'Perhaps he had a harder choice than any of the others?'

Father O'Connell looked at him. 'I have often wondered,' he admitted.

Lee paused a moment longer, then spoke quietly but with

101

great intensity. 'Something went wrong. If we could discover what, we might find out more about God's relationship with the world than we ever imagined. Wouldn't that be worth doing?'

The priest stared at him without answering.

'Possibly it's the key to our whole future, if any,' Lee concluded.

There was a long silence, during which the priest got up and gazed out the window. 'You'll have to let me think,' he said eventually, without turning around.

Lee stood up. 'Of course,' he said gently, 'there's no need to give me an answer now.' Father O'Connell turned to face him and Lee could see that his face was deeply troubled.

'Even if I decide to do it, I shall have to ask the bishop.'

Lee inclined his head. 'I understand,' he said.

'How long may I have?'

'As long as you need.'

'Very well.'

Lee paused a while longer, then said, 'It won't be as long as you think.' He took out a card and put it on the desk beside him. 'Perhaps you would phone me at this number?'

The priest nodded as Lee turned and left the room.

At Rockefeller Center, the auditions for 'Game of Life' were in progress. The producer of the show sat in a control room beside the studio manager, Joe Shand, a pleasant-looking young man in his late twenties, watching Anna read through a scene with an older actor in the large studio next door. They could see the two of them through a glass screen under a battery of lights, surrounded by cameras and equipment. They could also watch the pair from different angles in three of the half-dozen monitor sets on the wall above the screen.

The scene Anna had been asked to try was from one of the forthcoming episodes of the series. Set in a hospital ward, the scene consisted of a dialogue between a well-known politician who had just been rescued from drowning, and a nurse.

The actor was reading well enough, but Anna was stilted and unnatural as the nurse. Halfway through the scene, the producer turned to Shand and pulled a face.

102

'She's great as far as looks go, but she sounds terrible!'

Joe nodded. 'Perhaps she'd be better if she knew the lines,' he said. 'Some people just read badly.'

The other shook his head. 'I don't know,' he said. 'I never thought this stuff was Shakespeare exactly but she makes it sound like hell.'

They turned back to watch the rest of the scene, then Joe leaned forward automatically and touched the intercom switch for a few seconds to speak to the studio.

'Okay. Thank you. Just relax a minute, please.'

Anna sighed, turning to the man standing beside her. 'I hope I didn't spoil your chances,' she apologized. 'I was awful, wasn't I?'

The actor caught the eye of the nearest cameraman and raised an eyebrow eloquently. 'You'll soon find out, sweetie,' he assured her.

The producer thought for a moment, glancing down at his script. He turned to Joe. 'Well, I'm sorry, pal. I'd like to do your friend a favour, but you can see for yourself.'

Joe nodded, frowning. He glanced up at the studio clock. 'Look, what are you going to do now,' he asked, 'break for lunch?'

'I guess so. Why?'

Joe paused. 'Let me see what I can do with her until you get back, then give her another chance.'

The other looked at him curiously. 'Is it so important?' he asked.

Joe shrugged. 'No,' he said, 'I just think she's scared, that's all. I'd like to give her a break.' He paused, then added, 'You said yourself she looks great. So what harm can it do?'

The producer got up grinning and slipped his jacket from the back of the chair. 'None, I guess,' he admitted, putting it on.

Joe glared at him. 'And it's not what you think,' he said.

The other shrugged. 'It's your ulcer!'

The producer leaned forward and pressed the intercom switch. 'All right, everybody,' he announced, 'break for lunch. Back at two.' He then glanced in Anna's direction. 'Miss Princi, would you stay behind please?'

103

He went out, still grinning, leaving Joe by himself.

Joe looked at Anna through the glass screen in the now empty studio and reached again for the switch. 'Miss Princi, while the others are at lunch, I thought we might just run through that scene, if you don't mind?'

Anna looked back at him, trying not to seem too surprised. She had assumed she had been asked to wait merely to be told she was not good enough. 'Thank you,' she stammered. 'If you think it'll do any good?'

Joe nodded slowly. 'I think so,' he said, 'but first of all try to relax. There's no one else now, so have another look at the lines, then we'll try again. I'll read the other part from here.'

Anna nodded. 'I'll try,' she answered, but inwardly her heart sank. She knew, no matter how many times she tried, she would never be any good, but Herb's friend was evidently determined to help her. The least she could do in the circumstances was to go on as long as he was prepared to.

Upstairs, in Lee's office, Mary glanced at her watch, leaned across Lee's desk, and touched one of the keys on the intercom. A few seconds later Burgh's voice answered.

'Burgh.'

'Ray, I thought I'd go down and check the studio we're going to use now.'

'Fine,' she heard him say.

'They're using it for some auditions today but there shouldn't be anyone there now.'

'Okay, Mary.'

'Do you want to come?' she asked.

There was a moment's silence on the other end, then Burgh said, 'I don't think so. You know what Lee wants. If there's any equipment you need, just let me know.'

'Fine.'

'We've stuck out our necks this far!' Mary could tell he was smiling.

'You'll be famous,' she said.

'I should live so long!'

She heard the click as he switched off.

Mary smiled, flicking the switch back to the neutral position;

104

then she scribbled a note: *Gone to check Studio 3. Burnard's secretary rang to say he's flying in from Hollywood tomorrow and will let us know where he's staying.* She paused, looking down at the note, then bent down and added: *She's thinking of leaving him because he's growing a beard!* Mary grinned, then went out, taking the pencil and notebook with her.

Joe had turned off most of the lamps in the studio so that Anna was standing in a single pool of light. He read the other part with the aid of a small panel light, having also put the rest of the control room in darkness. She was reading a little better, but not much.

Mary walked along the corridor towards the studio. She stopped at the door, noting that the red light above the notice was still on. Turning to a janitor who happened to be passing, she asked, 'Phil, haven't they gone for lunch yet in Studio Three?'

The old man glanced up at the light. 'Yeah,' he said, 'broke about fifteen minutes ago. Must've left the light on by mistake, I guess.'

Mary smiled. 'Oh, right,' she said. 'Thanks.'

'You're welcome.'

In spite of his assurance, Mary opened the outer door carefully. There was a space between this and the inner one into which she stepped, letting the first close before opening the other. It took her eyes a few seconds to adjust to the darkness, then she saw Joe talking to a young girl standing by herself in the main part of the studio. She heard him say, 'Just have one more look, then we'll start from where we took it up before.'

The girl looked towards him. 'When I say, "Anyway, you were mad to go swimming there"?' she asked.

'Right. And this time imagine it's just you and me talking. You've never seen me before, but you've heard of me, and now you've come on duty at the hospital . . . and before you can say "Jack Robinson," we're having a fight!'

The girl nodded obediently. Mary stepped forward and Joe, hearing a sound, turned. When he saw Mary, he smiled.

'Hi, Mary!'

'Hello, Joe. What's going on?'

'I'm trying to help this kid loosen up a bit. Gerry thinks

105

she looks fine, but as soon as she starts to read she tightens up.'

Mary looked in Anna's direction again, this time more closely. 'Who is she?' she asked, after a few seconds.

'Anna Princi. She was sent over by a friend of mine.' Joe shrugged. 'I guess he felt sorry for her.'

Mary nodded. 'She does look a bit lost standing out there all by herself.'

'She can't have had much experience.'

'TV studios scare the pants off most people the first time.' Mary paused for a few seconds, then looked back at him. 'Why not try just talking to her?' she suggested. 'Get her to talk about herself.'

Joe looked at her gratefully. 'Yes,' he said, 'that might help. You mean improvise?'

Mary shook her head and slipped into the seat beside him. 'No . . . just be yourself.' She glanced at the script. 'Why not go on from where the script stops?'

Joe looked where she was pointing, then nodded and reached for the key.

'All right, Miss Princi, shall we take it again if you're ready?' He glanced down at his script as Anna began to read, noting that this time she was distinctly more natural.

' "Anyway . . . you were mad to go swimming there, of all places, when the tide was going out!" '

' "So I gather," ' Joe read.

' "Don't treat it as a joke, it's very serious." '

' "I'm sorry. I guess I've caused a lot of trouble." '

' "Yes, you have. But that isn't the point. A human life is the most precious thing in the world." '

Joe now looked directly at her through the screen.

'Is that what you really think?' he asked.

Anna looked back at him, startled, but very soon pulled herself together. She paused for a moment, thinking. Then she replied quietly, 'Human life *is* precious . . . but I don't think I'd call it the most important.' She hesitated, then went on, 'People give their lives for those they love. That must say something.'

Joe glanced for a few seconds at Mary, then back at Anna. 'Would you give your life for someone you loved?' he asked gently.

The girl looked down for a moment. 'I don't know. I hope I'd have the courage, if it was necessary. But perhaps I wouldn't.'

'Perhaps if you loved him enough?' Joe persisted.

Anna nodded slowly. 'Yes.' She hesitated again. 'My mother lost her life trying to save my father.'

Joe opened his mouth to say something, but Mary quickly put out her hand to stop him.

After a few more seconds the girl went on, 'He was knocked overboard by a squall when they were out sailing. Mother couldn't swim very well, but people in boats not far away saw her jump in after him.' She paused again. 'Neither of them was ever seen again.'

Joe found himself beginning to get caught up in something he didn't understand. He heard himself ask, 'Do you love anyone like that?'

Anna said slowly, 'The nuns who looked after me . . . and Our Lord, who sent his Holy Spirit to bring me back from the dead.'

Joe looked at her a long time. Suddenly everything had changed. 'Were you ill?' he asked after a while.

Anna shook her head. 'I locked myself away in a dark place at the bottom of my mind, so deep only the love of Christ was strong enough to find me.' Now she looked up to face him directly. 'That's why my dearest wish is to serve Him, and to bear the doubt that has sent me back into the world . . . until I can come home.'

Chapter
7

It was already dark as Anna walked slowly down the street towards the front door of the mission. Several people turned to look at her but she was oblivious to them until, reaching the steps, she looked up, paused for a few seconds to get out her key, then walked more purposefully up the steps and let herself inside.

At the same time Lee, slouched in his chair, was listening to Mary, who was perched on the desk in front of him in the darkened office, talking as if her life depended on it. Despite his relaxed position, he was listening intently.

'People came back from lunch, Lee, but she went on talking to Joe over the intercom, and one by one, they all fell silent, listening.'

Mary looked down through the window at the passing traffic. When she turned back Lee saw that she wore a wistful, almost sad, expression.

'She tried to explain what it felt like . . . to really love God . . . and feel his love coming back a thousand times more strong.'

'That's a tall order,' Lee said.

'But she succeeded. I don't know how.' Mary shrugged slightly. 'It certainly wasn't the clever use of words, but by the time she'd finished, even the most hard-bitten of us felt something.'

'I wish I'd been there.'

'I wish you had. Because I can't convey what it felt like – suddenly to be brought face to face with purity and goodness, right here in this building in the middle of New York.' Mary stood up quietly.

'What was she doing here?'

'Auditioning.' Mary took a cigarette out of the box and lit it, exhaling the smoke slowly. 'The head of the convent where she had lived since she was about sixteen insisted on her going back into the world before committing herself. Apparently, she trained to be a dancer before her parents died, so she tried that first.' Mary could see that Lee was thinking hard. 'Of course,' she went on, 'she didn't stand a chance, but she looked so lovely that a friend of Joe Shand's . . . '

'Who's Joe Shand?' Lee interrupted, looking up.

'He's manager of the studio we're going to use. Anyway, he sent her over to audition for a small part in that serial they put out every afternoon.'

Lee looked up at her again. 'Did she get it?' he asked.

Mary shook her head.

Lee paused and took a deep breath while Mary continued to look at him. 'I hope you're thinking what I am,' she said eventually. Before he could answer, the phone rang suddenly, making both of them jump. 'Because if not,' Mary went on, picking up the receiver, 'you'd better push me out the window right now!'

Lee smiled as Mary spoke into the telephone. 'Mr Harrison's secretary.' She paused for a few seconds, listening, then said, 'Just a moment, please, I'll see if he's still in his office.' Mary covered the mouthpiece and looked at Lee questioningly. 'It's Father O'Connell.' Lee stood up to take the phone from her.

'Yes, Father.'

The priest was in his study. The room was poorly lit, accentuating the lines of strain on his face. 'Mr Harrison,' he began, then stopped.

'Yes, Father?' Lee repeated, and waited for him to go on. When he did not, Lee said, 'You're phoning to give me your decision?'

'Yes.'

'You've been quicker than I thought.'

'I had to make up my mind. I couldn't rest with the matter unresolved.'

'Yes, I see.' Lee paused. 'Did you talk to the bishop?'

The priest nodded at the other end of the line. 'Yes,' he said quietly. 'I've just come from there.'

'I see. What did he say?'

There was a long silence before the priest answered. 'He said he'd pray for me.'

Lee frowned. 'Didn't he give a ruling?'

'He said it was up to me.' Again the other hesitated. 'I told him how much money you were prepared to give towards the rehabilitation centre if I did it.'

'Did that make any difference?'

'It's the only thing that justifies . . . taking such a risk.' O'Connell spoke so quietly that Lee could hardly hear him.

'I'm sorry,' he said, 'I don't understand.'

This time the voice was stronger. 'Do you think priests are immune from doubt, Mr Harrison?'

Lee shook his head. 'I never thought about it.'

The other went on, 'You're asking me to immerse myself in the character of a man who knew Our Lord far better than I – but lost his faith.'

Lee paused for a few seconds. For the first time he began to wonder if his hunch had been inspired after all. 'Now look, Father,' he began, 'I don't want you to do anything . . . ' but the priest interrupted him.

'No,' Lee heard him say, 'I've made up my mind. I'll do it. It's a test, I see that now. One I hoped, perhaps, never to have to face. But if I turn my back now, there will always be that doubt in my mind.'

Lee glanced at Mary quickly. 'Very well,' he said, 'of course, I'm delighted. I'll get my secretary to send you the rehearsal schedule first thing tomorrow morning.'

Again there was a period of silence before he heard the priest say, 'Thank you. There's just one thing. From now on, and until the programme is completed, I would like to be known as Mr O'Connell.'

Lee frowned, but he said, 'Yes, of course, I understand.'

'I hope so.' There was another pause before the priest said, 'Goodnight to you, Mr Harrison.'

'Goodnight, Father . . . ' Lee meant to add, 'You'll hear from us the day after tomorrow,' but there was a click as the phone went dead.

Lee handed the phone back to Mary who hung it up as he sat down again, looking suddenly tired.

'Is anything the matter?'

Lee shrugged. 'I should be happy,' he said, 'but suddenly, I'm not sure.'

Mary came to stand beside him and put her hand gently on the back of his neck. 'You're tired,' she said. 'Let's talk about Anna. Then, as I said, you can either blow my brains out or we'll go and have something to eat. Either will make you feel better.'

Lee looked up at her and smiled gratefully. 'Ah, yes,' he said, 'Anna. The last piece of the jigsaw puzzle!'

Mary took a deep breath. 'If you only knew how good it is to hear you say that!'

Lee took her other hand and kissed her wrist lightly. 'You're too young and far too beautiful to die!' he assured her.

At the mission, Sister Mary Pauline, with Anna at her right, sat at the head of a long supper table. At the other end, another nun presided. In between them, down either side, were two dozen girls of all shapes, colours and sizes, but all in their late teens or early twenties. Anna was looking around as the other girls burst into excited chatter, but Sister Mary Pauline chewed a piece of bread thoughtfully. Anna looked back at her expectantly. When she had swallowed her mouthful, the nun cleared her throat and automatically the chatter died into silence except for one or two stray giggles.

'And you want to know what I think?'

Anna nodded meekly. 'Yes, Sister.'

'Well, of course, no one's good enough to portray Our Lady properly . . . even as a very young girl, which she was, of course, when she gave birth to Our Lord.' Sister Mary Pauline almost glared around the table. 'A lot of people forget that,' she said. 'A very young and inexperienced girl – with nothing in her heart but goodness and love.' She paused for a few seconds, thinking. 'On the other hand,' she went on, voice lowered slightly, 'if merit is to be the qualification, we would never put on any Passion plays at all.' She glanced at Anna. 'And that's all this

111

sounds like to me, even if it is on the television – which would be a pity, because there are few better ways of bringing the Holy Scriptures to the ears of the heathen.' She glared at the girl on her left who muttered automatically, 'Yes, Sister.' The nun then turned back to Anna. 'So there's no reason on that score why you shouldn't take the opportunity.'

Anna's eyes widened. 'Then it's all right?'

'No, it is *not* all right, child,' the nun barked. Anna's face dropped and a muffled groan arose from the others.

'This woman offered you a thousand dollars, you say?'

Anna nodded. 'But the money's not important.'

'Nonsense, of course it's important!' Sister Mary Pauline banged on the table in front of her, then paused for a moment thoughtfully.

'Tell her in the morning . . . you wouldn't dream of doing the job for less than two!'

There was a moment's stunned silence. Everyone burst out laughing and got up to congratulate Anna. At this point Sister Mary Pauline's rugged face at last cracked into a smile.

'Fasten your seat belts, please, ladies and gentlemen. We shall be landing at Kennedy International Airport in just a few minutes.'

Burnard, now sporting a half-grown beard, glanced at Jenny, sleeping soundly beside him with her head resting against his shoulder, and marvelled, not for the first time, how she managed to sleep at all in aeroplanes. It had something to do with her faculty for trusting people – and things. It would never occur to her that some vital part of the aircraft might fail suddenly, plunging them all to their doom, or that perhaps the captain was trying a landing approach with one hand inside the skirt of the stewardess sitting on his lap. (He had actually witnessed such an incident once, while flying up front with a friend who had gone into civil aviation after the war.) Nor would it ever occur to Jenny that maybe one day he would send her away.

He looked out the window at the lights of Manhattan. In just a few minutes they would be down. Then it would all begin in earnest. He wondered what his father would have said.

112

'Willy . . . Willy . . . where are you hiding this time?' He remembered hearing his father's voice downstairs. 'Drat the boy!' Then a change of tone. 'Momma, why can't you teach him some manners? Twice the schoolteacher's called to see him and always he disappears!'

He heard his mother say something but her voice was more gentle and he couldn't distinguish the words. He felt bad for her, but not for him, that stiff, tight-lipped tyrant who ruled their lives with a tongue that could hurt like a snakebite. His father rarely used force – it wasn't necessary – and he didn't come home drunk like his Uncle Jake and beat his wife senseless, but he made their lives a misery just the same. Looking back down the long tunnel of time, he realized that his father's conduct stemmed from his own unhappiness. Poor relation of a rich man, all his life he had had to swallow condescension and a position of inferiority which had poisoned his soul and withered his undoubted talents.

'Say hello to your cousin Ben!' His father had pushed him forward to shake hands with the young man who had kept them waiting in the outer office for an hour and a half.

Willy wasn't looking at his father but he knew from his tone of voice that he would be wearing the ingratiating smile he often wore when talking to buyers. The boy hated him for his insincerity and for the humiliation that was now his to share. His father worked for his half brother as a travelling salesman and this was his employer's son who stared at him now with mild curiosity.

Willy's grandfather had died when his father was only a year old – killed in a construction accident while working on a block of cheap apartment houses in Baltimore. His grandmother had then moved back to Boston where most of her family came from and where one of her sisters could look after the child while she went to work in a department store. There she was noticed by a visiting salesman who invited her out to lunch. They discovered they had a lot in common, his own wife having recently died in childbirth, leaving him a son who had to be cared for by neighbours. Within two weeks they were married.

His father's new stepfather was kindly enough. He treated the boy and his mother well but, not unnaturally, it was his own son who received what little attention he could spare from his new business venture – a small factory that made men's shirts. When he died – worn out by work – he left his wife enough income to last her remaining years, but his entire capital went to his own son.

'So this is Willy,' the young man was saying. 'And you'd like to come and work for us?' Willy was thirteen at the time. There was nothing he would hate more, but his father answered for him.

'He's keen to start earning his living, aren't you, Willy?'

The boss's son looked at him with a faint smile. 'He doesn't look very keen,' he remarked. His father's smile turned to a snarl. 'That's just because he's a lazy good-for-nothing.' He stuck his forefinger viciously into Willy's ribs, at the same time switching on the smile again. 'But don't you worry, sir, I'll see he pulls his weight.'

'I hope so. We can't have any favouritism.' He now looked sternly into Willy's eyes. 'You know that, don't you?'

'Yes.'

'Yes, *sir*,' his father barked, poking him in the ribs again.

'Yes, sir.'

'That's better.'

His cousin then looked back at his father, and for the rest of the interview they talked about him as if he weren't there. At the end, his cousin nodded curtly. His father bowed and smiled his thanks while the other turned and walked away, without another word or glance in Willy's direction.

His first job was sweeping the floor of the cutting room. This was where wizened little men with huge scissors cut, from cardboard patterns, material for five or six shirts at a time, laid out on large wooden tables. Willy then carried the cut fabric to another part of the factory where women and girls sat in rows, sewing the pieces together. Then he went back to the cutting room for more.

Sometimes, when there was more work than the factory could handle, they subcontracted to one or the other of the

114

various sweatshops around the Irish quarter, and it was during one of these trips that Willy lost his virginity.

He was very good-looking. Women had always spoiled him, and by the time he was fourteen he was well over six feet tall and looked at least two or three years older than he was.

The manager of the sweatshop was a hard-bitten woman of indeterminate years who drove her girls like a galley commander and whose husband had run away, probably in self-defence, several years before. One afternoon she invited Willy to her apartment, over the sweatshop, after he had delivered the new material, then suggested he might like to do various other things for her.

Willy knew perfectly well what she meant from the outset, but he pretended to be slow until she became more explicit and offered him five dollars for a start. He held out his hand for the money. Somewhat taken aback at his alacrity, she gave it to him, then watched him put it away carefully in his back pants pocket. He finished the piece of cake she had given him, drank his coffee, and only then proceeded to comply with her request.

It was his first time, but he was pretty well up on theory, having talked at length with other boys in the factory. What he lacked in finesse he made up for in enthusiasm.

After that, he went back every week. Although the Irishwoman was only a taste of what was to follow, he always looked back on her memory with gratitude. Thanks to her, he secretly saved enough money – his father always saw to it that he gave all but a few cents of his official earnings to his mother – to enable him to leave, when the time came, without the immediate prospect of starvation.

In retrospect, it was easy to see how his father had become so bitter. He had possessed a wonderful tenor voice, and if there had been enough money and the opportunity for lessons, who knows how different life might have been for all of them. But even after forty years, understanding brought no spark of love to Willy – only the echo of hate for the sharp, nagging voice that had been the grey background of all their lives, sometimes an unbearable weapon of torment. So much so, that in spite of his love and pity for his mother, he had run away as soon as

115

he was able, knowing how it would grieve her but sure of her understanding.

He had never seen his father alive again. His mother, he saw twice. Once, at his father's funeral. She had sent a wire to the studios begging him to come and he went, although his going, he knew, would result in his being fired. When he got back to Hollywood, he was offered a small part by another company which led to his first big contract.

The second time was when he was on embarkation leave.

There was no need for him to have gone into the Air Force at all. By then he was an established star and the studio had had him exempted, but one day he got up quite early and signed on before anyone else knew about it. The studio was furious but made the best of it. The publicity people made him out to be a great patriot, which did him a lot of good after the war – he was even starred in a movie of his own wartime experiences – but it certainly wasn't true at the time.

What was the truth? Burnard himself never knew – except that if he had known what it was going to be like, he'd have turned over in bed that morning and gone back to sleep! Nearest to it was probably boredom. He was bored with making pictures, bored with those who called themselves his friends, but above all, bored with women and the prospect of going where they weren't appealed to him enormously. Of course, the feeling didn't last long, but by then it was too late.

Women had always been good to him. They had smoothed his path, fed him when he was hungry, visited him when he was in gaol. They had loved him, spoiled him, and practically suffo- cated him. He knew everything about them – and nothing. They offered themselves to him in endless shapes and sizes and in every conceivable manner, but he knew that inevitably they would all try to reach past him to the unattainable fantasy that was his screen image, brushing aside whatever was in reality there, as mindlessly as he used them in return. It was like the old cliché of the hero and heroine rushing towards each other with out- stretched arms from a great distance. But instead of meeting, their spirits pass on, leaving only unthinking flesh in blind collision. Only recently had he begun to think of a woman other than his mother – in fact, the girl who slept beside him now – as a fellow human being.

He had sent his mother money ever since he had first begun working in films, and she always wrote to thank him, giving him bits of news about his brothers and sisters; but before this there hadn't seemed to be any point in going back, and she had never asked – except that once.

His mother lived with his sister Effa and her husband. It was a nice enough house in the Italian district of Boston, since torn down to make room for a highway, but the visit was a waste of time. Friends and relations crowded into the house that evening to see the famous son, now a hero and leaving for the wars. He flew back to join his friends in New York early the following morning and made up for lost time by spending the rest of his leave throwing a party that went on for three days.

If he had been expecting some last minute outpouring of emotion during which his mother would embrace him and weep and tell him all the things she had been saving in her heart all these years – some reaching-out so that they would know each other once again, if only for a few moments – he was disappointed, or spared. She kissed him and told him to be careful, she even wept a little, but he knew she would have done the same for any neighbour's son going off to the war. He didn't know her at all. Whatever there had been between them had vanished. The woman he remembered was as dead as his father; in some respects, more so. She died in fact while he was in the prison camp.

The plane bumped a little as it banked into stacking order. Burnard glanced out of the window and saw the Verrazano Bridge a few thousand feet below them, outlined against the reflection of the moon on the narrows. The plane banked again to circle the city once more, and Jenny stirred but did not wake.

He had thought more than once about Jim Carson recently, the man who had tried to escape with him and who had been tortured to death by the Gestapo when they were caught. What would he, of all people, say now if he knew why Burnard had come to New York?

Jim had been a Christian. He had prayed a lot those last few hours. That they would be saved or, at least, that they would have the courage to stand up to whatever was going to happen to them. He had got to know Jim pretty well during the short time they had spent together in the cell just along the corridor from the interrogation room – probably as well as he had ever known anyone in his whole life. Years afterwards he would wake up in the night in a cold sweat, with Jim's screams still ringing in his ears.

'Jesus! Help me!'

That must have been when they poured boiling water on his testicles.

Jim had broken easily, and even then they had shot him, which had saved Burnard's life. Having got everything they wanted to know about who had helped the Americans since their escape, the interrogators let Burnard off with a beating and sent him back to the camp.

Jim hadn't been a very brave man. How had it helped to believe Jesus would save him? If only it had been different. If Jim had suffered bravely or had not been so afraid, the memory would help him now. But it had not been like that at all.

Amos Brown stood on the balcony and looked out over Central Park towards the skyscrapers further downtown. He heard the noise of the big jet overhead and glanced up before going inside, closing the balcony windows and drawing the curtains. He paused for a few seconds, then walked across the room and turned on the television set. After a moment, he turned it off again and flung himself into the corner of a large settee beside a pile of books that Lee had sent him. Suddenly he felt very much alone.

Perhaps he needed a woman? He dismissed the thought. There were still plenty eager enough to try and contain him, but he needed more – much more.

He looked slowly around the empty room again. It had all been here once – but he had thrown it away. What a fool!

The first meeting of those taking part in 'Christ on Trial' went smoothly, and there was no point in having the second and last run-through until the set was finished. As usual, Lee noted, this would give them only a couple of days at most before the first programme was broadcast, but there was nothing anyone could ever do about such things and he had to be content.

He would undoubtedly have been less so had he witnessed an incident at the end of the first rehearsal. O'Connell was leaving the studios with the others when Burnard caught up with him and touched him on the arm.

'Mr O'Connell?'

The other turned to him.

'Yes?'

'I understand you're a priest. Is that right?'

Father O'Connell hesitated for a moment, then he gave a short sigh. 'I suppose there's no point in denying it.'

Burnard said, 'I wonder if I could talk to you.'

'Of course. Here?'

'Which way are you going?'

'To get on a bus.'

'I'll walk with you, if I may?'

'All right.'

They walked in silence to the elevator, but once they were outside, Burnard said, 'Why don't you want people to know?'

'That I'm a priest?'

'Yes.'

O'Connell frowned slightly. 'Isn't it obvious?'

'Surely there's no harm in portraying the enemy in this sort of situation?'

'No, no.' The other shook his head. 'You don't understand.'

They reached a corner and Burnard stopped to face him. One or two other people glanced at them briefly before crossing the street but clearly none of them recognized Burnard, now that he was wearing a beard.

'There's a lot of things I don't understand, Father. That's what I wanted to talk about.' He paused for a second before resuming. 'Maybe it would help if you could explain your problem. Then I could tell you mine.'

119

The priest looked up at him without answering for a moment. In spite of his experience of men's frailty, he found himself surprised that this man, of all people, should seek his help.

'That is, if you can spare the time?' Burnard added after a few seconds.

'Yes, of course. I'm sorry. I'm just a little taken aback.'

'That I might need help?'

'Well,' and now Father O'Connell smiled faintly. 'You seem so confident. So . . . in command of the situation.'

'It's my job to put on a front, Father. But I know enough now to realize what's coming, what's expected of me, and for the first time in my life, I don't know how the hell I'm going to manage. I don't know what to do!'

Standing there at the corner of a busy street in New York, Father O'Connell suddenly felt the hairs on the back of his neck begin to tingle. There was something in the way the other looked and spoke that blotted out the noise of passing traffic; blotted out everything but the actor's eyes and the echo of his words. The priest shivered slightly, then said: 'Would you like to come back with me? We could talk quietly then.'

Burnard hesitated for a moment, then asked, 'Could I come this evening? There's something I have to attend to first.'

Ray Burgh's publicity campaign kept him out of Lee's hair most of the time. It was also Burgh's job to keep the sponsors happy, and Lee had to admit he was doing a good job on both counts.

The sponsors seemed as pleased as sponsors ever were with the way things were shaping up; but then, they had reason. Even though they had agreed to confine their advertising to the beginning and end of the programmes, public interest was already running high and there was every indication that audiences would set an all-time record. Lee did think, as they got nearer the time and everybody supposedly knew what he was doing, that things would quieten down, but what with carpenters, electricians, sound technicians, cameramen, company officials – not to mention the demands of the professional cast of actors and the daily arguments between Lang and Baal – Lee still found plenty to occupy his mind. In fact, as he freely admitted, if it

120

had not been for Mary, he would probably have gone clean out of it!

The last to arrive was Joseph Haald, the Norwegian high court judge who was visiting the United States to address the American Law Society, and whom Lee had persuaded to take part. Since the jurist refused to fly, he arrived too late for the first run-through. Thanks to Burgh, however, by the time the ship docked, the judge was already a national celebrity – which came to him as something of a surprise. In fact, he found so many press and TV men waiting for him on Pier 40 that it was necessary to hold an impromptu news conference. The press satisfied, Judge Haald proceeded to take his place for the final run-through on the set, which, as Lee had anticipated, had been finished just in time.

Chapter
8

Good Friday.

Lee knew that 'Christ on Trial' had already become a part
of the lives of dozens of people who had been strangers to each
other before it began; that it had permanently changed not a few
of them – his own and Mary's included. But he could never
have foreseen how many more would awake that morning little
knowing that the events of the next three days would tear apart
the accepted pattern of their lives.

By nightfall, everything was ready. As nine o'clock approached,
the sponsors and their wives began to arrive to watch the first
of the programmes in a special viewing room near the studio.
This was a gimmick dreamed up by Ray Burgh. partially to add
to the sense of occasion, but also so that he could be on hand to
pour scotch and gauge reactions.

Thirty minutes before broadcast time, the telephone rang in
Lee's office. He had been about to leave for the studio; in fact,
he had already reached the door and had to walk back to his
desk to answer the call. It was the callboy, phoning from a wall
telephone in the corridor outside the dressing rooms. His first
words made Lee's eyes widen with apprehension.

'Mr Burnard isn't in his dressing room, Mr Harrison,' the
boy reported. 'I checked and he hasn't arrived. At least, nobody's
seen him.'

Lee stood for a moment, his mind racing. Then he said,
'Well . . . go on looking.'

'Yes, sir.'

'And phone me the minute he arrives.'

Lee put down the phone, swearing under his breath. He
thought rapidly for a moment, checked the list of numbers on
his pad, and dialled the lobby.

'I haven't seen him, Mr Harrison,' the doorman told him.
'No, sir, there's always a bit of a stir. I'm sure he couldn't have

arrived without being seen.' The man listened for a few seconds, then nodded in answer to Lee's question. 'Yes, Mr Harrison. I'll let you know as soon as I see him.'

Lee's next call was to the Plaza Hotel. Within a few moments he was talking to the receptionist, who told him that the star had checked out just after breakfast.

'Are you sure?' Lee demanded. 'Yes, I see. But didn't he leave any message?'

Lee paused as the man assured him to the contrary, then he said, 'Okay. Thanks,' and was about to put down the receiver when he snatched it back up again.

'What about Miss Simak? Did she check out too?'

'Who?'

'Miss Simak. Mr Burnard's secretary.'

'Just a minute.' Lee waited, fuming impatiently. Then the voice came back on the other end of the line: 'According to our records, Miss Simak left a week ago.'

'A week!'

'We understood that she flew back to California.'

Lee put the phone down slowly without saying anything. He stood motionless, hardly daring to admit, even to himself, that Burnard might have run out on them. It was scarcely conceivable. Yet his absence now, coupled with his previous behaviour – checking out of the hotel, leaving no message – could hardly add up to anything else. And what about Jenny? John had never said anything about her leaving.

The more he thought about it, the more Lee's mind whirled. He was so preoccupied that he didn't hear the knock on the door, and it was a little while after it opened that he became aware of Father O'Connell standing just inside the doorway. Lee turned to look to him, his eyes still wide with shock.

'I was told you were here, even though you didn't answer,' the priest said.

'What do you want?' Lee's voice was harsh. He cleared his throat.

'I understand Mr Burnard isn't here?'

Lee took a step towards him.

'How do you know? Do you know where he is?'

123

The other shook his head. 'No. But I was half expecting this to happen.'

'You! Why should you have been expecting anything?'

'Please!' Father O'Connell held up his hand and Lee realized that he had been shouting.

'I'm sorry.' Then he went on in a more normal tone, although his voice still shook, 'But have you any idea where he is?' He glanced quickly at his watch and saw that barely ten minutes were left. If Burnard didn't show up of his own accord, it was probably too late anyhow.

'I don't suppose anyone knows.' Lee stared at him, and the priest continued, 'But I did promise to try and help him in any way I could.'

Lee's voice was bitter. 'It's we who need help right now, Father!'

'I know that, and I know he will come, if he can.'

Lee closed his eyes and took a deep breath.

'It's probably too late.'

'Then . . . ' Father O'Connell hesitated, then went on softly, 'Then . . . just for tonight . . . let me take his place.'

It seemed to Lee, for a moment, that he hadn't heard right.

'It's only necessary to answer the charge today,' the other went on. 'I know what to do.'

Lee paused a moment longer, gripped the priest by the arm, and stared at him intently. A few more seconds passed, then he said suddenly, 'It *might* just work . . . for tonight!'

'Then, that will give you . . . will give him another day.'

'You must tell me what you know afterwards.'

'I'll tell you what I can.'

'All right – later. Now let's get you down to makeup as fast as we can!'

In the studio, one side of which was filled with the courtroom set, all seemed chaos and confusion, but Joe Shand had been in the business long enough not to worry too much. Baal, Lang, and their assistants were already in position. In the control room, Joe himself, with two vacant seats beside him for Lee and Mary, was making a final check of equipment. On the other side of the studio, the members of the audience were filing into their places. Mary, oblivious of what was going on upstairs, was checking their passes with the help of an assistant, asking those holding the preselected numbers to sit in the jury box. She noted with relief that the prospective jurors seemed both excited and pleased.

Finally, the moment arrived. The studio audience settled down and those already on set held themselves ready.

In the sponsors' viewing room, Burgh ushered a few stragglers into their places just as the senior network announcer appeared on the monitor, without fanfare or music, and began: 'Ladies and Gentlemen: It is not often that a television network is privileged to present a series of programmes comparable to the one we are beginning tonight. Indeed, it is difficult to recall any real precedent. So that your enjoyment and concentration may be undisturbed, the sponsors have requested that there be no interruptions.'

In the viewing room some of those present looked at each other with modest smiles. In the control room Mary slipped quietly into her place and looked around for Lee.

'Nevertheless,' the announcer went on, 'we are sure you would wish to know the names of the firms whose generosity and public spirit have made our presentation possible this Eastertime.'

In the studio, the floor manager, who was wearing a pair of headphones, raised his hand. 'Stand by . . . in ten seconds.'

In the control room, all the monitors were now alive, including one showing the announcer.

'Camera one, forward slightly,' Shand breathed into his microphone. He glanced up at the appropriate monitor. 'That's enough.'

Lee arrived while the announcer was reading the list of sponsors. Mary put out her hand to touch his briefly. 'Good luck,' she whispered.

Lee nodded, but did not smile. He was still recovering his breath.

Now the announcer was looking straight into the camera. 'Ladies and Gentlemen,' he said, 'NBC presents "Christ on Trial." '

'Camera three,' Shand's assistant called. 'Four next.'

'Sound up.'

Everyone concentrated on the central monitor, which showed the picture being transmitted.

The scene was an exact replica of a modern American courtroom. The two attorneys were in their places, exchanging final words with the juniors. Various court officials were busying themselves with papers. Suddenly, the court clerk appeared at the back of the court and called out: 'Stand, please.'

Everyone obeyed, falling silent as Haald appeared, now fully robed, to take his place. When he was settled, the others sat down again. There was a brief murmur of conversation, which stopped as soon as the clerk of the court rose and began to read from a charge sheet.

'The People versus Jesus of Nazareth.'

He glanced behind him and Haald nodded. 'Bring in the Accused.' He spoke with the merest trace of accent.

Again there was a murmur of conversation, which rose as Father O'Connell, now made up to look as much like Burnard as possible, strode in. Lee looked around quickly and was amazed that not even Mary seemed to have noticed anything different – proving again that people see what they are expecting to see. Of course, those who had watched Burnard in rehearsals would realize the difference as soon as the priest opened his mouth, but now Lee believed that all concerned were professional enough not to betray their surprise. The one comforting thing was that it was not until the third programme that the Accused was due to take the stand – the same night that Father O'Connell himself was to appear as Judas. A lot could happen in forty-eight hours and until then they were safe – as long as everybody kept his mouth shut.

In the sponsors' room there was a murmur of satisfaction from some of those watching. Burgh smiled and nodded in acknowledgment, but his eyes darted to the deadpan expression of several others. He realized that his career probably rested on the ultimate reactions of these few.

The clerk rose to face the prisoner. 'Are you Jesus of Nazareth?'

Father O'Connell inclined his head. 'I am,' he said quietly.

126

'You are charged with fraud – in that, being an ordinary man, you deliberately led others to believe you enjoyed some special relationship with Almighty God, specifically, that you were his only Son.' The clerk looked up at him. 'How do you plead? Guilty, or not guilty?'

There was a long silence, until everyone but the clerk and Father O'Connell himself began to look restive. To keep the action going Shand ordered a camera to move in for a close-up. He glanced worriedly at Lee. 'My God,' he breathed, 'he's not going to wreck the whole thing by pleading guilty?'

Lee shook his head almost imperceptibly, but continued to stare at the monitor.

Haald bent forward. 'You must answer the charge,' he said.

After a moment longer, Father O'Connell took a deep breath, then said in a voice which just carried, 'I do not acknowledge the authority of this court.'

This caused something of a flurry. Haald banged his gavel for silence. Lee in the control room, breathed a sigh of relief. Then he turned to see Mary staring at him, her eyes wide with amazement. He glanced quickly at the others to see if anyone else had noticed. No one seemed to realize that the voice was not Burnard's. He looked back at Mary and shook his head slightly. He knew she would not say anything until they were alone.

'Quiet please!' Haald looked across at Lang. 'Will counsel for the defence please approach the bench?'

Lang stood up, glanced down at his junior, then went over to exchange a few words, unheard by the viewing audience, with the judge. A few seconds later, Lang nodded in agreement and returned to his place. The judge then turned to the clerk of the court.

'Enter a plea of "not guilty."'

The clerk bowed slightly. 'Yes, Your Honour.'

Haald then looked across at Father O'Connell. 'You may sit down,' he said.

'I prefer to stand.' The priest spoke quietly, without arrogance. After a moment Haald nodded again.

'Very well,' he said, 'if you change your mind later, you may

127

be seated at any time.' He then glanced in the direction of the chief prosecutor. Baal rose to his feet.

'Your Honour,' he began, 'I appear for the People in this case, assisted by my colleague Mr Kolok.' At this he glanced down and smiled at his junior. Haald nodded briefly, and Baal continued. 'We should like to begin by assuring the court that we do not seek to try to prove or disprove the existence of God; only to show that the Accused could not have been the "Son of God" in a way that made him different from any other member of the human race.' He looked at the jury. 'We think it necessary to make this point because so pervasive has the Accused's claim become that we members of what has become known as "Western civilization" might be forgiven for confusing the two issues.'

Haald inclined his head. 'The point is accepted, Mr Baal. Please continue.'

'Secondly, Your Honour, we accept the historical fact of the existence, and consequently, the identity of the Accused.'

The judge smiled faintly. 'That certainly simplifies the conduct of this trial,' he admitted.

Baal returned the smile, then continued. 'Lastly, the prosecution intends to take the line that the Accused was completely sincere in what he believed about himself; that although he did mislead others, he was, first and foremost, self-deluded.'

'I see.' Haald glanced at the clerk of the court, then briefly at Lang before turning back to the prosecutor. 'Can a man be guilty of fraud as defined by precedent if he acts unwittingly?' he asked mildly. 'Should not the charge be altered to a lesser one of, say, misleading without intent to deceive?'

At this, Lang hurriedly rose to his feet. 'Your Honour,' he said, 'with all due respect, such a charge is scarcely possible. The court might just as well bring in a verdict of "guilty but insane" and have done with it.'

Baal grinned. 'I agree,' he said, but Lang went on, ignoring him.

'Whereas our evidence will show that, far from being a simpleton, the Accused was a man of the highest intelligence who easily saw through every intellectual trap set for him by the best brains of his day.' He paused for a moment to look at the

128

prisoner, then turned to the jury. 'The defence cannot dictate to our worthy opponents what line of argument they ought to take,' he told them, turning back to the judge, 'but we ask the court to allow the original charge to remain – and to let our case stand or fall on that issue alone.'

Haald looked at Baal, who was still on his feet. The latter shrugged slightly. 'The prosecution is content with the original charge, Your Honour. But after hearing our case, the court may well decide that the verdict suggested a few moments ago by my learned colleague is appropriate.' He suppressed a smile.

Lang said, 'Your Honour knows I was suggesting nothing of the kind. I was merely pointing out . . . '

Haald raised his hand, interrupting the defence attorney. 'Mr Lang, the court appreciates the point you are making.' He then glanced at the jury. 'The jury will note that the defence strongly contests any suggestion that the Accused was insane.'

'In fact, quite the reverse,' defence counsel put in, 'he was probably the most sane . . . ' but again Haald held up his hand to interrupt.

'Mr Lang, you will have the opportunity to make your opening address in a moment. Mr Baal still has the floor.'

Lang bowed slightly. 'I beg the court's pardon,' he said, and sat down.

'Thank you, Your Honour.' Baal smiled. 'But I have no other points I wish to make at this time.' He sat down and the judge looked back at Lang.

'Very well. In that event, Mr Lang, you may proceed.'

Lang got to his feet. 'Thank you,' he said, then took a breath before beginning.

'Your Honour, the defendant is either who he says he is – the only begotten son of God the Father, a fact that I and literally billions of others down the ages have been taught to repeat each Sunday, firmly believing the words to be true – or he is the biggest confidence trickster and heartless blackguard of all time!' He paused while a murmur rippled through the court. When it died, he continued, 'From the dawn of the history of the Jewish people the coming of the Messiah had been foretold – the Chosen One, the Lamb of God whose blood would wash away the sins of the world, the Christ!' Lang looked deliberately around the court. 'Our evidence will show beyond any doubt that the man who stands accused before this court today, Jesus of Nazareth, could not possibly have been the deceiver I described, but was, indeed, Jesus the Christ.' He paused again to look directly at the jury. 'Indeed, if *he* was not the Messiah, why had another not appeared? Some Jewish apologists now contend that probably he will not appear in the flesh at all – that the millennium will just come about, gradually.' Lang's voice now took on an accusing tone. 'But is it coincidence that almost immediately after the rejection of the Accused by the Jewish people as a whole, Jerusalem was utterly destroyed – as foretold by Jesus himself; that the Temple, which had stood for a thousand years as the symbol of God's covenant with the Israelites – of which the sending of a Messiah was to be the crowning fulfilment – was razed to the ground, never to be rebuilt; and finally, most terrible of all, instead of the millennium of peace which was to follow the Coming, the Jewish nation was scattered to the far corners of the earth for twice that time, again, as Jesus himself foretold.'

Lang reached into his breast pocket, put on a pair of reading glasses, and taking a note from his assistant, began to read:

' "*For there shall be great distress in the land, and wrath upon this people. And they shall fall by the edge of the sword and shall be led away captive unto all nations. And Jerusalem shall be trodden down of the Gentiles . . . until the crime of the Gentiles be fulfilled.*" '

Lang removed his glasses. 'Who can deny,' he demanded, 'that these things came to pass?' He looked at the jury. 'The wrath of God has indeed been terrible. Fortunately, for all of us, his mercy is even more strong. But can anyone reasonably suppose the terrible retribution, only now coming to an end, has been for nothing – unconnected with those awful words uttered by the mob before Pilate: "His blood be on us and on our children!" '

The counsel for the defence paused, looked around the silent court, inclined his head briefly at Haald, and sat down. The silence continued for a few moments as everyone's eyes turned to the prisoner, who stood looking at the judge impassively. Then Haald nodded briefly. 'Thank you,' he said. 'Er, Mr Baal, would you please call your first witness?'

In contrast to the sombre mood engendered by Lang's speech, Baal bounced to his feet, smiling. 'Delighted, Your Honour,' he said, beaming. 'The prosecution calls Dr Hilda Rogers.'

Almost immediately, a middle-aged woman in modern dress came from the back of the courtroom and took the witness stand. She had iron-grey hair, which had obviously been specially coiffed for the occasion, and an intelligent face. Lee noticed also that she smiled easily.

The clerk moved forward to administer the oath. In the control room Mary touched Lee on the arm and said softly, 'They're *marvellous* – Lang and the others!'

Lee nodded. 'They're on home ground,' he whispered back. 'The real test is going to come when one of the actors takes the stand.'

Mary gave him a look, then squeezed his hand. 'Relax,' she whispered, 'it's going to be all right.'

Lee smiled gratefully.

The clerk retired and Baal stepped up to the stand to ask his first question.

'Would you please tell the court your name and what you do for a living?'

The woman inclined her head graciously as she answered, 'My name is Hilda Rogers. I'm a consulting obstetrician.'

'Could you tell us exactly what that entails, Doctor?'

'General practitioners consult me if they have any unusual problems on which they want a second opinion.'

'In connection with what?'

Dr Rogers smiled faintly. 'Why, childbirth,' she answered, 'as well as prenatal and postnatal problems.'

Baal nodded and glanced at his notes before asking the next question. 'Have you written books which are widely regarded as authoritative works on the subject?'

'Within the medical profession?'

'Of course.'

The witness hesitated for a moment before answering. 'Yes, I have.'

'In other words,' Baal went on, 'if I can put it in plain language, you are one of our country's leading experts in the science of human reproduction?'

Dr Rogers frowned slightly. 'That sounds a little immodest,' she protested.

Baal also frowned, rather impatiently. 'We're not concerned with modesty here, Doctor. We just want the truth.' He paused for a few seconds before continuing: 'Is what I have said a fair description of your standing in the medical profession at the present time?'

'Yes.'

'Thank you. Now, Doctor, would it be possible, in your opinion, under any conceivable circumstances, for a female human ovum to be fertilized without the presence of an equivalent male sperm?'

The witness shook her head firmly. 'No.'

'Not under any circumstances?' Baal persisted. 'Say – in the laboratory?'

'Human ova have been fertilized under laboratory conditions . . . '

'In a test tube?' Baal put in, and the witness nodded.

'Something like it,' she said. 'But a male sperm is still necessary.'

'What about artificial sperm? Is such a thing possible?'

Again Dr Rogers shook her head. 'Not in the foreseeable future,' she said. 'Although infinitely small, the sperm contains half the blueprint of an eventual human being, complete in every detail. It is programmed at molecular level, and I would say that if we ever reach that stage – and personally I hope we do not – we would be halfway to creating an artificial person.'

At this Baal himself smiled. 'I share your hopes, Doctor,' he said.

'But artificial or not,' the other went on, 'without sperm you cannot have a human being. It would be like trying to build a ship with only the plans of, say, the decks and engines – only worse, because without the whole plan of a living organism, you cannot begin at all.'

Baal nodded. 'Very well,' he said, 'then let us turn to the specific matter under investigation. Are you familiar with the gospel account of the virgin birth?'

132

'I have studied it again recently, as you requested.'

'And what was your opinion upon reading it again?' Baal asked.

'I'm afraid it's impossible.'

'Why do you say "afraid"?'

Dr Rogers smiled a little sadly. 'It's a beautiful story,' she said. 'I only wish it were true.'

The prosecutor returned her smile. 'Speaking as a human being, I presume,' he said, 'not as a scientist?'

'Of course.'

'Thank you.' Baal glanced up at Haald, said, 'No further questions,' and went back to his seat.

Lang got to his feet more slowly and walked thoughtfully towards the stand. 'Doctor,' he began, 'you have given us your opinion but, just supposing for a moment that the story we are considering happened to be true, how would you describe such an occurrence as the virgin birth in one word?'

The witness looked at him for a moment before replying. 'I should say it was a miracle.'

'A miracle?' Lang repeated.

'I just don't happen to believe in such things – in the literal sense.'

Lang raised his eyebrows slightly. 'Nevertheless,' he said, 'how would you define the word "miracle"?'

Dr Rogers hesitated for a moment. 'Something that defies natural physical laws.'

'Which has, therefore, no logical explanation?'

'Yes.'

'Yes, I see,' Lang paused for a moment, glanced at the jury, then turned back to the witness. 'How would you define electricity?' he asked.

'It's a current capable of generating power by the displacement of electrons.'

Lang smiled pleasantly. 'That's a precise description of what it does,' he said, 'but what is it?'

Dr Rogers returned his smile. 'Very well,' she said, 'it's an electromagnetic force.'

'And what might that be?' Lang asked, still smiling. He saw

133

her hesitating, then went on, 'Apart from being a current capable of generating power?' He paused again just long enough for her to open her mouth, then without allowing her to speak he demanded, 'Isn't it true, Doctor, that our knowledge of electricity is really empirical? That we have an excellent knowledge of what it does, and how to use it, without the faintest idea of what it really is?'

Dr Rogers looked up at Haald as if seeking his support. 'This is outside my field,' she began.

'Come now, Doctor,' Lang persisted, 'a person does not reach your eminence in the medical profession without gaining a considerable knowledge of physics, surely? Isn't it true to the best of your knowledge and belief, that electricity defies analytical description?'

The witness now began to look flustered and Baal jumped to his feet. 'Your Honour,' he said, 'the defence is trying to discredit the witness by this excursion into a field in which, as she has already made clear, she has no specialized knowledge . . . '

'Your Honour,' Lang tried to continue.

' . . . and which is, moreover, totally irrelevant,' Baal persisted.

'Your Honour,' Lang began again.

'Mr Lang,' Haald said, interrupting him, 'the prosecution does have a point.'

'I'm simply trying to establish the nature of a miracle, Your Honour. If the court would bear with me just a few moments longer, I feel sure it will be satisfied as to the relevance of my line of questioning.'

Haald paused for a moment, then inclined his head. 'Very well,' he said, and turned to the prosecutor. 'I think the prosecution must agree that the nature of a miracle has relevance,' he said. 'Not only to the circumstances of the Accused's birth, but also insofar as his ministry and subsequent death are concerned.' He turned back to Lang. 'Nevertheless,' he went on, 'the court would be pleased if the defence could reach the point as quickly as possible.'

Lang bowed slightly. 'As Your Honour pleases.'

Baal subsided into his seat as the attorney for the defence turned back to the witness.

'Doctor, I will repeat the question. Would you agree that the exact nature of the force we call electricity is unknown?'

During the previous exchange Dr Rogers had obviously regained her composure. She now said calmly, 'I believe that is so.' Lang saw Baal smile briefly but he went on, 'Then by your earlier definition, electricity is a miracle?'

A ripple of laughter ran through the courtroom, but the witness gazed at him blandly. 'Not at all,' she said. 'Electricity cannot be said to defy natural law; it is entirely predictable.'

Lang inclined his head slightly as if acknowledging the skill of her parry. 'Well, then,' he said, 'let us turn to your basic premise. Do you believe in God, Doctor?'

The other shook her head. 'No,' she said firmly.

'Then who made the laws which govern the universe – and to which you evidently attach such importance?'

Dr Rogers shrugged. 'That question presupposes the sort of answer you require,' she said. 'In reality, nobody made or ordered them as such. They just are.'

'They just happened?'

'They have always been.'

Lang hesitated for a moment. 'But you have no idea why – in spite of your certainty about their duration?'

Dr Rogers paused for a few seconds, trying to guess where this was leading. 'We shall understand one day, I have no doubt.'

'And in the meantime,' Lang persisted, 'you are prepared to accept them?'

'Yes.'

Lang glanced briefly at the jury as he asked his next question. 'Isn't that more illogical than supposing them to be the work of an intelligence so great we can understand only a very small part of His creation at a time – as and when He wants us to?'

The witness hesitated. 'I don't know,' she said eventually.

Lang smiled. 'Doctor, accepting the existence of that super-intelligence for the moment, which the prosecution does not seek to deny' (this with a brief glance at Baal), 'would it not be a comparatively simple matter for Him to alter one of His own rules?'

Dr Rogers shrugged. 'It is difficult to answer such a hypothetical question,' she said.

135

'Please try,' Lang persisted.

The witness paused for a moment. 'Very well. Then I should say such a being would be unlikely to break His own laws.'

'Not even in exceptional circumstances?'

It was the witness's turn to smile. 'The child who carefully builds a sand castle is the least likely to kick it over,' she said. This drew a laugh from many of those present, but Lang looked at her, blank-faced.

'I fail to see the connection,' he said, deliberately killing the laugh. 'May we return to an earlier answer?' He paused for a moment. 'You implied just now, if I understand you correctly, that although you do not understand the laws that govern the universe at the moment, you expect to one day.'

'Not me personally. Man as a species.'

Lang nodded thoughtfully. 'I see,' he said. 'Does that mean Man – or perhaps I should say *Woman* – does not fully under-stand them at the moment?'

'That's what I said.'

'Then is it not possible that the apparent miracle of the virgin birth was a perfectly natural extension of the presently under-stood operation of natural laws by an intellect who understands them more fully?'

'That's another hypothetical question.'

'Then answer something more specific,' Lang went on, almost without drawing breath. 'Is it not true that living cells reproduce themselves by splitting and that, until quite recently – on the time scale of evolution – this was the only way living organisms reproduced themselves?'

'Yes . . . but . . . '

'Thank you,' Lang said firmly, 'no further questions.' He turned on his heel at once and went back to his place.

The witness hesitated for a moment, clearly taken by surprise at the sudden termination of her ordeal, then left the stand.

Baal now rose to his feet: 'Please call Dr Collins,' he said.

'Another physician, Mr Baal?' Haald asked, frowning slightly.

'Dr Collins is a doctor of theology, Your Honour.'

'Very well.'

Dr Collins, a large gentle-faced man with a ruddy complexion, took the stand and was sworn in by the clerk. Baal then stepped forward.

'You are Dr Paul Collins?'

'That's right.'

'Are you senior professor of theology at St David's College, Oxford, in England?'

'In Wales, actually,' Collins answered with a smile. 'The theological college is affiliated with Oxford University but is situated in Lampeter.' He spoke with a pleasant but unfamiliar accent, which Lee took to be Welsh.

Baal nodded. 'Thank you for the correction.' He then went on, 'Doctor, what is the modern theological view of the virgin birth?'

Collins took a deep breath and let it out between his teeth, thoughtfully. 'Its belief is still widely held amongst many Christians,' he began, 'but in the light of modern developments, an increasingly large number are beginning to feel it is not an essential ingredient in believing in Christ as the Messiah.' He gave a brief shrug. 'Bishop Stevley of the Anglican Church, for example, and even Father Salt of the Order of Jesuits are among several prominent ecclesiastics who have expressed doubt on the matter recently.'

Baal nodded. 'And what about those who lived at the time?' he asked.

'Ah, yes,' the other smiled but went on seriously. 'It is evident from the Gospels and the Acts of the Apostles that early Christians attached little, if any, importance to the matter. Neither Mark, which was the first to be written, nor John, which was the last – written after many years in which to dwell on what was or was not significant – makes any mention of the virgin birth. Only Matthew of the original Gospels – I'm not counting Luke, who admits at the beginning that his version is largely a repetition tidied into some sort of order – mentions it at all.'

'I see.' Baal glanced in the direction of the jury. 'Tell me, Doctor, in your opinion, is it in order to qualify one's acceptance of the gospel in this way if one professes to be a Christian?'

'I believe so.' The witness hesitated for a moment. 'Clearly – or perhaps I should say, in my opinion – the main story is true, but certain traditions have grown up around the central core which I do not feel it is necessary to accept without question.'

'In other words,' Baal went on, 'one might simply accept Christ as a great teacher who lived an exceptionally wonderful life, but reject the idea of his being the son of God?'

Collins frowned. 'Certainly one could not go so far as that and remain a Christian,' he said, 'but that's exactly what the Moslem religion does teach.'

'So you believe the main part of the story, and without it, obviously you would not call yourself a Christian. But for the rest of us, if the account won't stand up as a whole, why should we stop with the virgin birth? What about the resurrection? Will you admit that this might not also be one of the traditions to which you referred?'

Collins shook his head. 'I don't think it is possible to dispense with the resurrection,' he said, 'but I understand the point you are trying to make.'

'What I am asking,' Baal said, 'is this: inasmuch as many leading Christians agree that the gospel story needs some qualification, is it reasonable to expect those of us who come to it with an open mind to reject only those items which leave the declared status of the Accused intact?'

Collins looked doubtful. 'Perhaps not,' he said, 'at least, not on those grounds alone.'

Baal nodded. 'Thank you, Doctor. No further questions.' He sat down and Lang took his place.

'I have only one question to ask you, Doctor,' the defence attorney began. 'In spite of all the analysis of what other people think and believe, which you and my learned colleague have just undertaken for the benefit of the court, do you personally believe in the story of the virgin birth?'

Collins looked at him for a moment, then said, 'Taken in isolation, I would reject it out of hand. But in the light of what followed, it could be true.'

Lang smiled. 'Which is, I suppose,' he said, 'as near to a direct answer as we're likely to get.'

Collins said, 'It remains, like many things, a matter of personal faith. On this particular point, I am simply uncertain.'

Lang nodded. 'Thank you, Doctor. You may step down.'

138

Collins left the courtroom and Lang went back to his seat. Baal rose.

'Your Honour, the last witness we should like to call at this time is Archelaus, eldest son of the king who ruled over Judea and Galilee at the time of the birth of the Accused. He is not so well known to us as his famous – or infamous – father, Herod, whom the Greeks called "The Great," but I have asked Archelaus to testify because he will be able to tell us, not only of events immediately preceding and following the birth of Jesus, but also of what happened after Herod's death, when the Accused was four years of age and reportedly living with his parents in the village of Matareah on the banks of the Nile in Egypt.'

Haald inclined his head and Baal turned to the clerk.

'Call Archelaus.'

Mary's hand tightened on Lee's arm. Lee stared at the short, effete-looking young man, dressed in the purple of a Roman aristocrat, now taking the stand, then whispered, 'Now we'll really see if it's going to work!'

'Camera four pull back a fraction,' Shand ordered quietly. 'Take in the faces of the jury.' Lee glanced up to watch the jury's reactions on the monitor. 'Camera one next,' he heard the assistant say, and almost immediately Shand cut to a close-up of the stand where the clerk was administering the oath.

The closer shot showed that although the witness's face betrayed the beginnings of flabbiness – reportedly from extreme self-indulgence – his mouth was hard and his eyes easily narrowed, giving the whole face a shrewd, calculating look that contained more than a hint of cruelty. He really looked, Lee thought, like someone who came from a family which had carried the art of subterfuge and political assassination to a point that made the Borgias of a later era seem like hesitant amateurs.

When the clerk had finished, Baal stepped forward.

'You are King Archelaus, son of Herod the Great?'

'I am.' The voice had a delicate, almost weak quality, which contrasted sharply with its owner's expression.

Baal said, 'Would you please explain to the court your relationship with the Roman Empire?'

'My relationship, or that of my country?'

139

'Both, if you don't mind.'

'Certainly.' The witness turned to face the jury. 'Israel was part of the Roman Empire, but as reward for welding its scattered chiefdoms and tribes into one law-abiding nation, my father was granted the right to rule as king, exercising power in the name of the Emperor Augustus.'

'In fief, as it were?'

Archelaus frowned. 'I am not familiar with the expression.'

'No matter.' Baal held up his hand for a moment, then lowered it and continued. 'Your father reigned for approximately forty years, I understand?'

'That is correct.'

'Was he loved by the people?'

The witness hesitated, then said, 'I think it true to say he was admired by most law-abiding citizens. Indeed, without the stability of firm government Israel could not have achieved the level of prosperity it did, prosperity which had never been achieved before as far as the ordinary people were concerned, not even in Solomon's time. Those in commerce certainly appreciated this.'

'But there was trouble?'

'Oh yes. God himself called us a stiff-necked people! Inevitably, the more fanatical were blind to the benefits my father's rule had brought – even to the entire rebuilding and refurbishing of the Great Temple in Jerusalem – and could see in his every action only the hand of Rome.'

'Were there any serious challenges to his authority?'

'To begin with, yes. But once the country had been unified, they never amounted to anything.'

'What about the period towards the end of your father's life?'

Again the witness paused, evidently weighing his words. Finally he spoke. 'As my father neared his death, he became progressively more afraid that advantage would be taken of his illness and a serious rebellion mounted.'

'Had he any grounds for these suspicions?'

'On one occasion, about a year before he died, a group of young Pharisees led by one Matthias stormed the Temple and took possession of it.'

140

'What happened?'

'They did a great deal of damage, but were eventually over-powered.'

At this point Lang rose to his feet.

'Your Honour, no doubt this is all very instructive, but we are here to try the prisoner, not take part in a history lesson.'

Haald nodded and turned to the prosecutor. 'Mr Baal, interesting although this is, we do seem to have drifted away from the point.'

Baal nodded. 'Indeed, Your Honour. I simply felt it would do no harm to acquaint the court with the historical background to the events with which we are concerned.'

'Our time is not unlimited!'

Baal bowed slightly. 'I apologize. I will endeavour to bring the witness's testimony directly to the point.' He turned back to the stand.

'Would it be true to say that during the last years of your father's reign, and during the thirteen years of your own rule, there never was a time when rebellion of one sort or another was not in progress or imminent?'

'They were always contained.'

'Nevertheless?'

'Yes. It would be true to say so.'

'And who, above all others, was the focal point of this discontent?'

'John, son of Zacharias.'

'Later known as the Baptist?'

'That is correct. Not even my father dared touch him, for he was venerated by the people as a holy man. He did not take up arms himself but constantly incited others to do so.'

'He preached sedition?'

'Not directly, or not even he would have escaped. He constantly referred to the Deuteronomic law of kingship, implying thereby that God did not approve my father's rule.'

'But how could that be? According to Christian reports, John was only six months older than the Accused. When your father died, that would have made him barely five years old.'

'Nonsense!' The witness's face now twisted with anger. 'I

141

myself came into conflict with him the moment I came to the throne – or rather, I clashed with the chief priests because of him.'

'How was that?'

'As an act of mercy I released ten thousand prisoners as my first act of kingship. Unfortunately, John took this as a sign of weakness and goaded the people into demanding his appointment as high priest instead of Joazar, my own nomination.' The look of anger now turned into a sneer of contempt as he continued, 'Scarcely the action of a five-year-old child, no matter how gifted!'

Baal allowed himself a brief smile, then went on. 'You are saying, in effect, that the Christian reports are incorrect?'

'If that's what they allege.'

'Thank you.' Baal paused for a moment, then said, 'If they are incorrect in such a fundamental matter, would you think it likely . . . '

'Objection, Your Honour.' Lang rose hurriedly to his feet again.

Baal raised his hand in acknowledgment and turned to the bench for a moment. 'I'm sorry. I'll rephrase the question.' He turned back to the witness. 'Do you know if the other accounts – those which concern the so-called miraculous birth of the Accused – are true?'

The witness shrugged. 'I know little of them, but if they are accurate . . . '

'Your Honour,' Lang protested. 'The prosecution is obviously leading the witness to express an opinion.'

Haald nodded and frowned at Baal. 'Objection sustained. The prosecution will confine itself to asking questions of fact.'

'I apologize to the court. It is a little difficult in this case to distinguish one from the other, but we will do our best.'

'Very well.'

Baal turned back to the witness.

'Then let us move on.' He glanced down at his notes. 'Please tell the court what happened when the chief priests came to you and tried to replace your own nominee for high priest with John.'

Archelaus straightened up and looked directly into the camera.

'Naturally, I refused.'

142

'What happened then?'

'There was a series of disturbances – which were suppressed. I had often thought my father unduly harsh in such matters, but this incident taught me a lesson I never forgot. In the long run, there was less suffering, less loss of life in being ruthless with troublemakers. In this particular case, far more people died than the ten thousand I originally spared. And that was only the beginning.'

Baal nodded. 'I was coming to that. What happened to John after this?'

'He ran away and hid in the desert. For a while, nothing was heard of him, then he began to make even more trouble.'

'How was that?'

'He began to preach the coming of the Messiah. And not in general terms – as had been the case from the beginning of history. John spread the rumour that the Messiah's arrival was imminent and began to baptize those who came under his influence, not only as a sign of repentance – there was no harm in that – but also as a bond between fellow conspirators sworn to overthrow the legal government.'

'Would you tell the court what happened as a result of all this?'

'With pleasure. At John's invitation, no less than three stepped forward claiming to be the Messiah and, after gathering armies, closed on Jerusalem.' Archelaus turned to the jury. 'The three imposters were Judas of Galilee, son of Hizgiah whose rebellion my father had crushed some years earlier; Simon of Persea, an escaped slave; and the shepherd Athronga.'

'What happened?'

'They were defeated.' There was a pause after the witness turned back to Baal, and Lee saw that his face had hardened. But he went on softly, 'Only Judas escaped. The rest were destroyed.'

Baal let the ensuing silence hang, then he asked quietly, 'Would it come as any surprise to you to learn that the Accused was also baptized by John?'

Archelaus turned to look at the prisoner while the prosecutor continued, 'He also claimed to be the Messiah and eventually led his followers to Jerusalem.' Baal consulted his notes again.

'According to the Roman historian, Josephus, the Temple was occupied and the depleted Roman garrison destroyed. Pilate, the governor, was with the main force at Caesarea, and when he heard what had happened, he made a forced march to Jerusalem and retook the city within hours – after which Jesus and all those who had not managed to escape were tried and crucified.'

Archelaus turned back to Baal and nodded slowly. 'They were troubled times.'

'There would be nothing out of the ordinary in such events?'

'Nothing.'

'Except, possibly,' and now Baal himself turned to the jury, 'the fact that as all Jesus' right-hand men managed to escape, they were able to carry on after he died . . . '

Haald interrupted. 'I am amazed the defence has allowed you to depart so far from straightforward questions without objection, Mr Baal, but I can no longer allow you to make what amounts to a speech at this stage.'

Lang rose.

'Your Honour, the defence is aware of this deliberate distortion by Josephus of my client's mission in the world, and of the events leading to his crucifixion. We knew that the prosecution would parade the travesty at some stage and felt it better that it be disposed of as early in the trial as possible, no matter how it emerged.'

Haald inclined his head. 'Very well, Mr Lang.' He then turned to Baal.

'I have the feeling your examination has come to its conclusion, Mr Baal. Is that so?'

Baal smiled and bowed slightly.

'I have no further questions, Your Honour.'

'Very well. Mr Lang, you may commence your cross-examination of the witness.'

The two attorneys changed places.

Lang paused for a moment to allow a buzz of conversation in the courtroom to subside. Then he turned to the witness.

'I understand that although you were the eldest son of your father, you did not succeed to the whole of his kingdom on his death?'

'That was not as he wished it. My cousin, Herod Antipas, made a pact with the Romans behind my back.'

'As a result, I understand, your jurisdiction was confined to Judea, whereas your cousin ruled over Galilee?'

'That is true.'

'And was it not to Galilee that John fled after you sought to put him to death?'

'After his attempt to usurp my authority, my soldiers sought him to bring him to trial, as was the law.'

'Nevertheless, he went where you couldn't touch him?'

'So?'

'So he was able to live in peace for a great many years.'

'Antipas was soft!' The witness spat out the words as if they were poison.

'Or perhaps, having better information, he saw little harm in what John was preaching?'

Archelaus stared at him with eyes as cold as those of a crocodile, but made no answer. Lang went on. 'According to one report the theme of his message was this, and I quote,' Lang glanced at his own notes and read, ' "A mortal shall not reign over you, but the Most High, who sent me." ' Lang looked up at the witness. 'Those words would seem rather to refer to the heavenly kingdom Jesus himself talked about later in his life, would they not?'

Archelaus again made no answer. 'Well?' Lang persisted. 'Do they or don't they?'

Eventually, the witness answered sullenly, 'I don't know.'

'Exactly,' the defence attorney went on. 'There's probably a great deal you don't know because both John and Jesus spent most of their lives keeping out of your way – and I don't blame them. It also means you don't know much about either of them, except what you heard other people tell you – and that was probably what they thought you wanted to hear – which makes the greater part of your evidence hearsay and, therefore, inadmissible.'

'I don't know.' For the first time the witness looked confused. 'I don't know what you're talking about.'

Lang smiled. 'Then permit me to help you tell the court

about something you possibly *do* know about.' He paused for a moment. 'Four years before your father died, he received at his court in Jerusalem a caravan of visiting Magi. I'm sure you remember. It caused something of a stir.'

Archelaus nodded curtly.

'I remember some such.'

'Splendid! Did you learn why they had come?'

'They said the sky was full of omens.'

'Of what precisely?'

'Something to do with the birth of a new king.'

'Ah! Now we're getting somewhere!' Lang took a breath, then continued.

'What happened after they left?'

'Nothing happened.'

'You mean they didn't return?'

The witness shrugged and began to look bored.

'They didn't return. Nothing happened – that's what I said.'

'In spite of the fact that your father had asked them to do so?'

'It didn't matter. He had spies follow them.'

'Then something did happen?'

'I meant something out of the ordinary. He had spies follow everyone – including me!'

Lang gave a grim smile. 'I don't blame him!' A ripple of laughter went round the courtroom and Archelaus flushed.

'He had no reason to distrust me!' he said, angrily.

'I thought you tried to have him poisoned?'

'It's a lie!'

Baal jumped to his feet, but Haald held up his hand.

'Mr Lang, the court will not tolerate the abuse of witnesses. No matter how much you may disagree with a witness, you will treat him with respect as long as I am presiding.'

Lee could see that the defence lawyer looked more than uncomfortable. With so strict a man on the bench, Lang's task would be considerably more difficult. Finally he said, 'Your Honour, while accepting your ruling, the defence would humbly ask the court to bear in mind that the imputation of practices that would undoubtedly provoke extreme reaction in modern times were so commonplace during the lifetime of the Accused

146

that questions concerning their happening or otherwise may be considered simply questions of fact – not implying anything out of the ordinary.'

Haald suppressed a smile. 'The court accepts your point, Mr Lang,' he said, 'and will exercise its judgment in each case on its merits.' He looked at the jury. 'There is, of course, nothing wrong in counsel attempting to undermine witnesses for the opposite side provided that it is done in a proper manner.' He turned and looked from Lang to Baal, the latter having now resumed his seat, and continued, 'I simply thought it an appropriate moment to express my opinion concerning future conduct.'

Baal rose from his seat for a moment to acknowledge the ruling and Lang inclined his head.

'Very well, Mr Lang. Please continue.'

Lang turned back to the witness and saw, to his annoyance, that Archelaus had completely regained his composure. The interruption had probably lost Lang the round. Nevertheless, he had no choice but to continue.

'Would you please tell the court what your father's spies reported?'

Archelaus smiled at him infuriatingly. 'I don't remember – if I was ever told, which I doubt.'

'Did anything happen as a result of their reports?' Lang persisted doggedly.

'Yes. I seem to remember that a company of foot soldiers set out with two officers for Bethlehem.'

'What did they do there?'

'I've no idea.'

'Then let me tell you. They murdered about twenty young children. Does that surprise you?'

'Not in the least. Just before my father died he had ten thousand heads of families imprisoned, with orders given that they were to be executed as soon as his own death was announced.'

'In heaven's name, why?'

'So that the event would be marked by a national day of mourning.' The witness shrugged. 'You can hardly expect him to have attached much importance to such a trifling matter as the death of a few children if he thought his throne in danger.'

'Then he did take the visiting Magi seriously?'

'Oh, yes. They were held in much awe throughout the East.'

Lang turned to the jury. 'And so, it would appear that, in this respect, the witness's evidence substantially corroborates the traditional Christmas story.'

Baal rose to his feet quickly. 'As a point of historical fact, perhaps, Your Honour. In my opening address I said that the prosecution accepted the existence of the Accused, but it says nothing whatsoever of the far more relevant part of the story which seeks to establish his special identity from the beginning and his relationship with the Creator.'

Lang said mildly, 'I seem to remember my learned colleague implying earlier that inasmuch as part of the witness's evidence conflicted with the Christian report in one particular, the rest of the story was in doubt. It is at least comforting to note that such logic can also be followed to suggest that as his evidence now confirms the gospel story, the rest of it is also probably correct!'

'Gentlemen, please! Sit down, Mr Baal.' Haald banged impatiently with his gavel and the prosecutor regained his seat. 'Have you any other *questions* to put to the witness, Mr Lang?'

The attorney for the defence nodded. 'Just one, Your Honour.'

'Very well.'

Lang turned back to the stand and, although he kept a straight face, Lee thought he detected a twinkle in the attorney's eye.

'You heard the prosecuting attorney refer to the report by Josephus concerning the Accused's last week in Jerusalem?'

'I did.'

'Were you aware that Josephus was the Jewish military commander in charge of the defence of Upper Galilee against the Romans during the rebellion of 68 A.D.?'

'Of course not.'

'Or that, once surrounded by the forces of the Roman general, Titus, he capitulated, changed sides, then did everything he could to help his new friend defeat and ultimately destroy his fellow countrymen?'

'No.'

Lang smiled grimly.

148

'I thought not. But it's important that the ladies and gentlemen of the jury be aware of the nature of the man to whose unsubstantiated reports the prosecution evidently lends such weight.' He then turned quickly to Haald who was just opening his mouth to say something. 'No more questions, Your Honour.' He returned to his seat.

Haald hesitated for a few seconds, sighed gently, and turned towards the witness stand. 'Very well. The witness may stand down.'

Baal rose to his feet as the witness left the courtroom. 'I have no more witnesses to call regarding this section of the trial, Your Honour.'

Haald nodded and turned to Lang. 'In that case, you may call your first witness, Mr Lang. But I warn both of you gentlemen that if there is any more departure from strict court procedure, I will call an immediate adjournment.'

Lang rose and bowed slightly. 'May it please the court, the defence would like to call Joseph, husband of Mary, the mother of the Accused.'

A murmur went through the courtroom as Joseph walked in. He was a tall, distinguished man in his mid-fifties and wore the traditional clothes of a village elder of the period. While he was being sworn, Mary turned to look at Lee to see if he was satisfied, but he seemed so preoccupied that she turned back to the courtroom scene.

The clerk of the court had just finished administering the oath and Lang moved to stand in front of the witness.

'Sir,' he began, 'would you please tell the court your name?'

'I am Joseph, a carpenter of the House of David.'

'Where were you living just before the Accused was born?'

At this, the witness glanced at the man standing silently on the other side of the courtroom, and although they barely smiled at each other, Lee was aware that for a few brief seconds they had somehow projected a strong bond of affection. Joseph then turned back to answer, 'In Nazareth.'

'Please tell us in your own words what happened.'

Joseph bowed slightly. 'My first wife died,' he began. 'It was hard for me to manage at first. I had a good business and two of the children were not really old enough to look after themselves. Then the elders of the synagogue asked me to take Mary into my house.'

'As your wife?'

'Yes. She was an orphan. Both her parents had died when she was quite young and she had lived in the care of the synagogue ever since.'

'How old was she?'

'She had reached the age of puberty.'

Lang said, 'I understand that created some difficulty?'

The witness nodded slowly. 'Yes,' he said. 'A woman was regarded as unclean during the time of her monthly period, and by law was not allowed within the synagogue precincts. Conversely, an orphan in temple care was not supposed to leave until an adoption or marriage had been arranged.'

'Do you know why Mary was not adopted as a child?' Lang asked.

'Adopting a boy was always more popular,' the other told him. 'Girls in such circumstances were often left until of marriageable age.'

'Then it was arranged as quickly as possible for the reasons you mention?'

'Yes. In fact, in such circumstances, it was common for the girl to stay with the family of her husband-to-be until the formalities had been completed.'

Lang paused a moment. 'Is that what happened in your case?'

Joseph nodded again. 'Yes,' he said. 'I was reluctant at first, but the elders said it was my duty as the only eligible man available. So eventually, I agreed.'

Lang looked at him for a moment: 'Why were you so reluctant?' he asked.

The other shrugged slightly. 'In spite of my need for a woman to look after my children, there was a considerable difference in our ages,' he said. 'In fact, my eldest daughter, who had already taken a husband herself, was two years older than Mary.'

'Nevertheless,' Lang persisted, 'you agreed to the marriage, and she came to stay at your house pending the making of the necessary arrangements?'

'Yes,' he said. 'Mary slept with the young children, Ruth, who was eight, and Simon, who was six.'

'What happened then?'

Joseph paused for a moment. 'One day,' he said, 'Mary disappeared. I received word that she had gone to visit her elder cousin, Elizabeth, who was expecting her first child.'

'Were you annoyed with her for going like that?' Lang asked.

The other smiled faintly. 'I meant to be,' he said, 'but by then she had become very dear to me.'

'In so short a time?'

Joseph continued to smile gently as if looking inwards. 'She had a quality of sweetness,' he said, 'of gaiety and love I had no right to expect again at my time of life. It was impossible to stay angry with her.'

'Did she say why she went?'

Joseph now looked at him directly. 'Yes,' he said, 'later. I thought it was because she had suddenly realized it would be difficult to get away once she was fully responsible for running the house.'

'Which she was not until after the marriage?'

'No.' He paused for a moment before proceeding. 'No one thought Elizabeth would conceive so late in life, having been barren until then, and I knew Mary longed to see her before the baby was born.'

Lang said, 'So you thought she had suddenly decided – and gone – on impulse?'

Joseph nodded slowly. 'That's what I thought at the time,' he agreed.

Lang paused for a moment, then asked, 'Would you have minded her going if she had asked you first?'

Joseph shook his head. 'Not for myself.'

'Didn't she tell anyone?'

'She told Ruth, but the child forgot to give me the message.' He smiled as if apologizing for her. 'You know what children are like – and that was really the trouble. Mary herself was little more than a child. I thought she had set her mind on seeing her cousin and had taken no account of the dangers of travelling alone.'

151

'How far was it?'

'About fifteen miles.' He paused, then added, 'God protected her.'

'What happened after she returned?' Lang asked.

'She came straight to me in the workshop.' Joseph paused, then went on slowly, 'I can't describe how she looked – afraid and elated – transfigured somehow, so I was half afraid to look her in the face.' He looked up at Haald. 'She said she had seen a vision – an angel sent from God – to tell her that she had been chosen to bear the Messiah, the living son of God, as foretold by the prophets.'

Lang paused a moment, then asked, 'Did you believe her?'

The other shook his head sadly. 'I wanted to,' he said. 'I couldn't believe she would betray me, but it was too much – in spite of her tears.'

'What was the punishment for fornication?'

Joseph now looked at him sharply. 'In the circumstances, the same as for adultery.'

'Which was . . . ?'

'Death by stoning.'

Lang glanced at the jury. 'Perhaps she was in fear of her life,' he said. 'Perhaps that was the reason for her distress?'

But the other shook his head. 'No. From that day, fear for herself never entered Mary's heart.' His voice dropped again. 'It was grief at my unbelief.' Joseph paused. 'In spite of what I thought must have happened, I could not bear the idea of her being hurt, let alone killed. So I told no one. I decided to go on a journey and leave her in the care of strangers.'

'Did Mary know what you'd planned?'

'Yes, I told her. But she begged me, rather, to denounce her so that others might judge her innocence.'

'Rather than be separated from you?' Lang put in.

'Yes, she . . . ' He stopped suddenly, and Lee could see he was fighting to control his emotions. 'She said . . . she loved me . . . ' he paused again before going on with obvious difficulty, ' . . . and that I needed her.'

Lang hesitated for a moment, then he queried, 'But, in spite of all this, you were determined?'

Joseph raised his head and looked again at the prisoner on the other side of the room. Then he turned slowly to his questioner. 'God forgave my unbelief,' he said simply. 'Jealousy would have destroyed me, but God, in his mercy, sent an angel to put my heart at rest.' His voice grew strong as he looked around at those watching. 'I . . . Joseph, the carpenter, the Lord of the Universe sent an angel to comfort me!'

'And he confirmed what Mary had told you?'

'Oh, yes.' Joseph nodded, and now his voice surged with confidence. 'And he was right. We had some hard times. Once we had to run for our lives, but God's hand protected us. And for the rest of my life, I watched the son of God grow into a man.'

Watching from the control room, Lee saw with amazement that tears of joy had started into the man's eyes. 'Nobody else can say that,' he went on. 'I missed the sorrow that followed. I watched him grow. He never forgot who he was, but it was I, Joseph of Nazareth, who taught him to be a man.'

He paused, and when he spoke again his voice was quiet but full of wonder. 'To think . . . I might have missed it!'

Lang stood silently for several moments, then he nodded quietly and said, 'No further questions,' and sat down. Baal now rose to his feet and approached the stand.

'Would you please tell the court exactly how this "angel" appeared to you?' The prosecutor's voice was deliberately pitched to jar the atmosphere that had been created. Joseph turned to him.

'In a dream,' he answered.

'I see.' Baal nodded. 'And do you attach much importance to dreams?'

The other looked at him, puzzled. 'Sometimes,' he admitted.

'But not always?'

'No.'

Baal paused for a moment. 'Was that how the angel appeared to Mary?'

The other shook his head. 'No, he appeared to her while she was awake.'

'I see. Can you account for that?'

Joseph nodded. 'I think so,' he said. 'Mary was without sin.

But for someone like me to look God's messenger in the face would have been too much.'

Baal frowned slightly. 'In what sense?' he demanded.

The other shrugged slightly. 'I was not of the right mind,' he said. 'Quite simply, I should have died of fright.' He now turned his gaze full on Baal. 'Just as you would!' Some of the jury laughed at this as Joseph went on, 'These things are not for ordinary men.'

Baal nodded, quite unperturbed at the laughter. He was, in fact, glad that they were not afraid to laugh; it was a weapon of much more danger to the other side. 'You said in answer to a question by my learned colleague,' he continued, 'that you were reluctant to take Mary to wife because of the difference in your ages.'

The other inclined his head slightly. 'That is so,' he said.

'Why?'

Joseph paused for a moment, thinking. 'I suppose I was afraid it would cause some difficulty,' he said eventually.

'And isn't that exactly what it did cause?' The prosecutor's voice took on an edge. 'What did you say was the punishment for adultery?'

Lee saw Joseph hesitate uneasily before answering, 'Death by stoning.'

'Wouldn't you agree that if your wife's story were not true, she was guilty of such an offence?'

'I myself had a vision.'

'Before or after she put the idea into your head?'

'After she told me.'

Suddenly Baal's voice became savage. 'Have you ever heard of wish fulfilment in dreams?' he asked.

'No.'

The prosecutor looked briefly at the jury to emphasize the point, paused for a few moments, then turned away from the witness as if in contempt. 'No further questions.'

In the control room Mary turned to Lee. 'Sometimes I hate that man,' she said, but Lee smiled.

'He's doing a good job.'

'Who's next?' Shand whispered, glancing sideways.

'Mary.'

Mary Bell suddenly got up. Lee looked at her in surprise. 'Where are you going?' he asked.

'I can't watch this,' she said, 'he'll destroy her.'

Lee reached out and took her hand. 'No, he won't,' he said, 'please stay.' Mary paused for a few moments before sitting down again, heavily.

'You may proceed, Mr Lang.'

Lang rose from his seat. 'No further witnesses, Your Honour.'

He had scarcely sat down when the prosecutor was on his feet, looking furious. 'Your Honour,' he began, 'did I hear my learned colleague correctly?'

'I imagine so,' Haald said mildly.

'But I understood the defence would call Mary to testify.'

'That was my impression also, Mr Baal, but if they now choose not to do so . . . '

'Is the witness unwell?' Baal interrupted and Haald glanced over at Lang.

'Mr Lang,' the judge said, 'I realize the defence is under no obligation to give an explanation, but in the circumstances the court *would* be grateful for further information.'

Lang got to his feet, looking faintly surprised, as if he had no idea at all why the prosecutor was so angry. 'As the court pleases, Your Honour,' he said. 'The witness is quite well and able to be called. But she is a young and sensitive girl, and in view of the obvious line the prosecution is taking, we do not wish to expose her willingly to questions we feel are bound to upset her.'

'Upset or not,' Baal stormed, 'I've exposed my witnesses to your questions. Either she appears or I refuse to go on.'

'Now you're being childish.'

'Gentlemen, please!' Haald cut in, 'you'll address your remarks to me – not to each other.'

The prosecutor turned to him. 'Very well,' he said.

'Your Honour,' Lang interrupted.

'We agreed to . . . ' stormed Baal.

'We agreed to adopt normal court procedure, Your Honour,' Lang interjected.

'We also informed each other which witnesses would be available,' retorted Baal.

'So what?' Lang demanded.

'So that a balanced picture might be presented to the jury in a mutual search for truth,' Baal snapped and swung back to face the judge. 'Now the defence is seeking to distort . . .'

'Your Honour,' Lang interrupted, 'the defence seeks to distort nothing.'

'Then produce your witness,' snapped Baal.

'She's here. As promised.' Lang paused for a moment, looking at the prosecutor. 'You produce her.'

Baal stared at him, then comprehension began to dawn. Haald smiled to himself, and cleared his throat. 'There *is* nothing to keep the prosecution from calling the witness if it so wishes,' he pointed out.

Lang smiled faintly. In the control room Lee turned to Mary, grinning. 'You see,' he whispered, 'he's forcing Baal to give him the last word.'

In court, Baal breathed heavily for a few moments, then said, 'Very well, call Mary, mother of the Accused.'

Anna walked in from the back of the courtroom and took the oath. She was always beautiful, but now, dressed in the simple clothes of the period, she was transfigured. An involuntary sigh rose audibly from those watching; even Baal's face softened when he saw her, but as the clerk retired and she turned to face him, he forced a more stern expression.

'You are Mary, wife of Joseph, mother of the Accused?'

'I am.' Anna's voice was barely audible. Haald bent forward.

'Would you speak up, please?'

'I'm sorry. Yes, I am Mary.'

Baal said, 'I understand you were orphaned as a child and brought up in the care of the synagogue?'

'Yes.'

'What did you do, exactly?'

'When I was in the synagogue?'

'Yes.'

'We helped to keep it clean. To polish the lamps and trim the wicks. We learned to read and write and to prepare food

156

for the priest and his helpers. A lot of the time we just played.'

Baal nodded. 'Quite so,' he said. 'Did you have access to the Scriptures?'

Mary frowned. 'The Torah?' she asked. 'No. Only men are allowed to read the holy books.'

'But you heard them read each Sabbath?'

The girl nodded. 'Sometimes, every day.'

'And what books were you allowed to read?'

'Not many. The synagogue was rather poor.' She hesitated for a moment. 'We had some chapters from the Talmud, I remember.'

'The Talmud being exposition of the basic law?'

'Yes.'

'So,' Baal went on, 'in one way or another you were pretty familiar with the law which governed your people?'

'Yes.'

'You knew what happened to those who broke its commandments?'

'Yes.' Mary's answer this time was almost inaudible, but the prosecutor nodded.

'Of course,' he said and glanced in the direction of the jury before turning to her again. 'Now tell me – when you came of age, you knew the synagogue elders would arrange a marriage for you?'

'Yes.'

'Did you think about it beforehand?' Seeing Mary frown, he added, 'Wonder about the sort of man he would be?' The girl smiled softly for the first time.

'Yes.'

'Like all young girls,' Baal said, not unpleasantly, 'I imagine you hoped he would be young and good-looking?'

Undeceived by Baal's tone, Lang was on his feet in an instant. 'Your Honour,' he said, 'the prosecution is leading the witness.'

'I'll rephrase,' Baal said, his eyes never leaving the witness. 'What sort of a man did you hope to marry?'

Lang sniffed disapprovingly and sat down as Mary answered, 'I hoped he'd be kind.'

157

'Yes?'

'And that I'd learn to love him.'

Baal nodded. 'That's understandable, but had you any pre-conceived idea of what he would look like?' Mary shook her head without answering.

'How old did you think he'd be?' Baal persisted.

Mary looked at him calmly. 'Older than I,' she said.

'Much older?' The girl looked down without giving him an answer.

'You certainly didn't expect him to be old enough to be your father?'

Mary looked up quickly. 'It was not for me to question the wisdom of those who cared for me,' she said.

'But you must have been disappointed?' Mary opened her mouth but the prosecutor went on, 'In fact, wouldn't it be true to say your feelings were a good deal stronger?'

'I don't know what you mean.'

'I mean, weren't you hoping to marry someone else?'

'No.'

'I put it to you that you were,' Baal said, hardening his tone. 'In fact, when you finally learned of the elders' choice, weren't you terrified?'

'Why?'

'Because you had taken it for granted they would choose someone else.'

'Who?'

'That's what I want you to tell us.' Again Baal looked at the jury. 'We know he existed, because whoever he was, you were so sure that you had already allowed him to make love to you.'

Mary stared at him, shocked. 'No!' she protested. 'How can you say such a terrible thing?'

The prosecutor turned back to face her. 'Because you were pregnant,' he said calmly. 'You don't deny that?'

'No.' Mary's voice shook slightly when she answered, 'But . . .'

'Wasn't that why you suddenly ran off to your cousin Eliza-beth?' Baal interrupted.

The girl shook her head violently. 'No,' she said. 'I wanted to see her.'

158

'I can well believe it.' Again Baal looked at the jury. 'Knowing the law as you did, you must've been very frightened.'

'No.'

'Betrothed to Joseph,' the prosecutor turned to face her again, 'you found yourself pregnant by another man, the punishment for which was death.'

'It's not true!'

Baal raised his eyebrows slightly. 'Didn't you run in panic to ask her advice?' He paused for a moment, seeing her eyes widen. 'She was a good deal older than you,' he went on. 'Wasn't she the only person you could turn to?'

The girl remained silent, and Baal continued, 'She must have been a clever woman. If anyone could help you, she could, and by a tremendous stroke of luck, she herself was unexpectedly pregnant. And that's what gave her the idea, wasn't it?' Mary shook her head dumbly. 'Why not?' Baal demanded. 'One more miracle here or there wouldn't make much difference.' He turned to the jury. 'And so began the whole lie.'

'It wasn't like that,' Mary managed to say at last, but Baal swung back on her.

'Elizabeth told you what to say, didn't she? And just to make sure, you concocted another story between you about her own child – which already had some substance in fact.' Now his voice became even more abrasive. 'And so, to escape your own punishment, the pair of you repeated the lie until your husband-to-be was so bemused with angels from God and holy prophecies that he couldn't distinguish fairy tales from reality!' He suddenly swung round and, with a complete change of expression, faced the jury. 'No wonder he had dreams!'

Some of the jurors laughed, as he knew they would. He turned back to the girl. 'Oh, yes,' he said sternly. 'It would have been funny. Not for the first time, a couple of clever women make a fool of a simple man.' He paused, then went on more reasonably. 'I don't think many people would blame you in the circumstances.' Now he dropped his voice dramatically, 'If it hadn't been for the consequences.'

In the control room, Lee thought the prosecutor would have made a marvellous actor, had he not chosen a different profession.

159

'... because once the lie had been told, you were stuck with it forever. And not only you, but the whole of mankind! Was that not so?'

Mary stared at him as if he were mad.

'Two innocent children were the first to suffer,' Baal went on, addressing the court as a whole. 'I expect you thought people would forget in time, but you hadn't reckoned on the way such stories spread.' He turned back to the stand. 'Above all, you had not reckoned on your husband, who took another man's child to his heart, believing him to be the son of God. How could *he* forget?' He paused for a moment before continuing. 'So the two children were brought up to believe in a special destiny. Each, when he was old enough, searched the Scriptures for confirmation. On finding it, as they would – for it was on an imaginary fulfilment that Elizabeth's sharp wit had constructed the lie – each struggled to live up to what he had come to accept as true. The result? One ended his short life by having his head cut off in prison, and your son,' Baal now paused for emphasis, 'was nailed to a wooden cross, like a common criminal!'

There was a long silence. Baal and Mary stared at each other, the latter's eyes wide with shock and wet with unshed tears. Finally, Baal continued, quietly this time. 'You know, in spite of everything, I feel sorry for you. How must you have felt, looking up at him on the cross that day, his life ebbing away, knowing he was there because of something you had done to save yourself so long ago? You couldn't tell anyone – not even afterwards. Nothing could undo the harm that had already been done.' He paused once more, then said slowly, 'Whatever your offence, the punishment was indeed terrible!' The prosecutor paused a moment longer, turned, and sat down.

Lang immediately took his place.

'Mary,' he said gently. He waited patiently for the girl to collect herself. Slowly, she turned towards him.

'Yes?'

'Is that how it was?'

There was another long pause, then she shook her head slightly.

160

'No.'

'Then tell us, in your own words.'

Mary struggled visibly to regain control of herself. When she began, her voice still shook, but it gathered strength as she went on:

'When I knew whom I was to marry, I *was* frightened. I had thought I would marry a man nearer my own age, and that we would learn to love each other. But when I heard it was to be Joseph, my heart sank.'

'Why?'

Mary looked at him and seemed to draw strength from his expression. 'Because he had already given his love to his first wife,' she said. 'I was very young. I didn't think there would be any room in his heart for me. Also, he was an important man in the village. He had been used to having his house well ordered by an experienced woman.'

Lang nodded slowly. 'So you weren't disappointed?' he asked.

Mary shook her head. 'No,' she said. She paused for a moment, then added, 'Just afraid.'

'You thought he just wanted a good housekeeper?'

'Yes.'

'Is that how it was?'

Mary hesitated a moment. 'Oh, no! It wasn't like that at all!' The words came out spontaneously, all at once.

Lang glanced quickly at the jury, then back at the girl. 'How was it, then?' he said.

'The children took me to their hearts at once, but Joseph was . . . ' Mary frowned slightly, 'I don't know . . . always kind from the beginning.' She smiled and brushed a tear away from the corner of her eye. 'I don't think he knew how to treat me any more than I him.'

Lang smiled sympathetically. 'You mean he was as nervous as you were?'

'Yes.' Mary returned his smile gratefully. 'Of course,' she went on, 'I didn't know that. The house was terribly untidy, but at the beginning he would barely let me touch anything. I thought it was because he resented my changing the way his first wife had left things, but I realized afterwards he felt guilty about making me do any work.'

Lang nodded slowly. 'He must have been a very unusual man.'

'He was. He used to come in from the workshop covered in sawdust . . . and shuffle around the house like a great bear!' She smiled again, as if at the memory.

'This was when you were still betrothed?' Lang put in.

Mary nodded. 'Yes. He was always so grateful for anything I did for him. The children soon took me for granted, but it wasn't until one day when he cut himself quite badly . . . ' her voice trailed away as though she were remembering.

'What happened?' Lang prompted.

'He didn't want me to see,' the girl said, looking back at him, 'thinking I'd be upset by the sight of the wound. But I could see he was never going to manage, and I made him sit down so that I could tend to him properly.'

'You ordered him?'

'I suppose I did.' This time she suppressed a smile. 'I never stopped to think. Anyway, he sat down, just like a little boy, and did exactly what I told him until the wound was cleaned and bound.'

'What happened then?'

'I realized he was watching me closely, but I couldn't take any notice until I'd finished.' She paused for a moment and said softly, 'Then he put his arms around me very gently, and I held his head against my breast.' Mary looked at the jury for the first time. 'From that moment, we never noticed the difference in our ages again. He was always someone I could look up to and admire tremendously.' She looked around the courtroom. 'Any woman would have felt the same way. From then on, I knew he needed and depended on me for all the love and care women can offer their husbands, love without which few men are complete.'

Lang paused for a moment, then asked, 'You loved him from that moment?'

She turned back to him. 'I think I had already learned to love him, but then I knew everything was going to be all right. From then on, I looked forward to the wedding with joy – and without fear.'

162

Lang paused again. 'But something happened?' he said eventually.

Mary looked at him. 'I had never known a man before,' she said. 'I swear before Almighty God I would have died before I deceived the one who was to be my husband.' After a slight pause, she resumed. 'There was no fear in my heart when I first thought of going to see Elizabeth – only that I might tell her how happy I was and that I wanted to share her own joy. I was going to ask Joseph if it was all right, but something happened that sent everything else out of my mind.'

She turned to face the jury.

'I can remember exactly what I was doing. I was preparing the midday meal. Ruth and Simon were playing outside and Joseph was working, when quite suddenly, the walls of the room seemed to . . . just disappear. It was all so unreal, I thought I must be dreaming, but then I looked down and saw that I was still gripping the knife I had been using to cut up some vegetables.' As she spoke, Lee saw her clench her right fist and look down at it. 'My knuckles were white because I was holding it so hard,' she went on slowly. 'Then I heard a voice call my name. I looked up, and there was someone quite close. He looked like a man, only very tall. His face was young and yet, it seemed, full of wisdom. His eyes had an expression – joyful, but full of compassion.'

She turned back to Lang. 'I couldn't look him in the face. I wanted to cry out. Then he said, in a voice I seemed to hear inside my head, "Hail, thou that art highly favoured! The Lord is with thee. Blessed art thou among women."' Mary paused for a moment, as if to be quite sure that the words were exactly right, then continued, 'He said, "Behold, thou shalt conceive in thy womb, and bring forth a son, and shalt call his name Jesus. And he shall be great, and shall be called the Son of the Highest. And the Lord God shall give unto Him the throne of his Father, David. And he shall reign over the House of Jacob forever. And of his Kingdom there shall be no end!"'

It seemed to Lee that her eyes glowed as she spoke the last words. She looked down at her hand and said, 'Then the room

163

was as it had been before: the knife was still in my hand; the vegetables were on the table before me; and I was alone.' She paused a moment longer, then looked Lang full in the face.

'So I went to see Elizabeth. And shortly after I returned, I knew God's promise had been fulfilled.'

Lee was aware that while she had been speaking a silence had developed – a deep silence that was almost a bond between the girl who spoke and those who listened. Lang asked, 'Weren't you afraid of what might happen?'

'No.' Mary shook her head. 'My only fear was that Joseph would be hurt. For the rest, I had no fear, because I knew that God would let no harm come to me or the child.' She continued to look at him as if trying to make him understand. 'You see, it *couldn't* have been like the other man said. Where there is such love, deceit cannot abide. And there *was* love. Oh, yes.' She looked up at Haald. 'In spite of all the wonderful things that happened, we were a real family. Joseph became my husband in the flesh, and we had other children. But Jesus, our firstborn, was always our greatest joy.' Now Mary's voice rang out as she turned to face the rest of the court.

'You heard how he brought happiness to my husband's last years. I have no doubt in my mind that this was Joseph's reward. Could such happiness have been founded on a lie? It is *true* he missed the sorrow which followed; but even that was swept away by God's mercy . . . terrible though it seemed at the time.' Lee saw her glance at the prosecutor before going on, even more vehemently, 'Could all the hope and joy my son brought to those who put their trust in him be an illusion – with no more basis than his mother's treachery?'

Silence greeted the challenge, then once more her words reached out to those who were listening.

'Have no fear . . . and pity those who cannot understand that to the Lord God of Creation, all things are possible.'

Mary took a deep breath, then said more softly, 'When the pain was over, and I looked down at the face of the warm, living child in my arms, I knew – beyond any doubt at all – that not only was he the son of man, he was also the Son of Almighty God!'

164

In the control room everyone stared at the monitor showing Anna in close-up. Mary Bell gripped Lee's hand as tears welled into her eyes.

In the sponsors' viewing room there was a long and total silence. The spell was broken by the close-up of Anna fading from the screen and the caption 'Christ on Trial' taking its place. At once, everyone crowded around Burgh, overwhelming him with congratulations, ignoring the announcer who now appeared on the screen to read the list of sponsors.

Chapter

9

After everyone had gone, Anna, now wearing her own clothes, sat in the semi-dark studio, in one of the seats that less than an hour before had been occupied by a member of the audience. She stared at the half-lit set of the courtroom before her.

In the control room, Joe Shand and one of his assistants were setting up for the following day. Joe glanced briefly through the screen without seeing Anna and turned to the man beside him. 'Okay,' he said, 'you can kill all the lights now.'

'Right.' The assistant bent forward for the switch, then stopped just as he was about to turn it, looking through the screen into the half-darkened studio. 'Somebody's still in there,' he said.

'What?' Joe followed his gaze, then got up and looked more carefully.

'Isn't that the girl?'

'Anna Princi,' Joe said, frowning. 'Yes.'

The other looked at him. 'You want me to tell her we're closing up?'

Joe glanced back at him quickly. 'No,' he said, 'that's all right, Ed, I'll do it. I don't suppose she's come out of it yet.'

Ed nodded gravely. 'I'm not surprised. That was some performance!'

'It was all right.'

The assistant looked around the control room. 'Well, I don't think there's anything else, so if you don't mind . . . ?'

Joe nodded: 'Sure, that's fine. You run along.'

'Okay. Thanks. Well, goodnight, Joe.'

'Goodnight, Ed.'

The other made for the door, then paused, looking in the direction of the studio. 'It was great!' he said. 'Tell her, from all of us.'

Joe smiled faintly. 'I'll tell her,' he promised.

'Goodnight, then.' The other nodded a last time and went out, closing the door behind him.

Joe glanced through the screen, slipped his coat off the back of his chair, and went out the door leading into the studio.

He found Anna staring at infinity. She didn't even notice him until he was almost beside her.

'The boys told me to tell you that you were great,' he said, smiling. The girl looked up at him questioningly. 'Your performance,' Joe explained.

'Oh.' Anna paused, then nodded. 'Thank you.'

He looked down at her. She seemed small and crumpled somehow. 'That wasn't acting, was it?' he asked quietly. Anna closed her eyes, then shook her head.

'No.'

Joe hesitated before taking the chair beside her. 'Look,' he said, after a while, 'I've got to close up.'

The girl looked at him, suddenly alert. 'Yes, of course,' she said. 'I'm sorry.'

He held up his hand. 'That's okay. There's no hurry.' But in spite of this, Anna got to her feet and Joe did likewise. Almost immediately she swayed slightly and he had to put out a hand to steady her.

'Say, are you all right?'

Anna forced a smile. 'Yes, of course. I'm sorry. I suddenly felt a bit dizzy.'

Joe looked at her carefully. 'When did you last have something to eat?' he asked after a moment.

'Breakfast,' Anna shrugged. 'I was too nervous to eat lunch.'

Joe nodded. 'I thought so,' he said.

'I'll go now.' Anna started for the door and Joe hurried after her.

'Look,' he said, 'there's a place to eat around the corner. I was just on my way there.' Anna paused, staring at him. Joe grinned. 'I'd be very happy if you'd join me,' he said.

Anna returned his smile. 'It's very kind of you,' she said, 'but there'll be something for me when I get back.'

'At the mission?'

'How do you know about that?'

167

'You told me,' Joe said, 'remember? At the audition.'

He saw her relax. 'Yes, of course.'

'And if I know anything about missions, supper was a long time ago!' He paused, then smiled again. 'I really do hate to eat by myself!'

Anna hesitated briefly. 'All right. Thank you.'

'Great!' He took a step back. 'We can go out through the control room, then I'll switch off the lights.' The girl nodded.

'All right.'

'I'll lead the way.' He turned and made for the door, glanced back for a moment to make sure that she was with him, then stepped to one side to let her go out first. Suddenly he felt almost uncontrollably happy.

Joe lit a cigarette, exhaled contentedly, and smiled at the girl opposite as he put the match into the ashtray. 'Feeling better?' he asked.

Anna returned his smile. 'Oh yes,' she assured him, 'thank you . . . much!' They faced each other across a table in an alcove, the remains of their meal in front of them.

Joe watched Anna's eyes sparkle with the reflected light from the candles. Finding himself beginning to stare, he forced himself to say, 'You've never had Chinese food before?'

Anna shook her head. Her hair was long and dark and soft. Joe ached to touch it.

'Never,' she was saying. 'You're very kind.'

'Not really,' he heard himself say. 'As I said, I don't like eating by myself.'

Anna looked at him, puzzled. 'Why do you say that?' she asked. 'Are you ashamed of having pity for me?'

Joe shook his head. 'It wasn't that,' he assured her. 'Sure, I felt sorry for you when I saw you sitting there all by yourself, but I very much wanted to get to know you better. I have – ever since you first came to the studio. But somehow, until now, I never dared ask you out.'

Anna watched him silently. Joe shrugged and went on, 'And that's not usual for me, believe me.' He grinned momentarily. 'I'm no Casanova – I never had the time – but I make out okay.'

He wanted to stop, to let her talk, but her silence led him on. 'Fact of the matter is, I was going to be married last year, but it didn't work out.' He paused again, looking at her, trying to read her expression. 'I haven't had a regular girl since,' he said. 'Just a few blind dates, and that's not really my style.'

'Why were you afraid of me, of all people?' Anna asked.

Joe looked at her. 'I guess . . . ' he stopped himself, then shrugged self-deprecatingly, 'because I knew you were too good for me.'

'Joe, I . . . '

'Besides,' he went on quickly, 'what would have been the point? I knew what you were planning, I would have just broken my heart.' He paused, then glanced around uneasily to see if anyone had overheard.

'Joe!' Anna reached impulsively across the table and took his hand. He saw with surprise that her eyes were swimming in tears. 'I don't know what I'm going to do now.'

'I wondered,' he said gently. 'Do you want to tell me?'

Anna shrugged and looked down at the table. 'It's not very important.'

Joe looked at her steadily, but when he spoke he heard his voice wobble. 'It could be for me.'

Anna looked up at him. 'Don't fall in love with me, Joe,' she pleaded, 'I don't want to hurt you.'

'I'm afraid it's too late. What I was telling myself about you was just talk.' He smiled wryly. 'Anyway, I never listen to advice – least of all from myself! But don't worry, you don't owe me anything.'

Anna looked around. 'It's getting so hot in here,' she said. 'Is there anywhere we can walk in the fresh air?'

Joe nodded. 'Sure. I'll get the bill.' He looked over his shoulder and raised his hand.

Later they leaned against a low wall, looking down the river from Battery Park.

'I was so sure,' Anna told him, 'then, as I started to think about Mary and tried to imagine what sort of person she must have been, something began to change.'

169

'In what way?' Joe asked gently, looking at her profile.

She continued to look out over the water as she replied, 'I guess I never really thought about her before – not properly. To me, she was the Holy Mother of God, someone to be worshipped, to pray to . . .'

'But not to think about too much?' Joe put in.

Anna paused for a moment, then nodded slowly. 'But when I did,' she went on, 'I began to realize I was wrong. My image of her as a serene being – almost without emotion, except a kind of perfect, motherly love – just couldn't be true, and did her no justice at all.' Now she turned to face him. 'After all, what merit is there in goodness without the possibility of evil? How can courage mean anything if you aren't capable of being deeply afraid?'

'You think she was afraid?' Joe asked slowly.

'Of course. There must have been moments in her life when she was terrified, particularly as a young girl. And later, how could she have felt anything but hatred for the mob who condemned her son, then drove nails through his hands and feet?'

Joe shook his head. 'But do you think she forgave them?' he asked.

Anna nodded. 'Later,' she said, 'by an effort of will – not because there was no alternative.'

Joe thought for a moment. 'What you're really saying is that, slowly, you realized Mary was a human being, not a plaster saint.'

Anna said quickly, 'I never thought her that, exactly.' She went on more slowly. 'But you're right in a way. And yet only today, when I tried to speak for her, did the full realization come to me.'

'And the implications?' Joe questioned gently.

'Yes.' Anna looked back over the water again. 'When everyone else had gone,' she said, 'and I sat there, by myself, I understood, for the first time, what the mother superior tried to tell me.'

'About what?'

'About serving God.' Anna's voice was small. 'I knew then,

170

for me, there was only one way . . . to be *in* the world – and to face up to everything that means.'

'As a woman?'

The girl nodded. 'Yes,' she said. 'Of course, I'm not saying it's wrong for anyone else to become a nun, not at all. I can see that for many it *is* the way to salvation, but only for those God chooses for himself.'

Joe looked at her, his heart full of compassion. 'Anna!'

'I'm so lucky,' Anna said, her voice trembling. She turned to him and Joe could see how her feelings belied her words. 'I know, one day, I shall have a husband to love and a child of my own to hold. But Joe – I'm so sad that I shall never be going back.'

'You'll visit them,' he said softly.

Anna nodded and bit her lip. 'Oh, yes.' She suddenly looked up at him, her eyes wet with tears.

'Joe,' she choked. 'Please help me!'

Now certain what he should do, Joe gathered her into his arms and held her very tenderly, stroking her hair while she sobbed as if her heart would break.

When Lee had apprised Ray Burgh of the situation and had explained how he proposed to do without the Accused altogether during the second programme, Burgh had at first seemed unable to grasp it.

'What do you mean, symbolic?' he stuttered.

When light finally dawned, Burgh just stared at the producer. This had the advantage of enabling Lee to explain without interruption how they could carry on for at least one more night without Burnard.

'Okay,' Burgh said hoarsely, when he eventually regained his powers of speech, 'but he'd better resurrect himself by the third day or we'll sue him for every penny he's got!'

'We'll find him,' Lee assured him.

Burgh, who had started to walk away, turned back savagely. 'You'd better,' he snarled, 'if you ever want to work again!'

Lee then took Baal and Lang into his confidence and they agreed to co-operate in getting through the second programme, but Baal emphasized what Lee knew already – that it was one thing to have someone stand in when all he had to do was say a few sentences, but if Burnard himself didn't take the stand on the third night – for the climax – the programme would collapse in disaster.

By the time they left the building, Lee was exhausted. Mary took him back to her apartment. Not until he had eaten and had a chance to simmer down did she ask him to tell her what Father O'Connell had revealed, both before and after the programme, when the priest had stayed behind to tell of his meeting in Jersey City with Burnard more than a week before.

He had told Lee first of Burnard's experience in the prison camp and of his friendship with Jim Carson – the savage termination of which had haunted him for years.

'I tried to explain that Christ was not a God of heroes,' Father O'Connell had told Lee gently, 'but of sinners, and rogues and weaklings. I tried to explain it to him in terms of his friend.

' "What difference did it make to *him*?" he kept asking me. "How can I begin to know what it must have felt like to have been the Messiah if I can't even understand those who profess to believe in him?"

'I told him that I believe faith in our Lord Jesus appeals to that in us which is best. It does not eliminate the weak, bad sides of us – at least, not straight away. But in time, like all things – good or bad – when we turn our backs on them, they tend to wither away. Of course, it can take a very long time indeed, and none of us achieves perfection. But if you believe, as I do, that death is not the end – that there is another life, promised by Christ himself – then it is possible to imagine this process continuing until, with his help, we do become perfect.

' "As for your poor friend," I told him, "it may have been that he was not very brave, but then neither were Peter and all the others when Jesus was arrested. They ran away and left him to face death all by himself. But that didn't keep Jesus from believing in them, and it didn't mean he had been mistaken in choosing them in the first place. He still called Peter his 'rock' – and on him, and on those others whose courage failed them utterly when he most needed them, *was* built the Church which first brought Rome itself to its knees and has since lasted for two thousand years."

'Then he said to me, "Maybe so. But Peter and the others were given a second chance. What about Jim and those others who died in despair?"

'I said, "I believe they have their chance." Then he looked at me for a long time before saying, "I wish I could believe you." He seemed sunk in gloom. I think, for the first time in his career, he was really frightened.

'I tried to ease his mind by telling him of my own fears; how I could understand how difficult the task facing him must seem compared to my own, which was only too easy. He seemed to be listening, but when he spoke again I realized his mind had gone on.

'"I know enough now to realize how much further there is to travel."

'I didn't answer. I knew he was thinking aloud.

'"I can't do it unless I can understand what it must have felt like to have read the Scriptures, then to have known, beyond any doubt whatsoever, that they were talking about *you*. To have been so sure you were the chosen one, that not only were you prepared to face death on the strength of it, but to inspire others to do the same."

'Then he turned to me and asked, "How did it happen? When and where did he know for the first time?"

'He stared at me, but after a while I had to shake my head.

'"No one knows," I told him. "It is one of the mysteries. Part of the unwritten story."

'Then, suddenly, he stood up, as if his patience was exhausted, and his eyes seemed to burn as he looked down at me.

'"Then I shall have to find out in my own way," he said.

'I got up, too, but he still towered over me. I said, "I don't know what else I can do to help you. I want to – very much."

'Then he smiled and held out his hand. It was like shaking hands with a bear!

'"You have helped me a great deal," he said. "At least I think I'm beginning to see what I must do."'

Lee had stood quietly leaning on the edge of his desk as

Father O'Connell had been speaking. Then he had straightened up and asked, 'And that was the last time you saw him to talk to – a week ago?'

Father O'Connell had nodded, then added, 'Of course, I saw him at the final rehearsal. He said hello to me, but we didn't talk again – and I had no idea what he was planning.'

'I wish I had,' Lee had said grimly. Then he had taken a few steps closer to the priest. 'And you've no idea at all where he has gone?'

The other had shaken his head. 'None.' Then he had added quietly, 'Except . . . '

'Yes?'

O'Connell had hesitated. 'Except I suspect it will be somewhere he can be completely alone.'

'Like where?'

The other had looked at him a little strangely for a moment.

'Like a desert, perhaps, like in the gospel stories.'

Lee had looked at him, his heart thumping. 'You really think . . . ' then, suddenly, he had clenched his hands and half turned away for a moment before turning back. 'You could be right!'

'I'm only guessing, Mr Harrison.'

'It's a damn sight better guess than I've managed to make so far – and it fits. It does make sense.'

'But it doesn't help you very much I'm afraid. A quarter of the earth's surface is covered with desert of one sort or another.'

'But it does mean there might be some hope of his coming back?'

The priest had nodded. 'As I said to you earlier this evening, I think he will, if he can.' He had then taken a step towards Lee. 'I don't think even you realized what a difficult, almost impossible, task you were asking him to undertake.'

'Perhaps not.'

'I believe he will only come back if he feels himself able to give what will probably be the performance of his life.'

'And if not?' Lee had asked. The other had paused for a moment before shaking his head.

'I don't know,' he had said quietly, half turning away. Then he had looked back at Lee and said, almost accusingly, 'But if

174

not, it will be because he cannot. In which case, you have no one to blame but yourself.'

'You!' Mary said, breaking into Lee's story. 'Why you?'

Lee shrugged. 'For asking the impossible, I guess. In any event, Father O'Connell was much more worried about what would happen to John in that case.'

He looked so strained that Mary got up from her chair, put her arms around him, and whispered, 'Why don't we forget all about it now for a while? Enough is enough. Let's go to bed.'

Lee stood up and held her against him for a long time.

Later, he shaved in her dressing room. As he examined his face in the mirror, he saw the door open behind him and then Mary was standing in the doorway, wearing the quilted house-coat he had given her as a birthday present. Her skin glowed from the bath she had just taken, and he knew she had nothing on underneath the robe.

They smiled at each other in the glass. She came up behind him and laid her head on his shoulder. After a few moments of standing there quietly together, Mary opened her eyes and Lee saw her gaze travel down his half-naked body. Suddenly her eyes widened with shock as she caught sight of the huge scar that ran from belly to ribs. It was an angry wound, but one which, he knew, would fade in time, along with the memory of the ordeal itself. He turned around to face her. Mary looked down, then up at him, her eyes full of compassion.

'Oh, my dear,' was all she could say. 'I had no idea!'

Lee smiled. 'I'm afraid it's not very pretty,' he admitted, 'but the doctor said it wouldn't look so bad after a year. I hope you don't mind.'

Mary looked down again and put out her hand to touch him. Shaking her head slowly, she sank to her knees in front of him and put her arms around his legs, burying her face in his stomach. For a moment she made no sound, but he could feel her whole body shaking; then she turned her head to one side and wept, 'Oh Lee, I love you so much!'

Lee knelt, facing her, taking her into his arms and covering her tear-stained face with kisses. Later they made love, and it was warm and wonderful and full of joy.

Chapter

10

A shaft of morning sunlight reached through the shutters and fell on John Burnard's face. He had always been in full possession of his senses the moment he awoke. (This faculty had, on more than one occasion, saved his life, as on the chilly night on the road from Fort Ruby when the hobo with whom he had shared a dinner fire tried to slit his throat for forty-two dollars.) But now, looking around the small but spotlessly clean bedroom, it took him quite a few seconds to remember he was in one of the guest rooms of Kibbutz Ein Gev on the shores of Lake Galilee.

He had been walking for two days. That is, walking mostly, only occasionally thumbing a lift to break up the bigger distances. He couldn't explain to himself why he wanted it that way. He didn't have to ride on the crowded buses – it was easy enough to hire a car – but if he wanted any chance at all of capturing some echo of truth in the time available, it seemed the only way.

First he had gone to Jerusalem, then on to Bethlehem, half a dozen miles beyond. Only six miles, but thirty-eight years in the life of Jesus, whom some called Christ.

No Jew needs anyone to tell him the significance of Jerusalem. Had Burnard not been brought up to believe there is no other city of its importance in all the world? Every Passover as a child, had he not during the Seder repeated the traditional promise: 'Next year – in Jerusalem'? And had not Jesus himself repeated those same words at that last Seder?

But in the Holy City, for all that it contained, there had been nothing to help him. In Bethlehem, too, there was nothing for him. The town seemed to have the atmosphere of a dime store. After little more than an hour there, he left and retraced his steps. Early the second morning, with a sense of urgency almost bordering on desperation, he set off on the road leading west, out of the city, then headed north – for Nazareth.

Burnard's father had sworn to come to the Holy Land – the

home of his ancestors – before he died. Like most of his ambitions, this one was never fulfilled. As Burnard journeyed on, he wondered what the old man would have thought had he known what had brought his son home at last. And then he wondered why he kept thinking about one so long dead – and unmourned.

Nazareth is principally an Arab town, but in the centre some Christian sect has built an elaborate church above an overdecorated cellar, the two parts of which are proclaimed, respectively, to be the carpenter's shop and the grotto of the Annunciation.

The setting struck no chord at all. Burnard glanced at the faces of a group of tourists as they listened to the improbable spiel of their guide, and shivered in the sudden dankness after the heat outside, wondering how it was possible to make these so-called Christian tours of the holy places and remain with any shred of faith whatsoever.

What had this tourist trap to do with the young man who, upon his father's death, had carried on the family business until his brothers and sisters were old enough to support themselves? How, in a place like this, could one recapture Christ's dreams of destiny, his frustrations and, more than likely, his self-doubts? Yet it was here that Jesus had been forced to bide his time until hatred of the Roman oppressors had burned away, and from the ashes had risen a vision of a greater Messiah – not man's image of a warrior prince, but God's requirement of a paschal lamb to wash away the sins of the world.

As Burnard remounted the steps, leaving the guide and his party to themselves, and walked out into the sunshine, for the first time he suddenly caught a fleeting impression at the back of his mind. He set out at once on the road for Capernaum where Jesus' cousins, James and John, had lived with their father, Zebedee the fisherman; where Christ had met Peter for the first time.

This was the road Jesus himself had trodden when he had first set out to begin his ministry. Although it was hot in the early afternoon sun, Burnard at last began to feel the atmosphere of the country soaking into his bones, and his skin tingled with excitement. This was what he had come for! An old truck going in the same direction passed and pulled up to wait for him, but he waved it on.

Despite his gesture, the truck stayed where it was, and when Burnard drew level with it a young man in his late twenties stuck his head out of the cab and said something to him in Hebrew. Burnard shook his head. 'I'm sorry, I don't understand.'

The other grinned, then said in a beautiful English accent, 'That's all right, old chap. Get in.'

'Thanks, but I'd rather walk.'

'You're an American?'

'That's right.'

'Where are you going?'

Burnard rubbed the back of his neck and frowned slightly. 'Well, if it's any of your business, Capernaum.'

The driver smiled again. 'Of course it *isn't* any of my business. But you might like to know it's more than twenty miles. You'll never make it before sunset.'

'Oh.'

'Moreover, it's inadvisable to wander around the countryside after dark. You're likely to run into al Fatah.'

'What?'

'Arab terrorists. Or failing that, one of our security patrols might mistake you for a terrorist. They're rather liable to shoot first and ask questions afterwards.'

'On second thoughts, I'll accept your offer!'

'Splendid. Jump in the other side.'

Burnard walked round and got in, the young man obligingly leaning over and throwing open the door for him. The door squealed painfully on rusty hinges. Burnard got in, slamming it shut again with a sound that set his teeth on edge. When he turned to grin at the other, he found the Englishman looking at him with surprise.

'Haven't you got a bag or something?'

Burnard shook his head.

'No. I came in something of a rush.'

'I see! Oh well . . . '

So saying, the other let in the clutch and the truck began to move forward.

After a short silence, Burnard said, 'You needn't worry. I'm not a vagrant. I've plenty of money. There's no need to report me.'

'My dear chap!' The young man glanced at him. 'I wouldn't dream of such a thing. It's not that – but we do have to keep our eyes skinned. You know.'

Burnard said, 'Would it make you happier if I showed you my passport?'

'Well, if you insist.'

'Okay.'

Burnard felt in his inside pocket and produced the document. He opened and held it up so that the driver could glance at it without taking his eyes off the road for more than a few seconds. Despite this the other stared at it so intently that Burnard didn't think they were going to make the next bend. The young man finally nodded and grinned, casting his eyes back to the road and wrenching the wheel around at the last second.

'Fine,' he said, when the truck, which had lurched violently from side to side, had regained its equilibrium. 'My name's Lawry.' He reached across the wheel to hold out his hand. 'My first name was Charles, but since we've been here I've changed it to Chaim.'

'Glad to know you.' Burnard took his hand. 'Mine's Burnard.'

'Yes, I know. I just saw.'

'That's right.' Burnard put the passport back into his pocket.

Lawry was silent for a while, apparently concentrating on his driving. Grateful for the silence, Burnard contentedly watched the scenery slipping past the side window. Some of the olive trees, he thought, must have been young saplings when Jesus passed this way. He wondered if *he* had had to worry about terrorists. Bandits, more than likely. He must have got the idea for the story of the Good Samaritan from somewhere.

When Lawry spoke again, his voice was so matter of fact that his passenger thought for a moment he must have misheard.

'And what's a famous Hollywood film star doing walking by himself around Israel – apparently without additional clothes or luggage?'

179

Burnard looked at him sharply and the other added gently, 'Please don't do anything silly.'

'How do you know who I am?'

The other shrugged and grinned. 'Well,' he admitted, 'I wouldn't have recognized you from your passport photograph!'

After a second, Burnard reached up to touch his beard, and the other laughed. 'It's just as well they did recognize you at Lod Airport, or your reception might not have been so friendly.'

Burnard closed his eyes and made an impatient sound. 'I forgot the beard.' Then he turned to the young man again.

'Are you from the police?'

'No,' Lawry shook his head. 'I was just asked to keep an eye on you.'

'Have I been followed?'

The other shook his head again. 'That wasn't necessary. Israel's a small country. And you don't exactly melt into the background!' His eyes twinkled as he continued, 'I understand there's no objection to your walking around here when you're supposed to be in the middle of a television show back in New York. As long as you obey a few simple rules, it's entirely your own affair. But it would help the chief of police at Haifa to sleep at night if you could let us know – roughly – what you have in mind. It would be so bad for the tourist trade if anything nasty happened to someone as well known as you.'

It took Burnard some moments to recover from the shock. A second ago he had been an anonymous traveller pursuing a purely private goal. Now, it seemed, he had been a goldfish in a tank since his arrival.

Lawry glanced at him a few times, then said, 'Look – they really don't want to interfere. As long as it's legal, all they want to do is see you're all right.'

Burnard took a deep breath, then nodded.

'I understand,' he said. 'You can tell your friends that in my stupidity I undertook a characterization – which they undoubtedly already know about . . . ' He glanced at Lawry. It was the other's turn to nod before Burnard continued, ' . . . only to find I had undertaken something I was totally incapable of doing.'

'You've run away.'

'I don't know.' Burnard looked out of the side windows again. There was a long interval before he went on. 'I'm still hoping to find the answer.'

'You're seeking – Jesus Christ?' The voice was soft, but Burnard looked back at him sharply.

'You *do* know!'

'From what I've been told, and from what you've just said, it's not too difficult to guess.'

There was another long pause before Burnard said, 'I suppose not.' Then he added, 'This is the only chance. Please don't let anyone know where I am.'

'You can take it that no one will interfere. And as far as what's going on back in your own country, that's no business of ours.'

'Thank you.'

Again, they drove in silence for a while before Lawry said, 'I hope you find what you're looking for.'

Burnard nodded. Then the other, apparently deliberately changing the subject, began to tell him how he and his mother and father had come from England ten years before to settle in Tel Aviv and how he had gone to the university in Jerusalem to study agriculture with a view to working on government-backed projects in various African countries. Then came the six-day war, and the government called for young men with the necessary training, like Chaim, to lead new frontier settlements – kibbutzim – and he had gone to one being founded just inland from Ein Gev on the southern shores of Lake Galilee. They were practically self-supporting and were just beginning to send oranges and grapefruit to Haifa for export. Also, within seconds, the kibbutz could be turned into an armed fort – a trip wire against infiltrators and covering a strategic field of fire in the event of an invasion of more serious proportions.

Chaim eventually dropped Burnard in Tiberias, but on discovering he had nowhere to stay, invited him to the kibbutz on the other side of the lake. It was arranged that Burnard would take a taxi the remaining few miles to Capernaum so that he could see it before nightfall, while Chaim would drive the truck back to Ein Gev, where he would borrow a boat and return across the water to meet his new friend in Tiberias at sunset.

181

The two men parted to go their separate ways. Burnard guessed the young man's first call would be to the local police station, but he was not worried. Chaim's attitude to him during the rest of the journey had convinced him he would be left in peace. He felt that in accepting Chaim's invitation, he was doing nothing to interfere with the quest that became more pressing with every passing hour. Indeed, some instinct told him that his visit to Capernaum was now a diversion, and that the identity he sought was already waiting for him on the other side of the water.

As they drove along the lakeside the taxi driver, who readily assumed that his fare was Jewish, told Burnard how lucky the actor was to be able to visit Israel.

'A lot of you people come over here expecting to find everyone falling over themselves in gratitude for the money you send us,' he said, belligerently. 'And we have to point out it is you who should be grateful to us.'

Burnard was hardly aware of what he was saying, but the tone was familiar enough. He had been in Israel only thirty-six hours, but that was long enough to register that the first reaction for waiters, taxi drivers and the like was very often a hostile one. At another time it might have worried him, or, more likely, made him angry. But now he had more important things on his mind.

'I guess you can't argue with that?'

He became aware once more of the rather unpleasant voice of the man driving the taxi. He looked at him, then said in a matter-of-fact sort of way, 'Look, buster, I don't know much about your problem, but right now I've other things to think about, so just keep your eyes on the road and your mouth shut and we'll get along fine.'

The driver looked at him in shocked disbelief before he spluttered. 'You can't talk to me like that here!'

'Alternatively, just stop the car and I'll walk.'

'Ah . . . I didn't mean nothing,' the driver said eventually, modifying his tone to innocent hurt. 'You don't want to talk – all right.'

Burnard suppressed a smile, and for the rest of the journey they rode in silence.

Capernaum was everything the other places he had visited were not.

Apparently having come to the conclusion that Burnard must be a Christian after all, the driver told the actor that the reason the place is so unspoiled is because it is one of the few Christian holy places over which the Israeli government has complete control. Burnard then left him and wandered down the date-palm-lined avenue to where a group of stone houses stood around a small square, almost at the water's edge.

The houses and the tiny synagogue, which must have once been the largest building, stood in ruins – blind, empty doorways and windows looking out over the calm stillness of the lake. Yet in his imagination – as he had been unable to do elsewhere – he could see this village as once it must have been at this time of day, with the evening sun sinking into the far side of the lake where the Jordan began its downward journey to the Dead Sea.

The fishermen would be tying up their boats and unloading the day's catch, probably surrounded by swarms of eager children. The potters, carpenters, and smiths of all sorts would be striking the last of the day's bargains, and the air would be scented with the aroma of a hundred evening meals being prepared by the mothers and daughters of the men who still lingered outside talking of the day's events, or maybe sitting in the synagogue itself disputing points from the Law.

Burnard saw it as a friendly place, a place where everybody knew everybody else. Because the town was tucked away in a corner around the lake, between the water and mountains, the people would have rarely seen a Roman soldier or official, so that there would have been none of the tension, the constant bubbling hatred, that soaked up so much of the energy of their fellow countrymen in less fortunate places, like Nazareth, for example, which lay across the main lines of communication between Jerusalem and Damascus.

The atmosphere, Burnard thought, must have been relaxed. Although the people had been concerned with the everyday business of living, they had had time to care for each other and to think about eternal things like the Law, and Yahweh's love for his people – a love which had stood the test of time, a love which not even the Romans could shake.

After having lived in the feverish atmosphere of the coast – having endured the rebellions on the death of the old Emperor Augustus and the ruthless suppressions by Tiberius, his successor – Jesus had no doubt come here to find his feet and choose his supporters in comparative tranquillity before turning to face the hot breath of Rome and the Sanhedrin.

An hour after his arrival at Capernaum, the taxi driver dropped Burnard at the jetty where he had arranged to meet Chaim, tried to charge the American more than they had agreed on, and finally drove off in sullen silence.

The small launch arrived on time, piloted by Chaim. He was accompanied by a blonde girl wearing a shirt and skin-tight shorts. Her face, arms and legs were burned the colour of pale honey. Chaim grinned as he introduced his wife, obviously conscious of the skin-tingling effect she was producing. Burnard, for his part, knew instinctively that, despite the warmth of Helga's greeting and the way she smiled into his eyes as they held hands for a few seconds while they were being introduced, and his recognition of the familiar, often subconscious, response to his own masculinity, no other man would ever succeed in provoking her beyond the most superficial flirtation as long as her husband lived. This was just the sort of challenge that had always made life worth living.

'I'm glad to know you, Mr Burnard,' the girl was saying. 'Chaim has been telling me all about you.' She spoke unfalteringly, but with the strong local accent that was reminiscent of German, but much softer. 'We are very glad you have decided to stay with us.'

'It's very kind of you.'

'Not at all. We've never had anyone famous stay with us before. Please sit down here, then we shall be – how do you say? – better balanced!'

He sat down obediently, and Helga settled herself opposite him. She had incredibly beautiful legs.

Chaim opened the throttle of the outboard motor. The

184

boat rose as it cut through the water in an arc towards the opposite shore about five miles distant.

Owing to the noise from the outboard, it was difficult to talk during the trip, and they seemed to realize, in any event, that he would prefer to be left to his thoughts. Presently he looked away and stared for a long time back along the shore line to where the ruins of Capernaum were still visible in the twilight.

Eventually, Chaim cut back the motor and Burnard turned around to see that they were coasting into a stone jetty, similar to the one they had left and just away from which several other boats and pleasure craft rode at coloured floats.

Helga said, 'Since the war, people have been able to go sailing more on this side of the lake, but before it was too dangerous.'

'I imagine so.' Burnard nodded and gazed up at the steep escarpment of mountains which rose above them into Jordanian territory but which he knew must now be secured by the Israeli army. Before, it must have been a sniper's paradise, and he said so.

Chaim nodded. 'We weren't here then, but hardly a day went past when someone in the village wasn't shot at.'

'Where our kibbutz is now was once a cease-fire line,' his wife added.

Burnard wasn't sure if it was the habit of those in kibbutzim to ignore visitors to their communal dining room, but except for those seated immediately around him, the rest took no notice of him at all. At any event, Burnard found the atmosphere completely relaxed, although half the time his dinner companions spoke to each other in Hebrew, so that he could only catch an odd word.

'You may notice that there are no children here,' Chaim remarked towards the end of the meal. 'That is because the area is considered too dangerous.' His eyes twinkled as Burnard had noticed they always did just before the kibbutznik was going to poke gentle fun at him. 'I hope you don't mind – about the danger, I mean?'

Burnard grinned. 'I'll let you know,' he retorted.

'Seriously,' Chaim went on, 'I shouldn't wander around by

myself, if I were you. Certainly not beyond the limits of the farm. We haven't had a raid in months, but you never know when the odd one is going to slip through.'

'I think I know how to look after myself.' Burnard was smiling but he couldn't help feeling a bit irritated by the other's apparent assumption that he was likely to faint at the first sound of gunfire.

'That's all right,' his host said mildly, 'as long as you know. Just remember it's only in films the hero doesn't get scared.' Burnard was about to protest, but Chaim held up his hand. 'Oh, I know you were in the World War, but that was different. Here, most of the time, it's the enemy who decides when to fight.' Now he smiled, self-deprecatingly. 'We don't have any heroes here, John. We just want to survive.'

'You get used to it,' Helga broke in.

Her husband turned to her and nodded.

'But you don't get less scared. You just get scared more often!' Those around laughed at this. 'At least, you learn to live with it,' Chaim went on, helping himself to another mug of coffee from the pot which stood in the middle of the table.

'You don't have to live here,' Burnard pointed out.

The other looked at him with an expression he couldn't read, then one of them said:

'We don't have to live in Israel at all. You can always live in someone else's country, and after a few generations pretend you belong, but they never let you forget. This is the only place where a Jew can be a man.'

Burnard shrugged. 'Well, I'm sorry. I don't want to start a fight, but I just don't agree. I think what you're doing here is good, but there have always been two sides to this forgetting business.'

'I thought you were a Jew,' one of the others challenged.

Burnard turned to him and his eyes narrowed. 'That's true,' he admitted. 'But I've always regarded myself as a human being first.'

Chaim suddenly smiled and said, 'Why don't we talk about something else? We must be the only people in the world who feel it necessary to keep convincing *ourselves* as well as everyone else that we have a right to exist!'

186

'That's hardly fair,' his wife protested. 'We hardly ever talk about it.'

'Not among ourselves,' Chaim agreed. 'But until we can have a stranger among us without at once starting to cross-question him about his attitude towards us, we can't expect other people to take us for granted – and that, above all else, is what we need.'

'Chaim's right,' one of the others nodded. 'What we want is less glamour. The honeymoon was exciting – now we should get used to sitting on separate chairs!'

Again the others laughed, and the tension collapsed.

They talked a little while longer, then Chaim and Helga walked him to the guest cottage, where they said goodnight.

Burnard lay on the bed, looking up at the ceiling of the little bedroom, musing about his impressions of the day. It seemed that at last he was getting somewhere.

He pulled a sweat-stained New Testament out of his jacket pocket, but remembered that he had promised to leave his laundry outside the door – Helga had said it would be picked up, washed, and returned to him the following morning. He got up to attend to the matter, then settled down again on the bed and began to read:

'And he came down to Capernaum, a village by the sea of Galilee, and on the Sabbath he went into the synagogue and preached, and they were astonished at the power of his words . . . but there was one man who cried out in a loud voice . . . "What have we to do with you, Jesus of Nazareth?" '

Suddenly all the peace was gone. He still knew nothing.

' . . . most ratings indicate that "Christ on Trial" captured a huge audience last night. Critics in the nation's papers this morning were universally enthusiastic and there is every indication that audiences for the second and third nights will beat all previous records.'

Amos Brown snapped off the radio, then glanced around the apartment for a second before closing the door behind him and walking to the elevator.

Once out in the street he turned right into St Nicholas Avenue, then lengthened his stride as he made for the gymnasium and his morning workout. He felt pretty good and one of the main reasons for his good humour was relief that the letter he had posted the day before yesterday had, so far, provoked no response. It could mean they were willing to let things be.

It was just past eleven o'clock when Smith, who was holding the punch bag, suddenly looked over his shoulder and straightened up.

'What's the matter?'

The older man nodded behind him. 'We got company.'

Amos turned to see two young men wearing turtle-sweaters and leather jackets standing a few yards away. One smiled, but there was little humour in his expression.

'Good morning, gentlemen.' Amos and Smith nodded without answering as one moved forward a few paces. 'We don't want any trouble. Simon would just like a word.'

Amos glanced at his trainer for a second and saw a glint of fear in the old man's eyes. He turned to the young man and said, 'I'll be glad to talk, any time.'

'He wants to talk now.'

Amos shrugged with studied casualness. 'He knows where I am.'

The other visitor stepped in front of his companion and said in a decidedly less friendly voice, 'We've got a car outside. Are you coming or do we have to tell him no?'

Amos paused, conscious of the stillness that had settled over the gymnasium. Everyone was now looking in their direction.

'Okay,' he said quietly. 'Give me time to change.' Then he glanced at Smith. 'You'll know where I am if anyone wants me?'

The other held his eyes for a few seconds, then nodded slowly. Amos turned and walked into the dressing room.

Neither of his companions spoke once they were in the car, and twenty minutes later they were driving over the George Washington Bridge. A short time after that, they drew up to a ramshackle wooden house in a run-down part of Englewood, New Jersey. One of the two men got out and opened the door for him, and without further invitation Amos walked up the wooden steps, across the porch and inside.

He was familiar with the layout of the house, but once inside the front door, he stood to one side to let one of the others precede him along the corridor to a room at the end on the left. He realized that it would have been difficult, if not impossible, for the two emissaries to have brought him in against his will, but if he had refused he would never have known when the organization might reach out for him. He had seen it happen to others. He thought of the young man whom the organization had discovered to be a plant. His wife had found him early one morning with his ears nailed to the front door and his throat cut. Amos knew that once they picked a target there was no escaping from them. No matter how fast or how far he ran, they would find him. And he could not, he knew, live the life of a fugitive. Better face whatever was coming now. There was still the chance they would let him go, and if the worst happened – maybe it didn't matter so much. Now, nothing seemed so precious as freedom from the organization which, above all, personified the hatred that until so recently had been the sum of his own personality.

The room was furnished like an office. Sunlight was pouring into the room, but Amos knew the blinds would never be drawn –

it was too important for the members to see what was going on outside. He knew also why the office was at the back of the house – in case of a raid, the back provided at least a chance of escape. Immediately another door opened and a tall, immaculately dressed man in his early thirties entered the room. He was followed by two other men and a beautiful girl in a mauve dress who carried a notebook and pencil. This was Rosemary, Simon's secretary. One thing Simon had always hammered into them – if they wanted to be taken seriously by their own people they had to be successful, and to be successful they had to be efficient. That was why the whole set-up was run like a well-regulated business – with accountants controlling the finances; public relations experts in charge of propaganda; and every other division from political indoctrination to smaller sections dealing with terror and extortion, all managed by professionals – masters in their own field.

Amos looked at the man who sat at the desk now and mar-velled yet again – even though he was now an outsider and, consequently, in mortal danger – that this seemingly mild executive could have achieved so much in so short a time. Everyone knew he had been out of the country for some years – although nobody outside the inner sanctum knew where – and when he had returned he had set about rebuilding from the pieces left by those who had had more enthusiasm than skill; within two years this man had brought every group with similar aims under his control – or had had them eliminated. The girl sitting beside him was, Amos knew, not only capable of taking dictation at two hundred words a minute in cypher, but also an accomplished assassin, noted for the originality of her methods.

'Sit down, please.' Simon waved Amos into the chair opposite, then nodded to the two who had brought him. They left the room at once, closing the door quietly behind them.

Amos saw a few grey hairs curling at the temples of the other as he bent his head over some papers. He glanced around the room. It was almost like having an interview for a new job, but the fighter wasn't deceived. He knew something far more important than a position was about to be decided – probably whether or not he was to be allowed to walk out of the house alive. He took a deep breath in an attempt to stop his heart from thumping uncomfortably against his ribs, and tried to calm himself with the thought that if they harmed him, Smith knew what to do – if the old man had the nerve.

'Have you got the letter?' Simon held out his hand. The girl beside him handed him the few pages of notepaper Amos recognized as his own.

'Thank you.' Simon read quickly, then looked up at him.

'You wish to resign?' Amos nodded.

Simon glanced down for a moment, turning the letter over. 'You state your reasons as conversion to the Christian faith?'

'Yes, sir.'

'And how did this come about?' The other sat back in his chair and prepared to listen with evident attention.

'I got another job,' Amos began. 'One that involved reading the Bible a lot. It didn't happen all at once, but gradually it came to mean more and more to me . . . '

'More than your friends?'

Amos stared at him for a moment. 'My friends mean more to me than ever. But I came to believe that more was to be gained from trying to understand our enemies than from defeating them.'

'I see. You think we are mistaken in our policies of fighting the whites with their own weapons?'

'I don't know. If you mean, will you achieve your objectives – maybe you will. I just don't believe any longer it's the way to make folks happy.'

'Happy!' For the first time, the other's voice became hard. 'What right has anybody to happiness when our people still lie in chains?'

'Surely, trying to help other people is the surest way to be happy yourself?'

Simon looked at him, and for the first time Amos thought he saw a crack in the other's composure.

'Are you sure you haven't just made some *new* friends?' he snapped. 'Like the FBI maybe?'

Amos shook his head. He knew this was near the crunch, but

although he was afraid, he said as calmly as he could, 'You have nothing to fear from me.'

'You could be a grave danger to us.'

'There is nothing in my change of heart which calls for treachery.'

'I wish I could believe that.'

'It's just that – what you're doing doesn't seem so important any more.' Amos paused for a moment, then continued softly, 'Someone I've got to know pretty well recently lived in times like these – only worse, if anything. He once said, "All flesh is as grass, and all the glory of man as the flower of grass. The grass withers, and the flowers fall away, but the word of the Lord endures forever." '

Lee knew instinctively that it was no use, but in order to satisfy Burgh, he and Mary spent the entire day inquiring as discreetly as possible at airports, railway stations and even hospitals, but the star of their show had apparently vanished into thin air.

Apparently no one outside had noticed the substitution the previous night – which was, perhaps, not so surprising in view of Father O'Connell's heavy makeup and the fact that he had only been called on to say a few sentences, but it was vital, while there was still the slightest chance of John's reappearing in time for the third and vital night, to keep his disappearance a secret. Above all, suspicions of the press must not be aroused.

By the time Lee took his place in the control room that night, the programme had started and both Baal and Lang were on their feet facing Judge Haald.

'Very well, gentlemen,' the jurist was saying, 'it is agreed that the court will continue to hear evidence in the absence of the Accused.' He glanced at Lang. 'Needless to say, his failure to appear on the third day will be heavily prejudicial to your case, Mr Lang.'

'He has promised to appear, Your Honour.'

'Very well. Today we shall be hearing evidence concerning the Accused's ministry.' He now looked at Baal. 'Would you please call your first witness, Mr Baal?'

192

Lang sat down as Baal bowed slightly. 'May it please the court, the prosecution would like to call the Rabbi Hillel.'

Ray Burgh took his seat in the viewing room as the rabbi, a tall, distinguished man in his early forties, with calm eyes and a beautifully deep, resonant voice was taking the oath. The sponsor next to Burgh glanced at him and nodded approvingly. 'Nice touch,' he said.

Burgh nodded back, smiling confidently. 'Thanks.'

Baal stepped up to the witness stand. 'You are the Rabbi Hillel?' he began. The other inclined his head graciously. 'Yes.'

'Rabbi, would it be true to say that the Pharisee school founded by you a few years before the birth of the Accused exerted a tremendous influence on the whole Jewish religion?'

'Nothing changes the relationship of God to his Chosen People,' the other answered serenely and, Lee thought, without a trace of false modesty.

'I'm sorry. Perhaps I put it badly. How would you describe the significance of your teaching?'

'The Torah – those inspired writings Christians refer to as the Books of Moses – covers every aspect not only of God's requirements concerning his service, but also his instructions about how his people should conduct themselves from day to day in their ordinary lives.'

Listening, Lee found himself calmed by the rabbi's voice, which was reminiscent of the deep hum of a hive of bees. The producer sat back to concentrate on what the actor was saying.

'Many of these instructions are quite detailed and precise,' the rabbi went on, 'but because Man is imperfect and, therefore, an imperfect medium of communication, some laws are open to more than one interpretation.' He gestured with his hands gracefully. 'And as life became more complicated, there grew up areas of new activity not specifically covered. It has been necessary, therefore, almost from the beginning, for the leaders of our people to sit down and try to understand God's intention in every new circumstance. In particular, as the nature of God himself became clearer in the course of our history, during which he gradually revealed more about himself to us, it was realized that earlier interpretations must be revised.'

'And what role did you play in this?' asked Baal.

'I founded a school.' The rabbi glanced in the direction of the jury. 'And let me make it clear exactly what that meant. It was not a place where pupils sat in silence listening to their teachers.' He drew himself up. 'Rather it was a place where teachers, like myself, put forward ideas concerning the nature of revealed truth, and these ideas were discussed and disputed at length by other teachers and by those who had come to hear our discussions.'

Baal nodded. 'Nevertheless,' he said, 'out of all this, I understand, emerged a line of thought that was carried away by those who had come to listen and participate – a line of thought which came to dominate Pharisee teaching of the day and over which, most people would agree, you personally exerted great influence.'

The rabbi inclined his head. 'It is true I made a contribution,' he admitted. 'Perhaps, being the founder, my views were given more attention than they deserved. It was far more an evolution of corporate thought by a group of men seeking truth.'

'But no one can deny the influence this had on what was being preached in practically every temple in the country?'

Lang rose to his feet. 'Your Honour,' he said, 'this is all very interesting, but has it any relevance to the case?'

The judge looked at him sympathetically and turned to the prosecutor. 'Mr Baal,' he said, 'we do seem to have rather wandered from the point.'

'Your Honour, the witness's modesty has made me take rather longer than expected to make the point I am trying to bring out, which is simply the fact that anyone living anywhere in Israel at the time we are speaking of, and going to temple each Sabbath as the law required, could not have failed to have been influenced by the teaching of this witness and his colleagues.'

The judge nodded briefly.

'If Your Honour will allow me to continue,' Baal went on, 'now that the point *has* been established, I hope to the Court's satisfaction, its relevance will quickly emerge.'

'Very well. You may continue.'

Lang raised his eyebrows eloquently, glancing in the direction of the jury. He then sat down as the prosecutor turned back to the witness.

'Rabbi, what I am going to ask you now is not easy. If you had to summarize your school's view of revealed truth in a few sentences, what would you say?'

The witness answered without a second's hesitation, 'That Man should serve God with love, not in fear. Nevertheless, he must always remember that beside the Almighty he is nothing, so that pride never enters his heart.'

'And what should a man's relationship be to his fellows?'

Again the reply came back without hesitation. 'He should treat others as he would wish to be treated by them in return – both friend and enemy, for all men are brothers in the sight of God. If he does both these things to the best of his ability, his reward is eternal life.'

'Thank you.' Baal paused to let the significance of these last words sink in. 'Just a few more questions,' he continued. 'Would a boy brought up in Nazareth in the orthodox faith during the lifetime of the Accused, and visiting the temple in Jerusalem, hear these teachings?'

'Undoubtedly.'

Baal paused again. 'Rabbi, are you familiar with the teachings of Jesus?'

'Yes.'

'Would you say they bore any resemblance to the summary you gave us just now?'

The rabbi nodded. 'They are similar in many respects,' he said.

'Yet his teaching is compared by Christians with what they refer to as the Old Testament to illustrate how much closer it was to God's real nature and intention?'

At this the rabbi permitted himself to smile. 'I hope it is,' he said.

'Because, in fact, it was based on your own?'

'Apart from the heretical claim to be the Messiah.'

'So, leaving that aside, there was nothing original in his teaching at all?'

Again the rabbi addressed the court as a whole. 'It is fair to

195

say that many of the ideas which Christians attribute to Jesus evolved in the course of many long years before he was born,' he said. 'In truth, they were the inspired vision of many men, not just one.'

'One last question. What do you think of the Accused's claim to be the son of God?'

Hillel turned to face him. 'But for that, he would probably have been accepted as a great exponent of the most advanced thinking of his day.'

'You don't accept it?'

The rabbi shook his head firmly. 'No,' he said. 'Many men before and since have claimed to be the Chosen One. But when he comes at last, there will be no doubt.'

Baal bowed to him slightly. 'Thank you,' he said. 'No further questions.'

Lang rose to his feet and approached the stand with a note in his hand. 'Rabbi,' he began, 'you are familiar with the prophet Isaiah, no doubt?' Hillel nodded without answering.

'You accept his prophecies as the inspired word of God?'

'Of course.'

'Are you aware, then, that he wrote the following concerning the Messiah?' Lang slipped on his glasses and began to read:

' "He shall be delivered unto the Gentiles and shall be mocked, and spitefully treated, and spat on, and they shall whip him, and put him to death." '

Lang looked up at the witness, removing his glasses and tucking them into his breast pocket. 'That hardly sounds as if there were no doubt?' he challenged.

'I was not referring to the Gentiles.'

'On the other hand,' Lang went on, 'it does sound like what happened to the Accused, does it not?'

Hillel shrugged slightly. 'Scourging followed by crucifixion was a common punishment under the Romans. It happened to many. When Titus put down the rebellion, the road from Jerusalem to the sea was lined with crucified rebels.'

Lang paused for a moment. 'Rabbi, are you aware that the Accused stated many times that he had come to fulfil the law, not to destroy it?'

196

'That is the very heresy of which we complain.'

'We – meaning the orthodox Jewry of the day?'

'We – meaning the majority of our people.'

'But in the light of that claim, was it surprising that Jesus chose to build on the best he found?'

The rabbi shook his head. 'It is not for me to say,' he said.

'Possibly not, but you will agree that the Accused often rebuked your sect for putting the law before common humanity?'

'No man is above the law.'

'No *man*, agreed, but what of the son of God?' He paused for a moment, looking at Hillel, but the other did not answer. He continued, 'Is not the truth of the matter that you and your colleagues took the law about as far as Man could. It required God himself to give it life?'

Hillel looked at him. 'These are just words,' he said.

'Quite so,' Lang admitted. 'The importance of Jesus was not so much in the words he spoke, but in what he was. As you implied, any enlightened man of the day could repeat the law, but it took the son of God himself to fulfil it. Not to speak, but to *be*. Is that not so?' He paused for a moment, then turned away before Hillel could answer.

'No further questions.'

Haald nodded in the direction of the witness stand. 'Thank you, Rabbi. You may stand down.' Hillel swept out, looking neither to right nor left, as Baal got to his feet.

'The prosecution has no other witnesses under this section of the case, Your Honour.' He sat down again.

'Very well. Mr Lang, would you please call your first witness?'

Lang rose to his feet again: 'Thank you, Your Honour. The defence would first like to call John the Baptist.'

As the witness appeared, the buzz of conversation that usually arose whenever a new witness was called died away into silence. The clerk moved forward to administer the oath.

Watching intently from the control room, Lee remembered the Gospel description: 'John had as his raiment camel's hair, and a leathern girdle about his loins, and his meat was fruit and wild honey. He was the voice of one crying in the wilderness, Make straight the way of the Lord.'

197

The witness was a man in his late forties with a long, unkempt beard and greying hair. He carried a short staff in his hand, there were no sandals on his feet and his cloak seemed to be falling to pieces. Yet this shabby appearance became insignificant when one looked at the eyes of the actor portraying this man who was a legend in his own time. They were of such a penetrating blue that one could, Lee thought, become mesmerized by them.

Lang posed his first question. 'You are John, son of Zacharias the priest?'

'I am.' The voice was deep, and perfect teeth flashed from what seemed the depths of his beard.

'Are you any relation to the Accused?' Lang demanded, and as John looked around, he added, 'No, he is not here at the moment.'

'You mean Jesus of Nazareth?'

'Yes.'

John nodded slowly. 'My mother and his were cousins.'

'Were you older than Jesus?'

'I think so.'

'By how many years?'

John thought for a moment. 'I don't know. We did not meet until both of us were past our first youth.'

'When was that?'

'Some ten years before he began his Ministry. He sought me out in the desert.'

Lang nodded. 'Thank you. We'll come back to that in a minute. Now, can you tell me one or two things about yourself? It has been said that you manoeuvred the chief priests to nominate you as High Priest on the death of Herod instead of his successor's choice, Joazar, and that when this plan failed, you incited a direct rebellion and had to flee for your life when this was crushed.'

The blue eyes turned on Lang with interest.

'Who says such a thing?'

'Herod's son, Archelaus.'

To everyone's surprise, John suddenly threw back his head and roared with laughter.

Haald bent forward. 'The witness will try to control his mirth until he has, at least, let us in on the joke.'

John looked at him, wiping his eyes with the back of his hand. 'You must forgive me,' he said. 'It is just that I don't think Archelaus could recognize the truth if his life depended on it.'

Lang said, 'Then perhaps you would tell us?'

'Very well.' John took a deep breath, which he let out as a sigh. 'It is true that when Herod died the people would have had me for High Priest, but even before I knew of Archelaus' wishes I had already refused.'

'Why?'

'Why?' John repeated the question softly, seeming to look inwards, then said, 'Because I was afraid of becoming proud.' He looked around the courtroom. 'Already a spring had arisen from under the threshold of the Temple in accordance with Ezekiel's prophecy concerning the last days. And over the portico of the Temple itself a golden eagle had been placed by Herod as a symbol of his homage to Rome, thus fulfilling Daniel's prophecy that in that time there would be an abomination in a holy place.' He turned back to Lang. 'The signs were there for anyone with eyes to see, and the Lord spoke to me in a dream saying: " . . . You shall be a voice crying in the wilderness, Make straight the way of the Lord. For one comes after you whose shoes you are not worthy to unloose. You know him not, but upon the same you shall see the Spirit descending, and he shall baptize with the Holy Ghost." '

Lang paused for a moment, then asked, 'Do you think that in any way you influenced Jesus to think of himself as the Messiah?'

John looked at him, then replied, 'He was the Messiah – and now sits on the right hand of God the Almighty Father.'

'You mentioned a meeting you had with him ten years earlier. Can you tell us about it now?'

The witness was silent for a moment. 'The preparation was long and hard. First, his earthly father died when he was quite young and he had to work to keep his mother and brothers and sisters until they were old enough to look after themselves. But

199

even then, the Lord led him in many places and showed him many things before he was judged ready.'

'The meeting,' Lang prompted gently.

'Oh, yes.' There was a long pause before John continued. 'It was evening by the time he found me high in the mountains of Judea, overlooking the desert, in a cave where I was living. I gave him some food, and we sat on either side of the fire while it grew dark outside. He told me first of the story of his birth, then of the flight to Egypt and of his parents' vow of silence to protect him.'

'What was that?'

'After Herod's death, Mary and Joseph were still afraid of Archelaus' spies. When they returned to Nazareth, there was no one who could associate them with the events in Bethlehem, but they told no one – not even Jesus himself until he was old enough to appreciate the danger.' After a moment's silence, John continued more slowly. 'Then, beginning with the Scriptures, he traced how all things seemed to point to him as the Messiah and how, as he became older, God spoke to him more clearly each day. Finally, he told me – almost unwillingly, as I remember – about his powers of healing, which he had discovered by accident and had always tried to keep secret.

'I said to him, "If this is true, what do you expect of me? I have long foretold the Coming – should I deny it now because I find myself related to the Chosen One?"'

John stopped, and when, after a few seconds he still showed no signs of continuing, Lang inquired, 'How did he answer?'

The other turned again to the attorney and said quietly, 'He wanted me to tell him what he should do.'

'What did you say to him?'

Once again John seemed to be looking inwards, and it was a long time before he answered, 'I said that once I had wondered if *I* were the Chosen One. But as God continued to make clear his purpose for me, I realized that I was the one about whom it was written: " . . . Behold, I send my messenger before thy face, which shall prepare the way for thee . . . " Then I said:

' "The Messiah is among us presently, of that I am sure. But if you ask me to say from what you have told me – although a

200

surge of hope at your words has filled my heart and turned these old and heavy bones into those of a young man – whether or not you are He, I cannot say." '

Lang waited, then prompted again, 'What did Jesus say then?'

'Nothing. He looked away, and I saw he could scarcely conceal his disappointment. I told him, "Everything points to you, except for the doubt in your mind – for it is not possible that there should be any in His. Nevertheless, the fact that such exists in your heart does not rule you out completely, any more than its absence would prove that you were He." Then I reminded him of Judas of Galilee, and the others many years before. As I spoke, and he listened quietly with his eyes never leaving my face, I felt his power, and even then I wanted to cast all caution to the winds and fall down and worship him.'

John's voice had gathered strength, but now he paused for a moment, and when he went on his voice was almost a whisper. 'How often in those lone years had I asked myself: "When? What else must happen before He comes?" Yet, now, I believed that at last I saw the reason: God had not made his Chosen One ready.'

John again lapsed into silence, then seemed to recall himself and said, 'After a long while Jesus said to me, "How, then, shall I know?"

' "Perhaps, never," I told him. "In which case, you are not He. But if you do at last know, then there will be no more doubt. When you are ready, God will give you wisdom, and knowledge and power, beside that which you have today are but acorns to an oak tree.

' "As to the power which He has already given you, you are wise to use it sparingly in the meantime. This is a generation hungry for signs, and if you use your powers too openly, then perhaps it will not be God who decides. The people might force your hand, and if that happened, be sure His choice would fall on another.

' "Remember also, that if and when the time comes that He calls you forth, it will be to a destiny that has no comparison – so do not look back. Not to the Prophets, nor David, nor even to Moses. For when the Messiah is crowned, it will be

201

something the world has never seen before – and never will again."

'He looked at me, then said, "My Father's will be done." '

A silence had settled over the courtroom that Lang was loath to break, yet it was evident that the witness would say nothing more without further prompting. 'And that was the last time you saw him until he came to you at the beginning of his ministry to be baptized in the Jordan?'

John nodded, but didn't answer.

Lang went on, 'How did he appear then? Was he changed?'

John looked at him and smiled.

'He was the same, in that everything that was in him before was still there. But now the tree was in full flower. There was no longer any doubt.'

'Thank you.' Lang turned to Haald and said, 'No further questions.' He went to his seat as Baal, looking thoughtful, proceeded to take his place.

'I have only one question I would like to ask,' the prosecutor said slowly. 'You repeated several times in the course of your admittedly moving story that the true Messiah would have no self-doubt and that in the end you yourself had no doubts about the Accused.'

'That is the truth.'

'But is it not a fact that when you were in prison you became disturbed at the reports of some of the things Jesus was doing and sent two of your own disciples to ask him if he really *was* the one that should come, or should you look for another?'

'Yes, but . . . '

'Yes or no.' Baal's voice suddenly cut across the courtroom. 'Did you or didn't you?'

The witness looked at him for a few seconds. There was no anger in his eyes – only pity. At last he said, 'If half the truth will suffice, then yes, I did.'

'Thank you. That's all I want to know.' Baal walked away and sat down.

In spite of his great affection for Baal, Lee felt angry in a way that defied explanation.

202

The witness left the stand as Lang stood up and said, 'The defence would now like to call a witness who will testify concerning the Accused's power over death itself.' He looked directly at the jury before continuing. 'Three times he raised the dead – the last occasion being his own resurrection; but the first was a man I now call to testify before you. Call . . . Lazarus.'

Burnard had spent most of the day sunk in thought. Chaim and Helga had left him alone except to ask if he would like to join them for lunch, but he had declined.

Now, as he walked through the cool of the orchards under a canopy of stars which stood out, almost unblinking, like diamonds on fine velvet, the prayers of another whose voice had brought hope for such a short time, long ago, repeated themselves in his mind:

'Mine eyes have seen Thy salvation which thou hast prepared before the face of all people. A light to lighten the Gentiles . . . and the glory of Thy people Israel.'

As he walked, remembering Jim's words, the sounds of singing and occasional laughter grew fainter behind him, and at last he reached the end of the cultivated land.

Without noticing, he walked on to where the ground started to rise steeply in front of him. Stopping for a moment to look back at the lights of Tiberias, which twinkled far away across the lake, he began to climb, conscious that each step took him further from that responsibility which had hung around his neck like a great stone, and nearer to that insight in which it seemed that all mystery would be revealed, and the self-doubt that remained would melt away.

They didn't miss him until, half an hour after supper had started, Helga went to the guest cottage to see if anything was wrong.

Perhaps there was nothing to worry about. He was probably somewhere inside the grounds, wandering around looking at the stars. But it was the time of the new moon, a favourite time for infiltrators. The look-outs would be on their toes. Chaim and Helga were afraid that he might be shot by mistake.

Shortly afterwards, Chaim and his friend David set out with one of the dogs to look for Burnard.

No one who knew Amos before, except Lee, could have imagined the transformation. It was not just the makeup and clothes. To Mary and everyone else it was evident, even by the time he turned to answer the prosecutor's first question, that he had *become* the first Apostle. When Baal had finished, the boxer paused for a moment before answering: 'He said to me, "You are Peter, and on this rock I will build my church." '

'And was that true?' Baal challenged.

'That's not for me to say.'

The prosecutor paused, looking at him, then said, 'He obviously thought you were the strongest, the most likely candidate. But he was wrong, wasn't he?'

'The Master was never wrong.'

'Oh, I think so,' Baal said, calmly. 'He certainly made a mistake about Judas.'

The attorney for the defence rose at once, but Haald held up his hand.

'Mr Baal, would you *please* confine yourself to questions?'

Lang subsided as the prosecutor turned to face the bench. 'I'm sorry, Your Honour. In any event, I don't want to anticipate the evidence that the witness will give the court tomorrow.'

'Then please do as I ask, and we shall both be content.'

Baal inclined his head. 'As Your Honour pleases.'

'He does,' Haald said dryly.

The prosecutor turned back to the witness. 'I meant to ask that, since most people attribute the spreading of the gospel story to Paul, would it not be truer to say the Christian Church, as such, was founded on his work and not yours?'

The witness looked unruffled. 'Paul was a comparative latecomer,' he said calmly.

'Exactly,' Baal accepted, nodding. 'In point of fact, your master had never heard of him, which undoubtedly prompted him to choose you, in spite of Paul's alleged ability to foresee the future.'

Peter shrugged. 'Paul was the traveller,' he said. 'He was also a great talker and writer.'

'Which was why he was more successful?'

The witness paused for a few seconds then inclined his head. 'In some respects,' he admitted.

'In the ones that mattered?' Baal persisted, and now the other began to show the first signs of anger. Lang and his assistant exchanged glances but the witness bit his lip and controlled himself.

'It is not true to say that the Master never knew Paul,' he said. 'He called him, after He had risen, to take the place of Judas. And as to his being wrong about me, it's true I let him down sometimes . . . '

'I was coming to that.'

'But that was my fault, not his.' Peter paused for a moment, then spoke directly to the jury. 'God gave us free will. How we use it is up to us. The Master expressed his intention concerning me; He knew I had the strength, if I could only use it in the right way. In any event – perhaps that's why He chose Paul later – but in the beginning, after He had sent the Comforter, it was John and I, or rather, the Holy Spirit acting through us, who gathered Our Lord's followers together into the first Church . . . '

'Yes, I see,' Baal interrupted. 'You're claiming, that you founded *the* Church as opposed to *a* Church?'

The witness turned to him. 'I simply tell you the truth,' he said mildly.

'Then tell me this: Didn't you and Paul have a considerable difference of opinion concerning the priorities of the early Church?'

Peter hesitated for a moment before replying. 'Paul was keen to carry the news to the Gentiles, but I felt we should convert our own people first, if possible.'

'Quite so,' Baal agreed. 'But did this not develop into a quarrel which almost split the first Christian Church in two?'

'It never came to that.'

'Because you agreed to differ?'

'Yes.'

'Paul went his way and you went yours?'

205

Again the witness hesitated. 'You could say that,' he admitted.

Baal drew himself up. 'Then as to the result,' he said, 'would it be true to say that Paul's efforts ended with the eventual conversion of the whole Roman Empire, whereas the Jews, with very few exceptions, turned their back on the new faith?'

Peter looked at him intently. 'There are none so deaf as those who will not hear,' he said.

'Nevertheless, isn't it the truth that Paul largely succeeded, whereas you failed?'

'It was our duty to go on trying to convert the Jews before it was too late.'

'Wasn't it too late once the crucifixion had taken place?'

The witness shook his head firmly. 'God's mercy is always there for those who call upon Him in the name of Our Lord Jesus Christ.'

'But in this case,' Baal observed, 'few did?'

Peter nodded. 'As was foretold in the Scriptures.'

'So – the Christian Church became accepted by the pagans, but not by the Jews?'

'That is largely true.'

'Which brings us back to the first point. Surely, as this acceptance was built on the efforts of Paul, would it not be true to say he was the rock, not you?'

Peter looked at him in silence for quite a long time before answering, 'You can twist words to add up to anything.'

'Don't the results add up to the fact that Jesus was wrong about the way his movement would develop after his death?'

'No.'

'Which in turn, demonstrates his fallibility – and thus the truth of the charge brought against him?'

'Jesus was and is the only begotten son of God the Father. He came down and dwelt among us for a short time as a man, to show us how we should live – and died upon the cross for the redemption of our sins.' Peter turned away from the prosecutor and his voice gathered strength. 'I saw him perform miracles with my own eyes. I heard the words of his mouth fall like balm across the troubled souls of thousands, and in the end,

206

I saw his body risen from the grave, triumphant over death, as he promised.'

'If that was so, why did you all run away when he was taken to be crucified?'

The witness barely glanced at Baal before turning back to face the jury. 'Because in spite of all the wonders we had seen, and the hope with which he had filled our hearts, we had not yet witnessed the resurrection and, being mortal, the fear of death lay on us.' He paused, and when he spoke again his voice rang across the room: 'I, Peter, the so-called rock you rightly pour scorn upon, failed, as he knew I would. If it had not been so, if our nature and the nature of all men had been different, why would a resurrection have been necessary?' He turned back to Baal. 'But once we had seen him afterwards, with the wounds still on his hands and feet, and the mark of the spear in his side – though we still made the mistakes of which you accuse us, for we were still men – our faith never failed again. And each one of us went gladly to our deaths proclaiming the Risen Lord!'

As the studio audience poured excitedly out of the main entrance of the building at the end of the second night, Ray Burgh stood just outside the door of the viewing room saying goodnight to the departing sponsors and their wives, most of whom looked extremely happy.

'Can't wait for the last programme!' one stopped to say to him. 'I shan't sleep a wink tonight!'

A small crowd gathered around the doorway, laughing and joking. Burgh spotted Amos, now dressed in his ordinary clothes, approaching them down the corridor.

'And here is tonight's star in person,' he announced.

Amos reached them but could not get through because of all the laughing and congratulations.

'Let me pass, please,' he said. But Burgh clapped a proprietary hand on his shoulder.

'I guess you're feeling pretty good, eh?'

'On the contrary, I feel stupid and inadequate!' His tone was such that the smiling faces faltered, and one or two of the women glanced uneasily at their husbands.

Burgh unwisely tried to force the mood.

'That's just reaction,' he said. 'Come to that,' he glanced around, forcing a grin, 'I feel pretty inadequate myself!'

One of the others nodded, trying to help. 'Yeah,' he said, 'how about that?'

The fighter stared at them, then stood back a pace. 'All right,' he said, 'tell me how I should feel?'

'It was a great performance, Amos,' Burgh said, still trying hard. 'I hope there'll be many more.' But the other shook his head.

'No, I'm finished.'

'You'll be going back to the ring?' the sponsor nearest to him asked.

Amos turned to him. 'Sure. Why not? That should be good enough for someone like me.'

The other flushed angrily. 'Now look, fella,' he began, but Amos suddenly took a quiet but firm hold of his coat lapel. 'Don't fella me, mister,' he said softly.

Burgh quickly put a hand on his elbow. 'Take it easy,' he begged, but Amos still stared at the other, who looked around helplessly.

'What did I say? Look . . . '

Amos let go of him as suddenly as he had taken hold. 'Listen,' he said, 'it ain't Christ on trial back there; it's everyone who gets up on that stand.'

The others looked at him in blank-faced silence as he glanced around, half amazed, half amused. 'It hasn't even crossed your minds yet, has it!' he said, shaking his head slowly. 'You're sitting in there, watching, wondering how much money you're going to make tomorrow. You don't even know what's going on!'

There was continued silence until one of the wives asked nervously, 'What do you mean?'

Amos turned to her and spoke, not unkindly. 'I mean what I say, lady. It ain't acting. Lee Harrison had a cute idea. What he didn't realize was, doing it this way, you can't help measuring yourself against the guy you're supposed to be.'

The woman shook her head. 'I still don't understand,' she said.

Amos paused, looking at her. Then he said, almost pathetically, 'I mean – there ain't no room for a guy like Peter in the world today, is there?'

They stood looking after him as he pushed his way through and eventually disappeared around the corner in the direction of the elevator.

Burgh smiled. 'Well,' he said, 'it takes 'em all ways!'

A few of the others laughed.

Amos walked out of one of the side entrances and across the deserted plaza, his hands thrust deep into his pockets. He walked on a few steps then stopped as a young woman wearing a white raincoat and carrying a furled umbrella stepped into his path. After a few seconds his eyes widened with recognition.

'June?'

They looked at each other for a long time. She was much prettier than he had remembered. Now she smiled nervously. 'I was watching in the apartment of a friend, not far from here.'

Amos nodded slowly. 'It's been a long time,' he said quietly.

The girl nodded as well. 'Yes, it has,' she said. She paused, then said simply and without bitterness, 'You said you didn't need me any more.'

'Yes. I remember.'

She hesitated again, then said, 'I hated you.'

'I guess I deserved it.'

'You were an arrogant, cruel bastard.'

Amos smiled slightly for the first time. 'I still am,' he admitted.

The girl returned his smile. 'Yeah,' she said, 'that's what I figured.' Then she paused before going on. 'Only . . .'

'What?'

She looked away before turning back to face him with a shrug.

'Maybe you need me – now.'

After a pause, he started to walk on slowly, and the girl fell in beside him.

'I need something.'

He stopped to look down at the fountain, then turned to face her.

'For the first time in my life, I know what I should do but they won't let me go.'

It wasn't necessary for her to ask who 'they' were, and he went on. 'They won't let me go, June. They said they'd give me another chance. That I could go through with what I was doing, but no one walks away just like that.'

She reached for his hand. 'What *did* you tell them?'

'I said that I still felt the same way. That I couldn't go back – not like it was before.' He paused, seeming to look through her for a moment.

'They said that I should think about it some more. Then they let me go. I guess I was just lucky.'

June looked at him solemnly. 'What are you going to do?'

He shook his head. 'I don't know.'

'Would it help if I came with you? If we talked?'

'I don't know if it's a good time for you to be with me.'

'Honey, I never stopped loving you.' She paused, looking up at him. 'Maybe, together we can figure a way out? I'm not afraid.'

He rested on a rock and looked up into the night sky, the words of his ancestor David ringing in his ears:

'When I consider the Heavens . . . and all the work of Thy hand, what is Man that Thou are mindful of him?'

And yet, the whole history of his people showed how much this was so. God had never abandoned his people – and now John said the Messiah was coming.

After a moment he gave a cry and buried his face in his hands.

Let God banish all pride and self-seeking from his heart, and show clearly if he was the One. Let him not be mistaken, and like so many before, lead his followers to disaster.

Let God enter his soul if he chose, and use him in whatever way he saw fit.

Let his own personality wither away and be replaced by God's Holy Spirit – no matter what the end, whether it be glory or suffering.

Let only God make his purpose clear.

He could never remember later whether he heard Chaim's

warning shout before or after a hail of submachine-gun bullets splattered into the earth around him, some ricocheting off the rocks and whining away into the distance.

He hit the ground, and a split second later a second burst passed directly over his head. Then he heard Chaim calling him from about fifty yards down the hillside.

'John! Run! We'll cover you. Now!'

He saw where they were from the flashes of their guns as they fired at a position just above him. His heart was pounding as he half stood up, ready to drop again in an instant, but the enemy's attention was effectively distracted and he began to run, keeping his head down as much as possible.

They were in a shallow depression. They must have been able to see him coming – or perhaps, in his flight, he cried out, but they stopped just in time to prevent him from running into their fire. He dived the last few yards, rolling alongside them.

A moment later they were caught in vicious cross-fire and had to press themselves face down into the earth to take advantage of what little cover there was. Some of the infiltrators were outflanking them.

He heard the dog grunt as it died, and when the firing stopped for a moment, Chaim said, 'We've got to get out of here. If they manage to get around any further, they'll be able to pick us off like fish in a tank.'

Even as he spoke a flare curled into the sky, lighting them up as if they were on a stage, and once more they had to press their faces into the ground until it died and the subsequent firing stopped.

David said, 'Our own people'll be up here soon.'

'Not soon enough.'

'I'm sorry . . . ' Burnard began hoarsely, but Chaim cut him short.

'No need to be. It's given them plenty of warning.' He glanced down the hill, then back at Burnard.

'Are you all right? I mean, can you run?'

'Sure.'

'You know the way down?'

'Yes.'

211

'Right. You go first while we cover you.'

'What about you?'

'We'll cover each other.'

There was another flare and again a hail of bullets. It didn't seem possible that they could survive, but when the light died and the firing stopped they were still unhurt.

'Go on, John. Now.'

He hesitated for an instant, and saw them both come up into a firing position.

'Now, damn you! Before we start firing, or you'll be seen.'

He could never remember how he made it. He fell several times, skinning his hands and bruising himself badly, but he never noticed the pain.

The firing reached a crescendo behind him, then there was another, different kind of sound. Almost immediately thereafter he ran into the advancing Israeli force and they sent him back to the camp while they put the insurgents to flight.

The firing stopped about the time one of the girls had finished bathing his hands, and he stood silently with the others while the first of the young men to return brought in the bodies of Chaim and David.

The strange sound he had heard had been an exploding grenade.

They laid the bodies down gently on one of the verandas while stretchers were sent for and a young doctor examined them. After a short time he stood up and shook his head.

Helga turned to him. Her eyes were dry but her voice was shrill with grief.

'How did *you* manage to escape?'

He looked at her. His mouth opened but no sound came from his lips. After a few more seconds, she turned and walked away.

Chapter

12

Ray Burgh's new secretary telephoned Lee the following morning to say that her boss would like to see him at ten o'clock. When he arrived, he found Burgh pacing about his office. He practically jumped on Lee, almost before the producer had a chance to close the door.

'I'm right in thinking there's still no sign of the star of to-night's show?'

'I'm afraid not.'

'What are you doing about it?'

'We've got people on the look-out everywhere. If he surfaces we'll see him. But even then, we can't force him if he refuses to appear.'

'We'll sue him for two million dollars.'

'You said that.'

Burgh went practically purple with rage.

'Then listen to something new. If he doesn't appear you can whistle for the balance of your own money. In fact I'll see that you never work again!'

Lee looked at him. It was neither fair nor legal but Lee knew he could beggar himself trying to fight a network in such circumstances. Burgh was still raging. 'If you think I'm going to let a jerk like you ruin me and just walk away, you're crazy!'

Lee took a deep breath and held up his hand.

'Look, Ray . . . '

'I had a hard time persuading the Board to let you have a free hand.'

'I know. I appreciate everything you've done for me,' Lee went on doggedly. 'But we're not going to improve matters by falling out amongst ourselves. I know how you feel, believe me. But you must see Burnard's running off like that was something no one could have foreseen.'

The other continued to glare at him, but Lee could see he

was regaining control of himself. 'We've put out two programmes so far that haven't exactly disgraced us.'

'That's not going to help much if the climax is a fiasco.'

'It won't be.'

Burgh looked at him hard, but Lee shook his head.

'No. I don't know anything I'm not telling you. I just feel . . . well . . . whatever's going to happen was meant, that's all. You'll just have to believe me.'

Burgh suddenly snapped his fingers and drew in his breath.

'*You* do it! I mean – who knows more about it than you?'

'Plenty of people, but that's not the point. We've built up an atmosphere because everyone who has testified so far has either been himself or has steeped himself in the character for months. Only John can do it. The whole evening's planned to hinge on his testimony. We'll just have to go on praying he shows up.'

'What about O'Connell?'

'Not him, either. Besides, if Burnard lets us down, it's even more important for us to make the most of the others.'

'Who else have we got?'

'For the defence, Peter again, and Mary Magdalene.'

'Who's she?'

'The first one to claim to have seen Christ after the resurrection.'

Burgh stared at him for a long time, then asked quietly, 'And if he doesn't appear?'

Lee paused before saying, 'Then he's guilty – as far as we and the hundred-odd million who'll be watching are concerned.'

The other's eyes widened. 'Is that what you want?' he asked.

Lee shook his head. 'I don't know,' he admitted. 'When I started this, I didn't know how it would end. I still don't. But would it be so terrible?'

'I don't know.'

'Isn't that really the verdict of the world today? Why else would people act the way they do?'

'But it's not up to us,' Burgh protested.

'It won't be,' Lee said, interrupting him, 'so relax.'

Burgh seemed to sink in on himself. He asked plaintively, 'What am I going to tell the sponsors?'

Lee shook his head. 'I don't know. But, either way, it's going to be a night no one's going to forget!'

After a few seconds, he turned for the door, half expecting the other to call him back, but eventually he found himself in the corridor without another word from Burgh.

Lee glanced at his watch. It was half-past ten. He made for his own office where Mary was waiting for him. As he came in, she looked at him anxiously.

'How was it?'

Lee shrugged, leaving the door open.

'He's calmed down for the moment, but if things don't work out, he'll pin it on me somehow.'

Mary nodded. 'I know,' she said simply. 'He'd be the last alive in any lifeboat.'

Lee looked at her for a moment, frowning slightly. Then he asked, 'Why did you say that?'

Now it was Mary's turn to look puzzled. 'Just a figure of speech,' she said. 'Ray's one of nature's survivors, that's all.'

'Yes, I see.'

He seemed lost in thought. Suddenly he looked at her and smiled. 'Let's get out of here for a while.' He held out his hand. 'There's nothing we can do here, and there is something I want to say to you.'

'Oh.' Mary took his hand, looking up at him. 'Good or bad?' she asked.

'You'll have to wait and see.' He looked at the rays of sun streaming through the window behind her. 'Come on, some fresh air will do us good.'

Mary smiled nervously. 'Back to the park?'

Lee nodded. 'If you like.' He stood to one side to let her go out first. She gave him another look as she walked past him out into the corridor.

'Sounds like where I came in!'

Lee didn't answer as he shut the door, and they walked to the elevator in silence.

Mary found her heart thumping.

They wandered arm in arm into the zoo, then sat on a bench

215

watching a keeper trying to wash down the elephants' yard while one of the animals kept coming up behind him and trying to get hold of the hose. Suddenly the great beast wound its trunk around one of the keeper's legs, making him yelp and drop the hose completely. Lee and Mary laughed as, honour apparently satisfied, the elephant sauntered off, waving his trunk from side to side and snorting in triumph. The keeper grinned at them, then picked up the hose and continued his task.

Mary turned to face Lee and found that he was already looking at her. She saw that the lines of strain had gone for the moment, as the echo of his smile still tilted the corners of his mouth.

'Well?'

Lee said, 'Mary, I love you.'

She looked into his eyes and answered steadily, 'And I love you, Lee.'

'Then there are things we should discuss.'

Mary sighed. 'I guess so.'

'Why do you look like that?'

She shook her head. 'I don't know. I think I'm afraid.'

'There's no need to be.'

Again they looked at each other in silence for a moment before Lee said, 'I've been doing a lot of thinking these past weeks – about us.'

'Oh.'

'Even before all this blew up, I'd definitely decided this was my last show.'

'I see.'

'I'm grateful to Ray in a way for what he said to me just now, although I was counting on the rest of the money.'

'He can't . . . '

Lee interrupted her. 'Either way,' he went on, 'I think I can scrape through – particularly as Maxwell Baal has offered to help by putting up most of the purchase price on mortgage.'

'Purchase price of what?'

'A boat.'

Mary's mouth opened.

'A boat!'

216

Lee nodded, suppressing a grin. 'If I'm going to earn a living for both of us, I'm going to need one.'

Mary took a deep breath. It was all coming too fast.

'I'm sorry,' she said eventually. 'Are you proposing?'

Lee nodded again. 'Yes,' he said. 'But, before you say anything, I want to tell you what's involved.'

Mary said, 'I take it you're part of it?'

'Of course.'

'Then I accept!'

'No, Mary, listen. This is serious.'

She looked at him solemnly.

'Lee, I've never been so serious about anything in all my life. I've been so frightened, as the end came in sight, that you were just going to walk out of my life.'

'Was that likely?'

She bent her head forward towards him and shook it slightly. 'I didn't know. I was just scared!'

She looked up and Lee saw that her eyes were filled with tears. 'I'm sorry. I'm being stupid.'

Lee took her into his arms and held her for a while. 'I couldn't walk away from you,' he whispered. 'But you've got a career. I've no right to assume you'd just throw it up – to marry me.'

Mary sat back and now Lee could see that she was laughing and crying at the same time.

'You big lug!' she said. 'Do you think I care about that, if I have the chance of marrying the man I love? Here!' She held out her hand. 'Lend me your handkerchief. And for heaven's sake try and help me stop making an exhibition of myself!'

Lee pulled out his handkerchief and handed it to her. Mary wiped her eyes and blew her nose hard. When she had finished, she looked down at the handkerchief.

'Have you got another?'

Lee nodded. 'Sure.'

Mary opened her handbag and put it inside. 'Then let me wash this one.' She sniffed as she snapped the bag shut and looked up smiling, then made a wry face.

'It can be symbolic of my new state!'

'Okay.'

217

'Good. Now that's settled, tell me where we're going on this boat you've decided to buy.'

'*We're* not going anywhere.'

Mary looked at him aghast.

'You're not going to turn me into a sailor's widow?!'

Lee grinned. 'No, no. Nothing like that. I'll only be taking it out on charter for the day.'

'Where from?'

'Miami. A friend of mine's got some moorings; the same one who sent me details of the boat. There's a good living to be made and the tourist season's just starting; so by the time it's over we should have enough to see us through till the beginning of the next.'

Mary's eyes were wide now. 'Do you know anything about boats?'

'I know more about fishing. But Peter – that's my friend – is going to keep an eye on me until I've learned the local tides. I won't go out too far until then.'

'Darling, it sounds marvellous! But why didn't you tell me about it before?'

'I wasn't sure I could manage. But when Max came forward ...'

'But I've got some money!'

'No!' Suddenly Lee's voice was hard. Mary's smile faded.

'Why not? What do you mean?'

'You told me you have some money. Otherwise this venture won't be possible.'

Mary looked at him now with a worried expression.

'I'm sorry,' she said. 'I don't understand. Do you mean you want to use my money for something else?'

Lee nodded. 'Yes. I want you to keep it so that if anything happens to me, you've got something to fall back on.'

'Is what you want to do dangerous?'

'I didn't mean that.' He took a deep breath, then went on, 'I meant, in case there's a recurrence of ... my illness.'

'Oh.' Mary looked away for a moment. 'Is that likely?'

'There's a better than even chance not. But I couldn't allow you to give up your job unless I knew your money was there.'

'Darling. I don't care . . . '

Again Lee interrupted her. 'But I do,' he said firmly. 'Unless you promise me to keep that money in reserve – no matter what happens – I can't marry you. Please try to understand.'

Mary looked at him for a long time, then she smiled gently and leaned forward to kiss him.

'All right,' she said. 'I want to be your wife more than anything else in the world. So, if that's the only way, I promise.'

'Thank you.'

'Where are we going to live?'

'I'm not sure yet. First things first!' He grinned, and Mary smiled as well.

'But of course.'

'We'll find an apartment somewhere. Peter will help us look. In the meantime, we'll just have to sleep on the boat.'

'And what am I supposed to do during the day?'

'Look after the children. What else?'

'Oh. There are going to be children, are there?'

Lee suddenly looked at her uncertainly.

'Well, is that okay?'

Mary sat back looking at him. Then she threw her arms around him and hugged him hard.

'Oh yes,' she whispered. 'That would be wonderful!'

Lee had his arm around Mary's shoulders as they walked back towards Rockefeller Plaza.

There was one thing neither of them had mentioned, but Lee knew Mary realized that the comfort and hope of the promises they had just made to each other in no way diminished his anxiety at what might happen that evening. Although strengthened to face whatever it might be, Lee was aware that his decision to leave New York forever made this last programme even more important, and that the rest of his life – of their life together – would be coloured by what happened. The knowledge that Burgh's wrath might descend upon his head – that he might lose the much needed second half of the fee – was nothing compared to the knowledge that whatever awaited them was the intended fate towards which – he had known, almost from the beginning – he and everyone else involved were being inexorably drawn; that whatever contribution he could still make was to that end. No matter how much the result was considered to be a failure by Burgh and the network officials, it would not matter; the hidden will that he knew had been the real driving force behind the project would be satisfied, and everything else would work out. If not, then no matter what accolades might be heaped upon him by the world, he would have failed utterly. The hand which had lifted him up when he had been in the depths of despair, and in whose shelter he had felt so secure ever since, would be withdrawn forever. Of this Lee felt as certain as if God himself had said so.

It was almost noon when they got back to Rockefeller Center. Mary went directly to the studios to make sure that everything was in order.

The receptionist in Lee's office told him that a Mrs Harrison was waiting to see him. The girl looked at him a little oddly.

'She said she was your wife, Mr Harrison.'

'My wife?'

'I hope I haven't made a mistake, but I thought – under the circumstances – you wouldn't want her to wait out here.'

Lee nodded briefly. 'Yes, all right, Jill.'

He strode towards his office, conscious of the girl's eyes on his back. When he opened the door, a woman holding a half-smoked cigarette turned from the window to face him. He stopped dead in his tracks.

She looked at least ten years older than the last time he had seen her.

'Dorothy!'

She forced a smile.

'I hope you didn't mind the little subterfuge. I thought you might not remember my married name, and I wanted to be sure of seeing you.'

Lee closed the door behind him.

'It doesn't matter.' He indicated a chair. 'Wouldn't you like to sit down?'

'I'll stand, if you don't mind. What I have to say won't take long.'

He glanced towards the cabinet. 'Would you like a drink?'

'No. Thank you, Lee.'

'I could send out for some coffee?'

'I need your help.'

'I see. You won't mind if I sit down?'

'Please yourself.' Dorothy stubbed out the cigarette in the ashtray on Lee's desk as he sat in a chair against the wall facing the window. Then she turned to face him, leaning on the desk slightly. For a moment she didn't say anything.

'What *do* you want?' Lee asked.

She continued to stare at him as if trying to read from his expression everything that had happened to him since they had last seen each other. Then she seemed to straighten up a little.

'The doctors say I need an operation.'

Lee paused, adjusting to the probable line the conversation would now take. He had been expecting something entirely different – some professional favour now that she probably thought he was re-established.

He said quietly, 'I'm sorry. Do you want to tell me what's wrong?'

She looked at him, then said huskily, 'Practically the same thing my mother had.' In spite of the front, Lee could see she was terrified. He stood up at once and moved towards her.

'I'm very sorry.' He paused again, trying to think of some way to comfort her. Finally, he said, 'These things are always tough – but try not to lose heart. They can do so much more now.' Then he forced a wry grin. 'Look at me!'

'You had money.'

So it *was* that. He knew she wouldn't lie to him, certainly not on such a subject.

'Hasn't your husband got any?'

'We split after a couple of years. I haven't seen him since. I don't know where he is.'

'I see.'

'I've got insurance, of course – but you should know how these things are.'

'Yes.'

221

'I wouldn't ask, Lee, if I didn't need it.' Her voice was becoming more shrill. 'I know how you must feel about me. I was lousy to you, I know that. But I never asked you for any money.'

'You left me for dead!' He couldn't resist that.

'But I could have objected when Helen needed my signature to cash those policies.'

'I don't know what happened.'

'Well, I could have.' Now she was crying. 'I tried to make it up to you in that way. And I wouldn't come to you now if I had some other way to turn.'

In spite of his pity, something inside Lee stopped him from putting out his hand to touch her. Dorothy buried her face in her hands, and just at that moment the door opened without a knock and Mary came into the room. She stopped at once, looking from one to the other.

'I'm sorry,' she began uncertainly. Lee looked at her solemnly, then shook his head. Taking the hint, she went out again, closing the door behind her quietly.

'Who was that?' Dorothy began to rummage through her handbag, which was on his desk, for a handkerchief.

'That was my secretary.'

'Oh, Lee.' Suddenly she straightened up, then half fell into his arms.

'Please help me. I'm so frightened!'

After a few seconds, his revulsion passed, and as he held her, she slowly grew quieter. When she seemed calm again, Lee asked, 'How much do you need?'

Dorothy sniffed, then said, 'Ten thousand dollars.'

That was the exact sum he had left, bar a few hundred. His shock must have shown because she went on hurriedly, 'Most of it is for nursing afterwards.' She paused. 'It's not so much to someone in your position, surely?'

There was no point in arguing. He could have told her he wasn't in *any* position. That the money represented his whole future. And he knew the answers. He knew that if she really couldn't pay, she could go to a municipal hospital where they would treat her for nothing. And he also knew that the care in

222

such places was, of necessity, perfunctory and the atmosphere appallingly depressing.

It could not be said that he gave the money gladly. His mind was almost numb as he wrote out the cheque and handed it to her – but he seemed to have no other choice.

Mary came after Dorothy had gone and listened quietly while he told her what he had done.

She didn't upbraid him, nor did she mention her own money. They both knew that if Ray Burgh lived up to his threat, they were finished.

Like most ordinary people faced with something too terrible to contemplate, they kissed and clung to each other, then went about preparing for the third and final programme as if nothing had happened.

Father O'Connell sat alone in his dressing room, staring at himself in the mirror. On the table in front of him were the false beard, moustache and skull cap which he should have taken down to makeup some time before. Behind him hung the costume of Judas Iscariot.

His eyes had a haunted look, and after a few seconds he lowered his face into his hands. Almost immediately there was a knock on the door and the callboy looked in. The priest looked up at once and saw who it was in the mirror.

The boy said, 'Say, ain't you supposed to be Judas?'

'Yes.'

'Well, you'd better hurry up. They're on the air.'

The priest nodded. 'Yes, of course,' he said, 'I'm sorry.'

The other looked at him more closely. 'You feeling okay?' he asked.

Father O'Connell turned to look at him directly and smiled. 'Yes, thank you,' he said, 'I'm quite all right.'

'Well, okay. But you'd better get changed and go down to makeup.'

'Yes, I'll do it right away.'

The other returned his smile and turned towards the door. 'I'll give you another call when the witness before you goes on,' he said over his shoulder.

'Thank you.'

The boy turned at the door for a final reminder. 'Be ready in about twenty minutes, okay?'

The priest nodded and forced another smile. 'I'll be ready,' he promised.

'Right.' The boy gave a final nod, then went out, closing the door behind him.

Ray Burgh slipped into his place in the viewing room and glanced up at the screen with the sort of feelings he imagined a condemned man must experience just before execution. **He** saw a medium shot of the prosecuting attorney who was on his feet addressing Judge Haald. Lang was also standing, but instead of arguing, the defence attorney seemed to be listening quietly to what the other was saying.

'Your Honour, in view of the continued absence of the Accused, with your permission, and with the agreement of Mr Lang, I would like to call an extra witness who will simply make a statement, without cross-examination by either of us, concerning her view of the events with which we are concerned tonight. We both feel – again, subject to your agreement – that such a statement will help put the rest of the proceedings in perspective.'

Haald said, 'This *is* most irregular, Mr Baal.'

He turned to Lang, who said, 'We *are* in agreement with the proposed course of action, Your Honour.'

Haald raised his eyebrows. Then, after a brief pause he nodded briefly. 'Very well, gentlemen. Call your witness.'

'Thank you, Your Honour.' Lang also bowed and sat down.

'Call . . . Mary Magdalene.'

The woman who answered the call was a gaunt, angular figure dressed in the unflattering costume of the period, suitable for a woman who was no longer young. She was obviously nervous and stumbled clumsily as she took the stand, then stood trembling while the clerk of the court administered the oath. Her eyes were set too far apart. She had big, coarse hands roughened from hard physical work, but when she spoke, her voice was low and had a warm tone that flatly contradicted the impression of her unattractive appearance.

When the clerk retired, Baal stepped closer and spoke to her with surprising gentleness.

'Your name is Mary Magdalene?'

Even before she answered, Lee suddenly found a lump in his throat, finding in Baal's tone renewed evidence of the attorney's compassion for the faith of those with whom he could never agree.

'Some call me Mary Magdala.'

'You knew the Accused very well, I understand?'

'Jesus?' Suddenly she smiled gently and seemed to lose some

of her nervousness. 'Not as well as he knew me,' she answered softly.

'How did you first meet?'

'I was ill – so that I did not seem to be in possession of my body. I knew what others said to me, but my limbs would not obey my commands and the sounds that came out of my mouth could not be understood.'

'How long had you been like that?'

'Since I was a child. Not all the time, but as I grew older, the times of tribulation grew longer.'

'And he helped you?'

'Yes. He laid his hands on me, and my spirit became quiet.'

'Yes, I understand. Of course, you were very attached to him after that.'

'I loved him – but not just because he helped me. I loved him even before he saw me. When I watched him helping others, I prayed, inside myself, that he would notice me. Even if he could not help me, I felt he would understand what I was trying to say.'

Baal stood quietly for a moment and Lee could see that he was visibly moved.

'I see,' he said eventually. 'It must have been terrible to have been . . . trapped, like that.' Mary looked at him in silence, and the prosecutor continued. 'After he made you well, you followed him?'

Mary nodded. 'Yes, I went with him wherever I could.' Then she hesitated for a moment, frowning slightly. 'Of course, there were times when he wanted no one around him but the chosen twelve.'

'But in spite of that, you stayed with him.' Now Baal lowered his voice slightly. 'Even when all the others ran away?'

'Only one betrayed him.'

'Quite so. But isn't it true to say that when he met his death there were only four present of all those who had given their allegiance to him: his mother, yourself and two other women?'

Mary shook her head. 'No,' she said. 'There was one more. John – the disciple the Lord loved above everyone else.'

Baal inclined his head. 'Very well. But you, at least, followed him to the end, and claim to have seen him afterwards?'

'Yes.' The answer was scarcely audible.

Baal went on. 'Would you please tell the court in your own words what happened from the moment he was condemned?'

'I will try.'

Lee saw her screwing up her nerve. Baal said gently, 'Take your time.'

Mary turned to the jury. 'After Pilate delivered him to the soldiers, he was led away. They made him carry the cross, but they had ill-treated him so much beforehand, and then began to hit him as he dragged the huge timbers up the hill that although he was a strong man, used to lifting heavy weights, he was crushed beneath the wood. It seemed especially terrible because most of his life he had spent making beautiful things from wood.'

Mary's voice choked, and her eyes filled with tears. For a long time she seemed unable to continue. The spectators watched in silence, until Haald leaned forward and spoke gently. 'Perhaps the witness would like a glass of water?'

At this Mary shook her head and bit her lip. After a few moments, she managed to look up at him and say, 'No . . . thank you. I'll be all right now.'

'Please take all the time you need.'

'You're very kind.' She looked up at him and said, 'You see, it is so often the little things, the ones that take you unawares, that seem the worst!'

Haald nodded sympathetically. 'We understand. Please go on, if you feel able.'

Mary wiped her eyes with the hem of her cloak.

'I'm sorry. Where was I?'

Baal said: 'You were telling us that he became unable to carry the cross.'

'Oh, yes.' She looked up at him, then turned back to the jury.

'They beat him to make him get up. But he couldn't. I saw him try many times, and I tried to push through the soldiers to help him, but they wouldn't let me pass. Then, at last, they realized it was useless and pulled a man out of the crowd and forced him to carry it instead.' She paused for a moment, then

227

added, 'Even then, God acted, for as a result, that man, Simon of Cyrene, later became a follower of Jesus and died a martyr's death.'

'So Simon took the cross to the top of the hill?'

Mary nodded. 'They crucified Jesus between two thieves but Pilate wrote a notice and put it on the cross. It read: "Jesus of Nazareth, king of the Jews." '

'Wasn't there some trouble over that?' Baal asked.

'Yes. I heard the chief priests protesting that the notice should have read: "He said, I am the king of the Jews," but Pilate answered, "What I have written, I have written." ' She paused for a moment, then turned back towards the jury.

'Then the soldiers divided Jesus' clothes among themselves, and while they were doing this Jesus saw his mother standing beside me, with her sister and Mary, the wife of his friend Cleophas. He also saw John, and he said, "Woman, behold your son." Then he turned his head to look at John and said, "Behold your mother." And from that time, John took her into his own home, as the Lord knew he would, and looked after her for the rest of her life. A little while after this, they gave him vinegar to drink upon a sponge set on the end of a spear. Then he bowed his head, and died.'

'Can you tell us what happened then?'

'The soldiers came to break the prisoners' legs.'

'Why was that?'

Mary looked at him grimly. 'Sabbath was approaching. The chief priests didn't want to spoil their holy day having to bother about dying men.' Then she looked away. 'But when they came to Jesus, they found he was already dead.'

'So they didn't break his legs?'

'No.'

'What happened?'

Mary faced him again. 'Joseph of Arimathea went privately to see the governor to ask for the Lord's body. He was afraid of what the chief priests would say, but Pilate gave him permission and arranged for soldiers to deliver the body to his house secretly after night had fallen.

'Nicodemus brought a mixture of myrrh and aloes, about a

hundred pounds in weight, and after we had anointed the body, we wound it in linen bandages, then placed it in a new sepulchre in a garden, close to the place where he had been crucified, and a huge stone was rolled over the mouth of the cave.'

'So that was that?' Baal said.

Mary shook her head violently. 'No. That was not all, by a long way!'

'Please go on.'

'Early on the first day of the week, after the Sabbath, I went to visit the sepulchre.'

'Why was that?'

'To bring flowers. And to sit and think about him.'

'Weren't you expecting anything to happen?'

'No.'

'In spite of his promise to rise on the third day?'

'He had said many things to us which we didn't understand at the time.'

'Very well. Please go on.'

'I found that the stone had been rolled away.'

'Didn't you realize, even then, what had happened?'

'No, I didn't! I ran crying to Peter and John and told them someone had stolen the body of Our Lord. And they ran back with me and saw for themselves.'

'Was there no sign of what had happened?'

'Only the linen cloths lying on the ground.'

'What did the others say?'

'They saw I spoke the truth. Then they went back to their house sorrowing, thinking not to see him again.'

'But not you?'

Mary shook her head. 'No. I stayed by the entrance, weeping.' She paused for a moment, then went on slowly, 'But, after a while, something made me look once more into the tomb, and there sat two angels in white, one at the head and one at the foot of where the body had lain.'

'You must have been very frightened.'

Again Mary shook her head and turned to look at him.

'No, I wasn't. Perhaps my grief was stronger than my fear.

229

Then one of them asked me why I was crying and I told them, "Because they have taken away the body of my Lord, and I know not where they have laid him." ' She paused again, then looked away, as if into a great distance.

'Then, something told me there was someone standing behind me, and I turned, blinded with tears, thinking it was the gardener and said, "Sir, if you have taken him away, please tell me where so I may tend him." ' Mary looked up, and her face became transfigured.

'Then, he spoke my name. That's all. He said, "Mary!" and I knew it was he.'

After a long time, Baal glanced up at Haald, who nodded briefly. The prosecutor held out his hand and led the woman from the stand. She walked slowly out of the court as Lee wondered how he had ever thought of her as ugly. She was beautiful!

Baal then returned to the stand and cleared his throat. 'Your Honour, we are grateful to the court. The prosecution would now like to call its first witness of the evening.'

Haald nodded. 'Very well, Mr Baal.'

'The prosecution calls Caiaphas, the high priest.'

The man sitting next to Burgh turned to him and smiled. 'You guys certainly know how to build up the tension.'

Burgh nodded and smiled back. The other turned back to the screen as Burgh glanced around at the content, interested faces and wondered grimly how long it would be before they turned on him. Then he looked back at the monitor to see a close-up of a short, bald man facing the prosecutor and giving his name in a slight, high-pitched voice. Burgh sighed inwardly. Whatever was going to happen now was beyond his control. But of one thing he was certain. If he went down, he would damn sure take Lee Harrison with him.

'Would you please tell the court why the Accused was arrested and brought before the Sanhedrin – the temple court?' Baal was saying.

'Certainly.' The witness smiled companionably. 'Because, in spite of repeated warnings, and after all allowance had been made for the fact that he was not a man of learning – a man, in fact, of very humble origin – the Accused persisted in the assertion that he was equal to God.'

'In summary?' Baal asked.

'Heresy. Under the laws of Moses there is no greater crime. Our nation had suffered grievously in the past from such as he.'

Baal leaned forward slightly. 'Can you give me an example?' he asked.

'Many,' the other nodded. 'Perhaps one of the better known cases occurred in the time of Moses – when Aaron made a golden calf for the people to worship.'

'What happened?'

'Only the most rigorous intercession by Moses himself prevented our people from being destroyed then and there.'

Baal paused for a moment and glanced at the jury. Then he turned back to the witness. 'Looking at it from a different point of view,' he said, 'would it be true to say that as it has been the worship of God – as laid down by the laws given to Moses – which held your people together in the face of all adversity, anything which struck at the root of that worship would lessen the bonds which united the Jews as a nation?'

Caiaphas inclined his head. 'Perfectly true,' he said.

'And that is another reason why heresy could not be tolerated under any circumstances?'

Again the witness nodded. 'Without God,' he said, 'we are nothing.' He paused for a moment then spoke directly to Haald. 'Throughout the ages, there have been men who have claimed to be the Messiah. Some led away a few hundred, like those who followed Theudas, and others, like Judas of Galilee, misled thousands, but all of them perished and their followers were scattered.' Haald nodded slightly, and the witness continued, 'The only reason the cult started by the Nazarene took such hold was because his followers secretly removed his body from the tomb and thus started the preposterous myth that he had risen from the dead.'

'Thank you,' Baal cut in. 'Finally, would you please tell the court why, having been found guilty of heresy, he was handed over to the Romans?'

'It was the feast of Passover,' the witness answered without hesitation. 'Moreover the right of capital punishment had become the prerogative of the occupying power.'

Baal nodded. 'And during the feast of Passover, the shedding of blood was not permitted except in the course of ritual sacrifice?'

'That is correct.'

Baal inclined his head. 'That all seems perfectly straightforward,' he said, and glanced in the direction of Haald. 'No further questions.'

Lang rose to his feet and took Baal's place. He paused for a moment, then said, 'Why could you not have waited until after the feast to do your dirty work?'

Baal sprang to his feet. 'Your Honour,' he protested, 'the defence is being deliberately abusive.'

'Wasn't it because you were afraid the people would turn against you?' Lang thundered on.

'Mr Lang,' Haald said sharply, 'the court would prefer your cross-examination of the witness to be conducted without the use of slang.'

The prosecutor subsided in his seat as Lang turned to the judge and bowed slightly. 'I apologize, Your Honour,' he said mildly. He then turned back to the witness continuing, however, to regard him with distaste. 'Would you like me to rephrase the question?' he asked.

Caiaphas answered sharply, 'That will not be necessary.'

'Well then?'

'There was no indecent haste, as you imply. However, it is true that the prisoner had a talent for inflaming the mob and, therefore, had to be silenced as soon as possible for the sake of those who would have been misled.'

Lang looked around grimly. 'I'm sure we are all sickeningly familiar with the philosophy,' he said. He then turned back to the witness. 'Very well. Let us turn to another matter. You asserted that followers of Jesus stole his body from the tomb?'

The high priest nodded curtly.

Lang continued, 'Are you aware of the despair into which the disciples of the Accused were thrown when their master was crucified?'

The high priest permitted himself a brief smile. 'Realization of the truth *can* be painful,' he said.

'And yet,' Lang continued, 'within a few days, that despair had been replaced by extraordinary confidence; confidence so deep that – as you have heard the witness Peter testify – many of his followers went cheerfully to their deaths rather than deny what they had seen with their own eyes. I refer, of course, to the risen Christ.' Lang paused for a moment before challenging, 'Could such confidence have been founded on a lie?'

Caiaphas thought for a moment, then said, 'It is quite possible. The most energetic disseminator of the myth was Saul of Tarsus, a Roman citizen who was not among those who claimed to have seen the . . . ' He shrugged momentarily, 'Whatever it was they claimed to have seen. Oh, except for some story about yet another vision.' The high priest glanced around the courtroom slyly. 'Upon which, if I may say so, much of the Accused's special claim seems, rather conveniently, to depend.'

'The witness will not make observations,' Haald said severely. 'Please confine yourself to answering the questions.'

'Very well.' Caiaphas inclined his head graciously in the direction of the judge but continued to smile faintly.

Lang asked, 'Were you present when Peter and John, followers of Jesus, were also brought before the Sanhedrin for preaching and performing miracles in his name?'

'Yes.'

At this point Lang's assistant handed him a note. 'Then you will remember,' he continued, 'what Gamaliel, one of the most respected of your number, said at the time in warning you not to act against them?' He looked up at the high priest but the other remained silent. 'Then let me remind you,' Lang said, and he quoted, 'For if they be of Man, they will surely fall away, but if they be of God, you cannot prevail against them.' Lang lowered the note and looked at Caiaphas directly.

The other shrugged slightly. 'I remember some such,' he admitted.

'Then are you aware that Christianity was adopted by the Roman Empire a comparatively short time after the crucifixion,

233

and quickly became the most widely accepted religion in the whole Western world?'

'I was not aware of that.'

Lang took a breath and turned away. 'No further questions.'

As Lang returned to his seat, the high priest opened his mouth to say something, but Haald leaned forward and said, 'You may stand down.'

Caiaphas shut his mouth and left the courtroom in obvious displeasure, as Baal rose again to his feet.

'May it please the court,' he said, 'the prosecution would now like to call the Roman centurion who was in charge of the crucifixion.'

Two floors below, the callboy hurried down the corridor, knocked on the door of Father O'Connell's dressing room and entered immediately. The words he was about to say died in his throat as the occupant of the room, now miraculously transformed into Judas, turned to face him. After a few seconds, he found his voice again.

'Gee . . . you look great!'

'Is it time?'

The boy continued to stare in awe for a few more seconds, then in answer to the question he had just been asked, he nodded vigorously. 'Oh yeah. You're next.'

The other nodded and made for the door.

The callboy stood to one side to let him pass, then started to follow. But before he went out he suddenly hesitated and turned back to look around the empty room.

'That's funny,' he murmured to himself, as the other disappeared down the corridor. 'What did he do with his clothes?'

In the control room, Joe Shand and his assistants were concentrating on the monitors and nobody but Mary noticed Lee slip into his place beside her. She looked at him questioningly.

He shook his head. 'Not a sign.' He paused, then said quietly, 'I really didn't think he'd do it.' Mary reached forward to take his hand and he looked at her and tried to smile.

In court, Baal was standing close to the centurion who had now completed the oath. 'You supervised the execution of the prisoner you knew as Jesus of Nazareth?' he began.

The other, a tall, deeply bronzed man with iron grey hair and wearing the uniform of a Roman officer, nodded briskly.

'Yes, sir.'

'Had you ever supervised a crucifixion before?'

'Yes.' The centurion looked around the courtroom. 'It was the usual way of putting common criminals to death.'

Baal nodded. 'So we have heard.' He paused for a moment, then went on, 'So there was nothing particularly unusual about this one?'

The other shook his head. 'Not in the execution itself,' he began, 'but I do remember the crowd seemed more than usually excited.'

Baal glanced down at a note in his hand before continuing, 'Do you remember the prisoner's last words before he died?'

'The Accused, you mean? There were two others with him.'

The prosecutor frowned slightly. 'Yes,' he said, 'we're concerned only with him.'

'Well, he said something like, "My God, my God, why have you deserted me?"'

'And what did you understand from this?'

The officer shrugged slightly. 'That he was in despair.'

'You wouldn't say it was a remark consistent with absolute confidence that he would rise from the dead?'

'Far from it. As a matter of fact, although we were used to seeing men die on the cross, it gave us all a strange feeling when he suddenly shouted out like that.'

For a moment Baal glanced at Lang before turning back to the witness. 'You heard the stories put about later that Jesus had risen from the dead?'

'Yes.'

'But you didn't believe them?'

The other smiled faintly. 'When a man's dead, he's dead,' he said. Then he opened his mouth as if to add something, but hesitated.

'You were going to say something else?' Baal prompted.

'Well . . . I thought about it a lot afterwards; I reckon it was just possible his followers saw him alive later.'

At once there was a buzz of conversation in the courtroom. Mary glanced at Lee, puzzled, as Haald banged his gavel for order.

'Quiet, please!'

The prosecutor waited for the noise to die down before going on. 'Would you explain to the court why you thought such a thing might be possible?'

'Well . . . he seemed to die very quickly. The Jews were in a hurry for us to get it over with so they could get on with their festival, or whatever it was, and we were ordered to break the prisoners' legs.'

'But you did not break the legs of Jesus?'

The centurion shook his head. 'No. He was dead already. We eventually took them all down before the usual period had elapsed.'

'How long was the usual period?'

The centurion thought for a moment before answering, 'About fifteen hours, unless we were to leave them up as an example.'

'Why was fifteen hours considered necessary?'

'To make sure they were properly dead.'

'Then what are you suggesting?' Baal asked with deceptive mildness.

'Well,' the witness shrugged, 'I fought in battle many times and saw men wounded and left for dead who were found to be still alive later.'

There was another buzz of conversation. Again Baal waited for silence before continuing.

'You mean a man can give every appearance of being dead, yet still recover?'

'Sometimes, if he's properly looked after.'

'I see.' The prosecutor paused for a moment, then he asked, 'What happened to the prisoner's body when it was taken down so prematurely?'

At once Lang was on his feet. 'Your Honour . . . '

Haald held up his hand and looked reprovingly in the direction of the prosecutor. 'Try not to qualify the witness's testimony, Mr Baal.'

236

Baal bowed and Lang sat down again, making a face. 'I'm sorry, Your Honour. I will rephrase the question.' He then turned back to the witness. 'What happened when the prisoner's body was taken down?'

'I was ordered to deliver it to one of his friends.'

'Can you remember his name?'

'Yes. Joseph of Arimathea. I understood he went to the governor and asked his permission.'

'And was this man, this Joseph, one of those who later claimed to have seen the prisoner alive again – risen from the dead?'

'I don't think so.'

'What do you think would have happened if on getting the prisoner's body back home he discovered that some flicker of life remained?' Baal glanced quickly at the judge, who was opening his mouth to say something, and added quickly, 'What would you have done?'

'If I had been his friend, of course, I should have done everything in my power to nurse him back to health.' The centurion glanced up at Haald. 'I understand Joseph was a rich man. He could have afforded the best doctors and medicine.'

'And what about the body in the tomb?' Baal challenged.

'That would not have been too hard to fake.'

The prosecutor allowed himself a brief smile. 'Precisely,' he said, 'thank you. No further questions.' He sat down and Lang stood up to take his place.

The defence attorney picked up a Bible from his desk, then moved toward the witness stand.

'May I ask if you are aware of the opening line of Psalm twenty-two?' he asked.

The centurion frowned and answered sharply, 'I'm a Roman, not a Jew!'

Lang glanced up at Haald. 'Then I should like to read it, with the court's permission.'

Haald inclined his head. Lang then put on his glasses and, finding a marked place, began to read aloud: ' "My God, my God, why have you deserted me?" ' He lowered the Bible and removed his glasses to look at the witness. 'Will you accept that that is what it says?'

237

The other shrugged. 'If you say so.'

'Thank you.' Lang closed the book but continued to hold it. He asked, 'Were you aware that, contrary to the insinuation of the previous witness, the Accused was a rabbi well versed in the Scriptures?'

'No.'

'Then you will also be aware that it is the habit of both Jews and Christians to repeat appropriate verses from the Bible to help them in times of difficulty?'

'Yes.'

'Or,' Lang continued, 'that this particular psalm goes on to restate the faith of the writer in the mercy of God?'

The centurion began to look annoyed. 'I have already told you, I know nothing of these things.'

'Exactly,' Lang said mildly. 'Which puts you at something of a disadvantage in commenting on the significance of what you heard.'

The other opened his mouth to protest, but Lang pressed on. 'What happened immediately after he spoke those words?'

'He died,' the other said after a few seconds' hesitation. 'At least . . . '

'In other words,' Lang interrupted, 'he was released from his ordeal? One might almost be tempted to assume that his prayer was answered?'

The other shrugged. 'Maybe *you* would,' he said.

The attorney for the defence paused for a moment, then said, 'Let us deal with the possibility of the Accused not being completely dead at the time he was taken down from the cross. You say his legs were not broken. Was nothing done to make sure he was really dead?'

The centurion thought for a moment, then he said, 'Yes. One of my soldiers thrust a spear into his side.'

'Did you examine the body afterwards?'

'Yes.'

'And?'

'He appeared to be dead.'

Lang nodded slowly. 'And this was not a snap judgment in the heat of battle, but after careful examination?'

'I've just said so.'

'And you were used to judging such matters?'

'I suppose so.'

'You had done it many times before?'

'Yes.'

Lang smiled faintly and glanced at the jury. 'And none of the others had come back to life?'

'No.'

The defence attorney paused for a moment, then asked, 'When did the idea that Jesus might have done so cross your mind?'

The centurion hesitated. 'When I heard the stories.'

'But you had no fresh evidence?'

'No.'

'You would agree that Roman soldiers are not accustomed to dealing with the miraculous?'

'Of course not.'

'So,' Lang said, raising his voice slightly, 'coupled with your admitted ignorance of the Scriptures, you were really not in a position to judge, one way or the other?'

'I don't . . . '

'Thank you,' Lang said firmly. 'No further questions.'

The witness strode out, scowling, as Lang sat down and Baal stood up. Haald looked at him.

'Yes, Mr Baal?'

'Your Honour, the prosecution would like to call its last witness. One who, if I may say so, will remove any doubt that may remain in the jury's mind.'

Haald smiled faintly. 'That may be taken either way, Mr Baal.' The prosecutor inclined his head and returned the smile.

'It was intended so, Your Honour.' He glanced at Lang for a moment, eyes twinkling. 'I would not like my learned friend to feel the prosecution was taking unjust advantage.'

'Very well. Call your witness.'

Baal paused for a moment to make sure everyone was listening, then he turned and said, 'Call Judas Iscariot.'

There was at once a murmur of interest, but when Judas himself appeared and walked to the witness stand, the murmur

239

faded to complete silence. There was something about him that made him different from and more compelling than any of those who had gone before. Perhaps the difference was in his eyes, perhaps it was in the way he walked, then stood in silence waiting for the oath. Whatever it was, even Haald and the two attorneys found themselves staring at him until the court clerk stepped forward and placed the Bible in the witness's right hand.

In the control room, Lee suddenly rose to his feet, staring at the monitor. Mary glanced up at him in alarm.

'What's the matter?'

Lee said, 'That's not him; it's not O'Connell. It's not the same man!'

Mary looked at him, eyes wide. 'What do you mean?' she gasped. 'It must be.'

'Quiet!' Joe glanced at them. Lee suddenly turned on his heel and pulled open the door leading outside. Mary got up at once to follow him.

She came out into the corridor just in time to see him disappearing round the corner. She called after him, 'Lee, where are you going?' But he didn't stop.

She eventually caught up with him as he was flinging open the door of the priest's dressing room. He looked quickly around the empty room.

'What are you doing?' Mary demanded.

'Looking for some clue.'

'I don't understand. What's got into you?'

Lee turned on her, eyes burning. 'Listen,' he said, 'whoever's on the stand now isn't Father O'Connell. Which leaves three questions: Where is O'Connell? Who is taking his place? And why?'

Mary put her hand on his arm, half afraid that his ex-wife's visit, on top of the strain of Burnard's disappearance, might have unhinged him. 'You'll have to wait till afterwards,' she said as calmly as she could. 'If it is someone else, we'll soon find out,' but Lee again turned for the door.

'No,' he said. 'By then it might be too late!'

When they returned to the control room, Lee saw that the

240

lighting had been altered to throw more concentration around the area of the witness stand.

In contrast, the rest of the courtroom was in semi-darkness.

'Would you please tell the court when you first met Jesus?' Baal was saying.

Lee stood at the back of the control room staring at the man on the stand, trying to decide what to do. But what could he do, even if he *was* an imposter? Mary was right. Now he felt her squeezing his hand and leading him back to his seat.

'It was in Capernaum,' he heard the witness answer, 'on the shores of Galilee that I first met him face to face. In the house of Simon called Peter.'

'Had you seen him before then?' the prosecutor asked.

Judas smiled with surprising gentleness. 'Oh yes,' he said. 'We had heard in the hills of Judea that the Messiah had come out of Bethlehem, born of the line of David, as the Scriptures had foretold.'

'That was important to you?'

'Yes.' The smile faded from Judas' face. 'We had lived under the heel of Rome too long. Some of us who had been arming and training secretly for months were soon to make a stand.'

'Against Rome?'

'Yes.'

'Wasn't that a pretty desperate measure?'

'We were desperate men. That was why the news of Jesus came like the answer to all our prayers.'

Baal paused for a moment before asking, 'What happened?'

Judas turned to face the jury. 'I was sent by my companions to listen, and decide whether or not the Chosen One had really come at last,' he began. 'For many days I followed, listening to him preach and seeing the power which seemed to flow into all those who heard his words. I, myself, began to fall under his spell – even though trying to keep my mind clear in order to give those who waited my best opinion.' His face softened. 'But soon all doubt vanished. His words thrilled my mind; being near him and seeing the marvellous deeds of mercy he performed, simply by stretching out his hand to the poor and suffering, thrilled my soul. No wonder the multitude flooded out to see him wherever he went!'

The witness's eyes seemed to have been looking into the far distance, but now he turned back to speak directly to Baal. 'So strongly did I feel myself drawn to him, I could not bear to leave, and sent word by another. Perhaps the greatest joy I had ever known was when I managed at last to get close enough to speak to him. He suddenly turned to me . . . and put his hand on my shoulder and bade me follow him – just like that!' Judas smiled at the memory, then took a breath and went on. 'I knew from that moment that I would gladly die at his side.'

Baal waited for a moment before asking, 'But that's not how it worked out, was it?'

The other shook his head sombrely. 'In spite of my love for the Master, I could not understand why he chose so many of the others as his close companions. Peter – he was right enough, but John and Philip and some of the others seemed to go around half the time in a trance.'

'What do you mean?'

'Well,' Judas shrugged slightly, 'they seemed to have no will of their own. I could appreciate, at least to begin with, that the Master did not want to be bothered with day-to-day irritations; he had more important work to do. But if it had been left to the rest of them, he would have starved to death before our journeying had ever begun.'

'Why?'

'All they ever did was sit around listening.'

'You were the only practical one?'

Judas shrugged again. 'As it transpired,' he agreed. 'Of course, I didn't know that to begin with. But eventually I had to take charge of everything.'

'You held the purse strings?'

'Yes. And not only that. I had to buy food and arrange where we should spend the night. A lot of people gave us money. Any surplus I was supposed to give to the poor, and I did – except for some I put to one side in case of emergencies.'

'Did Jesus know you did this?'

'Some of the others told him.'

'What did he say?'

Judas paused for a moment, then he replied, 'He was angry. He said we should give no thought for the morrow.' He glanced around the courtroom. 'But somebody had to.'

'Was that the beginning of the trouble?' Baal asked quietly. The other shook his head.

'Not really. I got used to the others looking down at me. I didn't mind. We got along well enough most of the time, and as long as I was helping the Master fulfil his destiny, nothing else mattered.'

Again Baal paused before asking carefully, 'When did you begin to realize that his conception of that destiny and your own were different?'

Judas frowned. 'After about a year,' he said eventually.

'Please tell the court.'

The other turned again to face the jury. 'Throughout our history, leaders, inspired by God, have risen to save Israel from destruction: Moses, Joshua, David, and the Prophets; but all pointed to that ultimate saviour who would come from God himself to establish his chosen people in the forefront of the nations of the earth – to lead the world from wickedness into a thousand years of peace.'

He paused for a moment and Baal put in, 'Is that what you thought Jesus would do?'

Judas nodded slowly. 'Yes,' he said. 'I was not impatient to begin with. I knew the Master had to gain the people's confidence, and in the meantime his power was there, day by day, as a promise that his kingdom would soon be established.'

'But it was not to be?'

'It was not.' Judas paused, then said quietly, 'As a result, we all perished.'

Baal took a breath, paused, then asked, 'Why did you betray him?' The witness turned to look at him. 'Was it for the money?'

'Of course not!' Judas spat out the words contemptuously. 'Would I risk my life for three years – do everything in my power to help and protect him, then betray him for thirty pieces of silver?'

243

Baal shook his head. 'I don't know,' he said, 'unless your love had turned to hate.'

The other paused, then said gently, 'I could never hate him.'

'Because you felt he had let you down?'

Again the witness shook his head.

'Then why?'

Judas raised his eyes to look at his questioner. When he spoke, his words were slow and painful. 'Because . . . I had staked everything on him. It was too late to make a fresh beginning – already reinforcements were on their way from Rome. If he would not save us . . . we were all done for.'

'What did you do?'

Judas hesitated again. 'I had seen his power save others. I tried to force him to save himself.'

'But you failed,' Baal persisted. 'Why?'

The answer came almost in a whisper. 'Because he could not.'

'And for you, who had followed him as closely as anyone all that time, that could only mean one thing?'

The witness closed his eyes as if trying to shut out the memory, but he nodded slowly. There was a long pause, then he looked up at Baal and the prosecutor could see torment in his expression.

'He could not,' he said, as if each word were a nail pushed into his flesh, 'because . . . he was not the Messiah!'

Baal looked around the silent courtroom, then back at the witness. He said quietly, 'No further questions.'

Lang changed places with him in complete silence. Judas seemed to have turned in on himself. He did not even raise his eyes to the defence attorney as he took Baal's place beside the witness stand. Lang paused for a moment, looking at the man in front of him. Then he began to speak, his words principally for the benefit of the jury, but his eyes never leaving the witness's face.

'When I heard you describe your first meeting with Jesus, I was moved,' he began. 'You, and those with you in the hills, arming against Rome, had a preconceived idea of what he would be like. But when you came face to face with the son of God, your heart was filled with joy. Not because of some great manifestation of power that would put Israel where you felt she

244

belonged, but because love is the strongest force in the universe, and that day, long ago in Peter's house in Capernaum, you stood in the presence of the one who had been sent to show that, in spite of all its wickedness, God still loved the world and wanted nothing but its love in return.'

Lang now paused before asking gently, 'Could you not have said, therefore, that instead of joy, love filled your heart?'

There was a long silence which Lang knew he could only interrupt at his peril.

Eventually Judas raised his eyes to look at him. 'With love?' he repeated, then paused again. At last he said slowly, 'Yes. I loved him. Even at the end, when I knew we were all finished. Nothing could change that.'

'You loved him?' Lang persisted, 'and yet, you betrayed him?'

'No!' The witness's denial rang suddenly across the room. 'You don't understand!'

It was like a cry of pain. Lee, watching, felt himself go cold inside, and whether it was his imagination or not, the contrast between the pool of light concentrated on the witness and the darkness surrounding him seemed to grow more intense.

'None of you understand,' Judas cried out again. 'I couldn't change. It was too late!'

Lang, sensing victory, pressed on remorselessly. 'So you expected God to change instead?' he demanded. 'You *knew* Jesus was the son of God. There was no doubt in your mind, right to the end, or you would not have tried to force his hand.' He paused a moment before continuing. 'You could not change, but neither could he – because he was not the warrior king you had imagined.'

To Lee's horror the witness had begun to weep. For a few moments Judas held both hands in front of his face, then he lowered them slowly and said in a voice breaking with emotion, 'All right. He was the son of God. How could he have been anyone else? But how could I, Judas, live with that?'

Again his body shook with grief and his head turned from side to side before he was able to go on. Eventually he managed, 'I couldn't be what he wanted me to be. What choice did I have but to try and change him in turn?'

Lang began to feel he was losing control of the situation, but he had no choice now except to go on. 'You betrayed him,' he said doggedly, 'whatever else you may prefer to call it.'

'You don't understand!'

'What is there to understand? What do you want from us . . . pity?'

'No!' Again, the cry of pain as Judas opened his arms wide and faced the court.

'Recognition!' He looked around like a man in a nightmare. 'Look at me,' he begged. 'Don't you know who I am?'

In the control room Mary clutched Lee's hand. She looked frightened. 'What's happening?' she whispered. Lee shook his head without answering, his eyes glued to the monitor. The voice rang out again.

'I am *you*! The reflection of your own souls. For what have I done that each one of you has not done in his heart?'

Lang opened his mouth to say something but he seemed to have lost his power of speech as the witness rushed on, his words spilling out now like water through a burst dam.

'Are we to blame for being what we are? Repent from wickedness and live?' Lee saw Judas turn to the live camera as if reaching out to the invisible millions. 'Where?' he demanded. 'On some desert island where there is no opportunity for sin? If God is the Creator, he is responsible for the way we are.' Now the voice dropped suddenly. 'If I make a vase that cannot hold water, whose fault is it, the vase's or mine for making it so?' The note of anguish returned. 'And then having made us imperfect he sent his son among us to teach us perfection – knowing full well it is beyond our reach!' Judas paused, then smiled mirthlessly.

'Take no thought for the morrow! That sounds fine for a few, a very privileged few, but what would happen to the world if we all tried to live like that?' He looked round, trying to penetrate the darkness. 'I tell you, there would be famine and plague, the like of which the world has never seen!'

He pushed a lock of hair from his forehead impatiently. 'My sin,' he continued, 'was that I was the only one of the Apostles who was typical in any way of the rest of mankind – of you!'

246

In the control room Lee saw him point his finger at the camera.

'He must have known at the beginning I could not live as he wanted me to; that was why he condemned me to a death as certain as his own. Of *course* I fought to bring him down to my level. God created Man in his own image, but Man must do the same in return, or despair.' Judas paused, looking around him, and Lee saw that he had now regained complete control of himself.

'So what are you to make of the ramblings of the despicable creature you see before you?' he went on. 'Is Jesus here on trial to prove his claim to be the son of God? If so, it is not sufficient. Let him answer a more serious charge: not that he misled, but that he led where no ordinary man could follow – and so brought untold grief where there might have been, at least, some contentment.'

There was a long, long silence, then Haald spoke, his voice betraying his obvious emotion.

'You charge God himself?'

Judas looked up at him, 'In the name of all Mankind – yes. Let him speak, or admit forever the truth of my words.'

Lee saw, as Judas looked around slowly, almost triumphantly, that everyone, including the judge and two attorneys, seemed to have been frozen into silence.

'Now,' he breathed almost to himself, and at once another voice cut through the silence.

'Judas.'

Every head turned, and there, standing at the back of the court in semi-darkness, was the figure they had last seen on the first day. Judas, himself, looked as if he could not believe his eyes.

'Master!'

The figure walked to the centre of the court into the light, then stopped, still looking at the man on the stand. He said softly, 'What would you have me say?'

Judas paused for a long time, then shook his head. 'It doesn't matter,' he said, the note of despair returning. 'It's too late now.'

'No.' The figure of Jesus approached and stood in front of him. 'I know you,' he said slowly. 'I chose you for what you

247

were, because I *needed* somebody like you, that is true. But I did not want to lead you to condemnation.' He paused, then went on. 'Remember, it was not I who condemned you – that was left to others. And above all, Judas, you condemned yourself.'

Jesus looked around the court, then turned back to the Apostle and said, 'Were the words of the prophets ringing so loudly in your ears you could not hear the voice of truth?' Judas did not answer, and Jesus went on, 'Did I not tell you that God so loved the world he gave his only begotten son so that whoever believed in him should *not* perish, but receive everlasting life?' He paused again, looking at the man on the stand, before saying softly, 'You know me – you called me the son of God.'

Judas slowly raised his eyes. 'I know you,' he said quietly.

'So it is not I, but God himself you try to reject? But that is not possible. There are no exceptions. He that receives me, receives the one who sent me.'

Judas continued to look at him. 'You have not answered my charge,' he said eventually.

Jesus looked back at him solemnly. 'That the example I set was impossible to follow? Do you think Our Father does not know that?' He raised his eyes to those watching.

'Why was I sent? To impose God's will on a rebellious earth? If that were so, it would have been a different story, and a different Lord.'

He turned back to Judas. 'Surely you remember how often I was rebuked for breaking laws demanding obedience? Obedience of itself is nothing. All I asked was that you loved the Father as he loves you.'

Judas shook his head. 'No,' he said, 'it is too hard.'

'Then love one another.'

Again Judas shook his head stubbornly. 'It is still too much,' he said harshly.

'Then . . . accept only that I died for you.'

Jesus turned and to Lee it seemed that he spoke to the whole world. 'The light shineth in the dark. And the dark comprehendeth it not.' And again, 'For though a man sin, yet shall he live who puts his trust in me.'

After a moment, Jesus turned back to the witness and went on slowly, 'No man falls so far he is beyond the reach of the one who sent me.' He paused again, then said softly, 'Judas, do you repent of your sins?'

There was a long silence during which Lee felt his heart thudding against his ribs before Judas answered thickly: 'I cannot . . . except for what I did to you.'

Jesus inclined his head as if he had expected the reply. He took a breath, then asked, 'Will you promise to try and sin no more?'

Lee saw Judas shudder for a moment. He shook his head and answered miserably, 'Not if I am honest.'

Jesus looked at him for what seemed a long time. Lee could not read what lay hidden in his expression until, slowly, he held out his hand, and smiled – was it sadly?

'Then . . . love me anyway,' he said gently. 'Come, let us begin again.'

Although seemingly frozen into immobility, after a long while Judas stumbled out of the witness stand. He hesitated for a few seconds longer, then, taking the outstretched hand, fell to his knees, weeping. Jesus lifted him up, then, letting go of his hands, he turned and walked out of the pool of light into the darkness.

Judas watched him go, then looked into the camera for the last time.

'You see,' he choked, 'it doesn't make sense . . . but what else . . . ?' He seemed unable to finish.

He paused for a few more seconds, turned, and stumbled after the man who had just left.

There were a few moments of utter silence, then all the lights in the studio came on, followed by a complete uproar which Haald was powerless to control.

In the control room, Lee jumped to his feet and shouted at Joe, 'Fade out now. Run the closing announcements!'

'Lee!' Mary tried to attract his attention as Joe looked up at him and said, 'What about the verdict and everything?'

'Never mind. We just had it. Go on! Do as I say.'

Joe paused for a moment, shrugged helplessly and spoke

into the microphone: 'Stand by, announcer. We are fading out now.'

Lee stopped to watch for a few more seconds, then he tore open the door leading into the corridor, conscious that Mary was calling something after him, but then the door slammed behind him.

He reached the main entrance to the studio just as the first members of the audience were beginning to come out. The atmosphere was still electric, but Lee saw one of the technicians and grabbed hold of his arm.

'Is Burnard still in there?' he demanded.

The other stared as if he were still in a daze. 'No,' he said, 'he walked straight out, followed by the guy who played Judas. Weren't they terrific?!'

'Did you see which way they went?'

The man shook his head as he began to be swept away from Lee by the press of the crowd. 'Back to their dressing rooms, I imagine,' he called.

Lee waved. 'Okay, thanks!'

He turned and started to push his way back down the corridor, vaguely hearing the other shout after him, 'By the way, congratulations!'

Lee managed to get clear of the departing audience and rounded the corner only to run straight into Burgh followed by a crowd of sponsors, their wives and hangers-on.

Burgh positively beamed. 'Lee!'

'Here he is,' one of the sponsors' wives called out excitedly.

Lee groaned inwardly but it was too late to avoid them. Burgh seized him by the hand, almost tearfully.

'Lee, it was great – just great!'

A sponsor grabbed his other hand and began to pump that, too. 'Young man,' he said, 'that was the most moving thing I have ever seen on television.'

'I shan't forget this,' Burgh assured him, digging Lee in the ribs. 'Even though you did keep us all in suspense!'

Mary had managed to fight her way through the crowd surrounding Lee and now she flung her arms around his neck. 'Darling,' she said excitedly, and hugged him until he thought

250

his neck would break, while the others watched, laughing and clapping them on the back.

'How did you guess when he was going to appear?' Mary asked breathlessly after she had let go of him.

Lee saw Burgh's eyes widen.

'You mean it wasn't arranged?'

Lee shook his head. 'I was just on my way to try and find out what had happened myself,' he admitted.

'But you *did* know,' Mary insisted, 'you said so.' But Lee turned to her and shook his head seriously.

'No,' he said, 'I wouldn't fool you. I only knew if he didn't appear then we were dead.'

'Well, I must say!' Burgh began mildly, but Lee interrupted him.

'If you'll excuse me,' he said, 'I was on my way to the dressing rooms.'

The other seized on this. 'That's a great idea,' he said. 'Let's all go!' And before either of them could say anything, Lee and Mary found themselves being swept along the corridor towards the elevators.

In the corridor outside the dressing rooms, an excited crowd was gathering. Lee made a beeline for the star's dressing room, only to find the door wide open and the room empty except for the dresser.

'Has Mr Burnard gone?' he asked, while the others pressed in behind him.

The dresser looked disgruntled. 'No,' he said, 'I ain't seen him.'

'What do you mean?' Mary asked, frowning. The man turned to her.

'I've been standing around here for two days doing nothing,' he whined, 'but that ain't my fault. If the company thinks they ain't goin' to pay me . . . '

'Just a minute,' Lee interrupted, 'do you mean he didn't change here tonight?'

'That's what I said,' the other nodded, turning back to him. 'I ain't seen him since the day before yesterday.'

Lee and Mary looked at each other quickly as the others behind them excitedly exchanged this piece of news.

251

'Which means he's probably gone already,' Lee said.

Burgh pushed his way forward. 'But why?' he said. 'It was a great perfomance. Why should he want to run away?'

Lee shook his head. He paused for a moment, then said, 'Well, at least let's find out who took the part of Judas at the last minute.' He turned and pushed his way back out into the corridor as Burgh, wide-eyed, turned to Mary.

'What's he talking about?' he demanded. 'I thought that young priest . . . '

'Lee thinks someone else did it,' Mary interrupted quickly. She hurried after Lee who was now moving towards Father O'Connell's dressing room, but Burgh paused, frowning for a few seconds.

'Yeah,' he said, mostly to himself, 'come to think of it, he did look bigger.' He nodded. 'I thought so at the time.'

Lee pushed open the door of the priest's dressing room without ceremony, then stopped just inside. The figure of Judas sat at the dressing table. Their eyes met in the mirror. Once again the others crowded into the room behind him.

'What happened to Father O'Connell?' Lee demanded. The other shook his head slightly. 'He couldn't go through with it.'

'So you took his place?'

'It seemed more appropriate.'

Burgh arrived just in time to hear the last exchange. 'Well,' he began, 'whoever you are, I'd like to say on behalf of the network . . . ' but Lee held up his hand to silence him.

'Did you see what happened to Burnard?' he demanded.

The other paused for a moment, his eyes still on Lee in the mirror. 'He's still here,' he said eventually.

Lee glanced around the empty room, then turned back. 'What do you mean?'

'He's still in the building?' Mary prompted, but the other shook his head.

'No.'

The figure of Judas reached up to his face and began to peel off some thin pieces of rubber, then he took off the wig and stripped away the moustache and beard.

252

Lee began to feel the hairs on the back of his neck tingle as they silently watched the face of John Burnard slowly begin to emerge.

When he had finished, the star turned to face Lee directly for the first time. 'I'm sorry, Lee,' he said solemnly. 'I tried. But it was beyond me. Then, in despair, I set out looking – and I found Judas instead. One of these days I'll try and tell you about it.'

At this, he stood up and removed the outer cloak of the costume. 'I knew I'd cut it pretty close,' he went on. 'By the time I got here you had already started, but Father O'Connell didn't need much persuasion to let me take his place.'

Lee shook his head. 'I still don't understand,' he said.

'Well, I had some idea in my mind about finishing it all with a big speech. You know, something along the lines that every one of us is part Jesus, part Judas.' He shrugged and smiled faintly. 'Not very original, I'll admit, but better than nothing. Of course,' he smiled at Lee, 'I should have known you'd have an understudy up your sleeve!'

Lee stared at him, then he said slowly, 'You mean whoever played Christ?'

Burnard: 'Yeah. You should have had him in the first place. He was great! I meant to congratulate him. I thought I followed him down here but I guess he must have gone somewhere else.' Burnard frowned and shook his head slowly as he looked around at the others. 'The strange thing is, I'm not too sure how we made out. I seemed to be in a bit of a daze.' He turned back to Lee. 'I've never felt like that before. It must've been the lights.'

There was a moment's silence, then Lee said, 'We didn't have understudies, John. It wouldn't have been any good. As far as we knew, there was only one person who could be Jesus Christ.'

New York the following morning was just the same. Lee realized it was absurd to expect to be able to tell from people's faces whether they had watched 'Christ on Trial' or not – and of those who had, to try to discern what it meant to them. But

253

at least for him, and some others, he knew for sure, Easter would never again be the same.

Lee and Mary drove Burnard out to Kennedy and saw him on to the two o'clock Pan American fight to Los Angeles, where Jenny would be waiting for him. He told them he planned to return to Israel almost at once, pausing only long enough to tie up a few loose ends and to persuade Jenny to go with him. Maybe they'd be coming back one day, maybe they wouldn't, but at least, he had a lot of unfinished business and it would take a long time.

Burnard didn't open the paper he bought at the airport until after the plane had taken off. When he did, he read it cursorily and so missed a piece down in the bottom left-hand corner of the front page which reported the death of middleweight champion Amos Brown and his former wife June 'in an accident on the subway late last night. Brown had apparently slipped off the platform and fallen in such a fashion that he hung his head downwards over the track, his feet jammed into the ironwork, until a passing train decapitated him. His former wife had evidently fallen on to the track trying to rescue him. The autopsy showed that both had been drinking heavily, and foul play was not suspected.'

Lee turned the car off the main highway just after they emerged from the Lincoln tunnel. Mary looked at him with surprise. 'Where are we going?' she asked.

Lee smiled. 'You'll soon see.'

Within a few minutes he had brought the vehicle to a stop outside a small church. Lee cut the engine, then turned to her. 'Just something I wanted to show you,' he said as he got out. He crossed to the other side and opened the door for her.

He stood with Mary beside him looking up at the wooden image of Christ nailed to a cross, the wood of which had once been polished brown, but was now blackened by the fumes of factories and the procession of steamers up and down the Hudson River. He knew instinctively that this was the last time he would ever stand here. He was leaving New York and Mary was coming with him; that was why he wanted her to see where he used to stand as a child looking up at the tortured face; to tell her how he used to wonder what the son of God was doing in a side street in Jersey City.

Mary didn't say anything when he finished, but he could tell from her expression that she understood. He opened the car door again for her, and Mary got back inside.

As he was about to enter the car, Lee paused to look in the direction of the young priest who had come out of the side entrance of the church and now stood motionless, looking at him.

Lee hesitated.

The two men continued to look at each other from a distance. Lee raised his hand briefly. He saw the other incline his head to acknowledge the greeting, then turn slowly and walk back inside.

Perhaps it was just as well. Maybe there should always be one last question unanswered.